HONOR'S HEIR

Also by C. J. Brightley

Erdemen Honor:
The King's Sword
A Cold Wind

A Long-Forgotten Song:
Things Unseen

HONOR'S HEIR

C. J. BRIGHTLEY

9/26/15
To Nancy
CJ Brightley?

Egia, LLC

ISBN 978-0-9891915-2-4

Published in the United Sates of America by Egia, LLC.

www.cjbrightley.com

Cover design by Ivan Zanchetta

For Stephen

ONE

ELATHLO

My people have sixteen words for wind. There is the howling wind from the north edge of the world that carries the song of rage and lament of the banished gods. There is the small swirling wind on an otherwise still day, carrying eddies of snow up into a man's face. There is the gusting wind that changes direction, and the gusting wind that maintains direction, generally coming from the northeast. There is the loud, screaming wind of a blizzard and the wailing wind of a snow gale. Only one of the winds, the *hansha*, is gentle, and it comes from the south.

When I was five years old, my father took me on my first hunting trip. A snow gale was coming, and we dug a depression in the old snow. Father showed me how to force one of the dogs into the depression, and how to huddle against the dog while piling snow around us against the coming wind.

For long minutes, I felt the soft thuds as Father shoveled more snow on top of us. The dog, Ita, growled and squirmed beneath me. I clenched my legs tighter around his ribs, stuck like a bur, and gripped the leather strap I'd wrapped around his muzzle. Ita and I hated each other, and the strap was to keep him from whipping his head around and biting me.

The thuds stopped, and I expected a shout from my Father. He'd dig in beside me, wiggle through the snow until he could touch my foot or we could even speak to each other, and when the storm blew over, which might be an hour or a day later, he'd help me dig my way out.

I heard nothing. I shouted, but it made Ita thrash like a hooked fish. I tightened the strap around his muzzle again and waited in silence.

Hours passed. It was dark as night inside the snow mound, and I couldn't hear the howling wind. I waited. At first my heart beat fast with fear, but that faded into anger. I wasn't worried about Father; he would be fine. He must have left me.

As time crept onward, I began to shiver, even inside my many layers of wool and fur. Ita growled at intervals, reminding me that if I let up on the strap even for a second, I'd lose a finger, if not a hand or my nose. That happened once, to a boy in another clan. His dog bit off his nose. I had no doubt Ita would do the same, if given half a chance.

My stomach growled, and I managed to extract the last piece of dried horsemilk cheese from my pocket without losing control of Ita. I ate it, but then I wanted fresh milk or water, anything to drink. I ate a little snow, but it's dangerous to eat much. It steals the heat from your body, and I was already cold.

I shivered and waited. I thought of my mother and how Father beat her sometimes. More often than he beat me, to be fair, but then she was strong and I was weak. She rarely cried, and I almost always did. I didn't hate him though. I feared him, yes, and disliked him. But generally he had a good reason to beat me. I cried when I burned my hand on a coal. I cried when Otso-ka, my father's father and the high chief, told me that I was more like a mewling puppy than a proper chief's son, and then again when Father sighed his own disappointment.

Mother was the soft, bright light in my days, and even she was fading by then. Father's constant irritation and demands wore her down, and she sniped at him and brushed off my cowardly clinging at her skirts. I resented her for that; why could she not be more kind when I needed her? Still, she was the kindest person I knew, and most times she gave me at least a little comfort.

How many hours had it been? Too many. I debated with myself, and finally scratched slowly toward the surface, Ita grumbling beneath me, grunting as my knee dug into his ribs.

My head broke above the snow to see fading sunlight, and I almost shouted for joy. But I couldn't be too careless. I dug us out carefully without letting go of Ita until we were both fully free of the snow cave that had sheltered us.

He snarled, lips raised, then turned and set off for home. I called, but I didn't really want him to come back, so I wasn't disappointed when he didn't look over his shoulder. I followed his tracks, trudging through the twilight and the bright, cold moonlight that followed it. The sun is never far above the horizon in the beautiful north, and in autumn daylight is short but moonlight lasts for hours. I was fortunate that night was bright. I reached home close to midnight and fell into my mother's arms in exhaustion.

She patted me and fed me a very late dinner. Father said I'd been slow; Ita had been home long since. He laughed at me when I told him how long we'd stayed beneath the snow, and he told me the storm had lasted only for a few hours, not even all night. He mocked me for my brief tears of relief at finding myself safe at home.

The next morning, he pulled me in to my grandfather's tent. Otso-ka terrified me even more than my father did, and I trembled inside my parka while my father told him the story. My father did not say that I'd cried in my mother's arms when I finally stumbled into their tent. I knew better than to shoot him a grateful look, even at that age.

Otso-ka grunted his approval. "Good. He'll do."

My father nodded, then steered me out before any of the other chiefs could argue with Otso-ka's decision. Over lunch, he murmured that Otso-ka's approval meant that I was still allowed to be in line for the chiefdom after my father. Otso-ka was high chief over the scattered tribes, and my father was the chief of our clan, next in line for the high chief. The -ka after his name indicated his status. My father's name was Jerenth, and he was addressed as Jerenth-ko, the -ko denoting that he stood to replace my grandfather. He was brave, and strong, and smart like the wolf. In this role, my father kept the chiefs in agreement. He was quick with his words, his fists, and his knife.

I didn't see many of the arguments between the chiefs or how they challenged Otso-ka and my father. I did know that when I was ten, Father came back from a meeting with blood on his parka. He seemed satisfied, and he told me, "*That's* how you settle arguments,

Elathlo. Some men just can't be convinced. You have to make them see."

We feed our dead to the wolves and the carrion birds. It is civilized to let our bodies go back to the earth from which they came. We are born, we eat of the flesh of animals and the plants we can find, and then we provide food of our own when we die.

After that meeting, three dead men were left behind to feed the wolves when we moved our camp.

A few days later, my father showed me how to use a knife. How to keep it concealed in the palm of my hand with the blade resting flat against my wrist. Where to aim in a man's back. How to twist the blade once it was in, so that the hole would be enlarged and the blood would flow freely. He made me practice on a piece of wood.

Mother didn't approve of me learning such things at ten, but her opinion had little power, even within our tent. She approved even less when Father took me out for next test that Otso-ka decreed.

Tarvil boys become men by passing a series of tests, and then serving a warrior as an *aloka*. The tests are difficult, but they are only preparation for service as an aloka. That time is the most dangerous and most terrifying period of a Tarvil's life. The warrior is called a sponsor; he trains his aloka in combat and in anything else he deems necessary to be a man. A good sponsor might even teach his aloka to read if his father hasn't taught him already, although we have few texts and little need to read. My father had already taught me to read, and he and Otso-ka had taught me to speak Common, although later I learned that none of us spoke it well. They were more concerned with selecting a warrior who could teach me combat.

My father had trained me a little, but our lessons frequently devolved into shouting and beatings. I avoided them as much as possible, and Father did as well; I don't think he enjoyed beating me, but saw it as a necessary step toward toughening me into a man. He was constantly irritated by everything I did. Otso-ka once called me a *torethsha*, the word for a warm breeze that promises spring but fades into the icy *karetsha*. In other words, I looked promising but proved a disappointment.

The series of tests lasts for years. The summer I turned twelve, my friend Tirta, his cousin Dathlo, and I were given the fourth significant test. Otso-ka decreed that we would steal wolf cubs. They would be raised until they were nearly adults and then killed for their pelts. Wolf fur is thick and warm, a fitting tribute both to the ferocity of the animal and the courage and cunning of the man who killed it.

Raising a wolf cub was perhaps less courageous than killing an adult, but the cleverness was greater and so the honor was considered comparable. Besides, it was part of the test. A warrior must prove himself both fierce and wily.

First, we had to find a wolf den. In the distant past, our ancestors hunted wolves. They used horses and dogs and lasso poles. Sometimes they used bows, but often the wolves were too fast, or too tough; they could survive long enough to kill a man, even after a direct hit. The better method was to use lasso poles. They would catch a wolf around the neck and hold it in place while a man could advance close enough to club it over the head. Arrow holes in the pelt lessened the value considerably. The dogs were not allowed to kill wolves caught in the lasso poles unless human lives were in danger; they would destroy the pelt. Dogs were essential to the hunt, though. They helped track the wolves when the men were hunting, and they guarded the men and horses while they worked.

That was then. We had long since lost that skill, and our dogs had lost their thirst for wolf blood. The Erdemen soldiers had come often enough onto the tundra to keep the wolf packs in check, and we had not been forced to defend our flocks as often as in the past. Our flocks were smaller now and kept within the camp among the tents. Even the boldest wolves would rarely venture between the tents themselves, and we kept watch at night. We killed wolves, of course, lone wolves scouting around the tents or even small packs that roamed across the tundra. But we had not been on a grand wolf hunt in thirty years.

Although our dogs were no longer in the habit of wolf hunting, they could still follow a trail. Tirta, Dathlo, and I took three of the largest, fiercest dogs with us. They led us some eight leagues northeast, into some of the rolling hills at the base of the mountains.

The dogs sniffed and searched, and hours later we found the entrance to a den. The dogs were excited, but not howling with rage, and we guessed the mother wasn't inside.

We tried to get the dogs to crawl into the hole first, but even the smallest didn't get much past his hips before wriggling back out again. A torch revealed a narrow tunnel, but I thought we could make it. We threw a luck piece to see who would crawl inside.

Dathlo won, or perhaps lost. He stripped off his coat and outer tunic and shivered for a few seconds in his undershirt, gathering his courage. We tied a rope around his waist; in case something happened, we could pull him back out. He shoved the torch into the hole, then slithered in after it, knife in hand.

We could see the light in the gaps between his body and the edges of the wall. Then the tunnel turned, and his body blocked the rest of the light. Farther. We heard some muffled sounds, and then grumbling as he slid back out.

He shook a few bits of dirt from his hair and sat back on his heels.

"It's too narrow. I can't fit. But they're back there! I could smell them. I heard a tiny sound before they got quiet."

Tirta and I stared at each other.

"I'll go," I said. I didn't want to. But if I was to be chief, I should be brave. I was smaller than the other two, and I had the best chance of fitting through the narrow hole. Tirta nodded, looking a little relieved.

I stripped down to my own undershirt and shivered. The wind gusted, a few forlorn snowflakes icy against my bare arms. I trembled while Tirta tied the rope around my waist, making sure it was tight enough to catch on my hips.

Dathlo tied his parka closed again. He gave me a re-assuring clap on the shoulder. "Go on. Make us proud."

I crouched down in front of the hole and took a deep breath. The scent of wolf found my nose, musky and strong. I was still trembling, and only a little bit because of the cold. On my belly I shimmied inside, pushing the torch ahead of me. The thick smoke choked me, almost overpowering the smell of wolf that seemed to seep into my very pores from the walls. I crept forward. The dirt was not as well-packed as I had expected, though the tunnel was old. And if the dogs couldn't fit through, how could a wolf fit? I wasn't entirely sure, and I was afraid to think about the answer. I kept going.

The wolf cubs were silent, and I could guess how close I was to them only by the smell. The tunnel took a turn downward, though the slope was shallow. I slid down carefully, edging forward and listening for any little mew or coo or growl that might indicate the cave was occupied. Nothing but scent, although I thought the air might have been getting a little warmer.

An open space ahead. I pushed the torch through and then, when no wolf leapt out of the darkness to bite off my hand, I peered cautiously into the den itself. I gasped, my eyes wide.

Three cubs lay in a little pile, their eyes barely open. They were fat and round, with hair coarser than that of our dogs. Mostly black, with little streaks of grey and brown on their faces and legs. I set the torch down and reached forward to lift one cub. It squeaked when I picked it up, and I froze.

I heard another sound, a deep growl that made me tremble with fear. I started to shimmy backwards, but then, with a surge of courage, reached out to grab the other two cubs with one hand. They squawked in protest at the rough treatment, and I began to scoot backwards through the tunnel.

"Get me out!" I shrieked, my voice cracking. The rope jerked and tightened against my waist painfully and I began to slide backward faster than I could crawl. The cubs wriggled in my hands.

The light from the torch abruptly disappeared, replaced by blackness. The wolf mother was in the tunnel with me! There must have been another entrance, larger and more often used, and she had returned from her hunt. I was whimpering with fear, crawling backward as fast as I could. Her growling was deafening in such a small space, punctuated by blood-curdling snarls. I could hear her claws scrabbling against the sides of the tunnel and the soft fall of dirt. She was too large for the tunnel I'd used, probably larger than the dogs, and she was forcing her way through. Gaining on me. Hot breath brushed my face for a moment and I heard the almost-silent snick of teeth closing only inches from my face.

Hands grasped my ankles and jerked me backward before I could cry out again. We sprinted to the horses and vaulted on, galloping away as the mother wolf burst from the tunnel and flew at us. She was no longer growling, lost in a silent, murderous rage.

The dogs raced beside us, weaving back and forth and darting at the wolf when they had a chance. She leapt at Dathlo, trying to pull him from his horse, and he cried out as her teeth caught his pants leg. It jerked him sideways, and he righted himself only when one of the dogs caught the wolf's side in his teeth. The wolf let go to whip around and sink her own teeth in the dog's throat.

The dog was dead in moments, the wolf's mouth bloodied. She was behind us now, but she could run as fast as a horse and farther, so we were hardly safe. She stopped for a split second, sniffed at something on the ground, then launched herself after us again.

I groaned aloud as I realized I'd dropped one of the three cubs in the confusion and chaos. I hadn't even noticed.

Dathlo split away from Tirta and me and circled back. The wolf followed us, risking the flying hooves of our horses to try to bring us down. My horse was bleeding from a deep bite on one haunch already, and Tirta was fending off the wolf's snapping teeth with the end of his lasso pole. The two remaining dogs had fallen behind.

We circled back just enough to see Dathlo lean precariously down from his galloping horse, hanging from one hand and one leg. Nearly upside down, he swept up the cub in one hand and righted himself with a lurch, then shot after us.

We were fortunate. We fled all the way home, running like a demon was on our heels, as indeed it was. The wolf slowed and stopped some distance from our camp. I looked over my shoulder to see her looking after us. She was tired, sides heaving, but I didn't think she stopped from fatigue. She glanced over one shoulder and then back at us. Perhaps she didn't realize we had gotten all the cubs, didn't know Dathlo had retrieved the last one. Out in the open, the cub would be an easy meal for a golden eagle, a vulture, or a wolf from another pack. She stared after us, and I could feel the hatred and fury in her gaze. Then she turned and loped away.

All three of us breathed a sigh of relief. We trotted into camp with tears of relief in our eyes. Even Father smiled when he saw us.

"You got them?"

"Yes." I dropped the two cubs I carried into his waiting hands. They were half-crushed in my parka, and I could barely muster a bit of sympathy for their frightened mewing. I was trembling with fatigue and the aftermath of terror. Tirta and Dathlo were much the same.

"Who did it?"

We hadn't been expecting that question, and we glanced at each other.

"I got them out, sir, but I dropped one when we were fleeing the mother. It almost killed us. Dathlo went back to retrieve it," I said.

Otso-ka nodded. "Good."

I slid down.

Father merely nodded at me, but clapped a congratulatory hand on Dathlo's shoulder. "Had to fix my cub's mistake, didn't you?"

"Maybe a little." Dathlo smiled back, ignoring me as my mouth dropped open in protest.

Later Tirta and I grumbled about it between ourselves, but Father and Otso-ka had already decided to honor Dathlo rather than me. Tirta, who had barely done anything aside from flee with us, was somehow exempt from their barbs and insults. At least he took it gracefully. Dathlo managed to transform his moment of courage into a heroic epic, in which my admittedly fearful theft of the cubs was only a brief introduction.

THE WAR BEGAN before I realized it. The men went south for days or weeks at a time and returned with tales of plunder and pillage. This was not entirely new, although I had not listened much to their stories when I was younger. This year I listened. I preferred the chores I could do for Mother to listening to my Father's tales of bloodshed, but I was not immune to the excitement of combat. The stories frightened me, but they were thrilling too. I lost my taste for them when I began to hear of rape and other cruelties.

Perhaps I was soft, because the other boys my age listened with wide eyes, eager for every lurid detail. I tried to hide my blushing and bit my lip to keep from crying out when one of the men mimicked a girl's panicked pleas for mercy. He gave her none, of course.

My father had trained me a little in the arts of war. I knew how to wield a sword with tolerable skill, how to protect myself with the small shield, and how to use a bow with some accuracy, but my father said I was far from ready to join battle. Perhaps I should have been ashamed by that. I was ashamed that he found me wanting, but I was almost relieved that I was not yet allowed to fight.

The men said the fighting was easy, but even the soft Erdemen farmers could sometimes knock a man from his horse with a well-thrown rock or an arrow. Still, the casualties were few. The men stole grain and even kidnapped some Erdemen women.

I didn't see them; they were sent off with the various warriors who took them, or others to whom Otso-ka owed favors. When Father was gone, I asked Mother, "Why are they taking women?"

"Because so many died last winter. You remember how hard it was here. The western tribes had it even worse. They need women to bear children." Mother's voice was soft. "It's not something I'm happy with, but not something I can do anything about, either."

"So... they'll just make them have babies?" I wasn't well-informed on how babies were made, but I'd seen how our dogs, sheep, and horses mated. I assumed people did something similar.

"Something like that." Mother kept her eyes on the roasting mutton and I had the feeling she was avoiding my gaze.

"Will Father get one?" I tried to imagine an Erdemen farm girl sharing our tent and grimaced.

"No. There are too many men without wives now for Father to get a second woman." Her lips twisted in a bitter smile, but she said nothing else.

A few months later, everything changed. First, we moved north, with no explanation, or at least none that Mother and I heard. Father and Otso-ka were grim and irritable, and we knew better than to ask anything while they stomped about in such moods. The weather worsened, and even before the winter solstice, it was colder than it had been the previous winter. We moved again, north and to the east, toward the mountains. By then I could guess that the fortunes of war had shifted, and we were fleeing.

Tirta was in my clan, so we usually traveled together, but Dathlo was in my uncle's clan, and normally we would not see him often. But since we had begun our flight north, our clans had traveled in larger groups in order to better protect ourselves against the much-feared southerners. I heard little from my own family, but Tirta and Dathlo kept me well informed on the rumors they heard in their tents.

Dathlo had been honored with the task of caring for the wolf cubs, and we visited his tent often to see the cubs as they grew. They had to kept away from the dogs, although for six weeks we forced one of the new dams to nurse the wolf cubs. Her own cubs were dispersed among other litters, because the three wolf cubs ate as much as seven puppies. They ate until their little bellies were stretched tight as drums. Dathlo, Tirta, and I had to hold her down while the cubs nursed; we sat on her head and her hips so she couldn't turn and kill them. She hated it, and each time the cubs ate to the steady sound of growling as she protested her mistreatment.

For the next month, we made a paste for them of meat, milk, and flour. It would have been better to feed them nothing but meat, but already we ate only one or two meals each day ourselves. There was no surplus to feed to hungry wolf cubs who served no purpose.

The next month, Father killed two of the three cubs. He said they cost us too much meat that the men needed for their own strength. By then, the men who went to fight got meat every other day, and those of us who stayed behind got a bit of meat every week or ten days. Mother considered butchering a sheep once, but there were few enough that Father would not yet let her kill even one ewe. We did, however, eat the meat of the cubs in our stew for the next few days.

The Red Tarvil, who lived a little to the south and west, had fled to us, begging for help, telling of lost grazing land and the steady, relentless advance of the Erdemen army. They split off from us some weeks later, preferring to head west and north again rather than stay and fight. But their plea told us more than their words; they had never liked Otso-ka and had not been friendly with our clan in many years. They were desperate indeed to seek our help.

From their men, I heard the rumors of the Erdemen fighter, Sendoa, a giant who fought with the fury of a thousand demons. The Red Tarvil said he had been connected with the ascent of the new Erdemen king, but no one knew how. It probably didn't matter. We knew little of Erdemen politics and cared less.

My father went to a battle with some other men and returned with only two others. A sweeping cavalry charge had taken them unawares, arrows at their backs and Erdemen cavalry decimating them. He spoke to my mother after they thought I was asleep, and for the first time in my life, I heard fear in my father's voice.

"Their chief is one of the old demons. Either a demon or a god."

"You believe those stories?" My mother also sounded frightened.

"I didn't until now. He's not human."

Their voices subsided into murmurs, and I could no longer make out their words over the howling of the blizzard outside. Tirta told me the next day that he'd heard much the same from his father. The Erdemen chief, whom they called a general, had inhuman strength and speed and glowing green eyes. Some even said he could turn men to stone by looking at them, but Tirta and I agreed that was probably only a rumor. If he could do that, the Erdemen army would already have extinguished us. Instead, they were going about it the ordinary way, with swords and arrows, pushing us north until we fell off the edge of the world.

The one remaining wolf cub killed Dathlo about a week after we began our last flight into the snow. It lay in wait near the stake to which it was tied, so that it was hard for Dathlo to judge the length of its chain. To be fair, though, Dathlo had hardly been unwise. We had been cautious with the cub for months, but it had never yet attacked us.

Perhaps it did not think of it until that morning. Perhaps it was biding its time. By then it was nearly as heavy as he was, taller and leaner than many of our dogs, though still with the clumsy gait and big paws of a cub. Its face was still softer than that of a full-grown wolf, the muzzle not yet entirely elongated and the teeth smaller than they would be later. It didn't matter. If it acted as wolves always acted, it would have sprung at Dathlo in silence, with no warning growl, and killed him with the first bite in his throat. No one saw it, and the wolf cub settled down to eat its fill.

At some point it pulled the stake from the ground and disappeared. Later someone found the stake and the chain later some distance from our camp, half-buried in the snow. Dathlo's mother found him near dusk, a frozen body in a frozen puddle of blood, torn half to shreds. I saw the body later, when we cleaned him up before leaving him for the wolves. The corpse didn't really look like Dathlo anymore. I tried to think of Dathlo being gone, and the bloodied meat before me as unrelated to my friend.

I didn't cry until long after Mother and Father were asleep that night. Tears filled my eyes. I brushed them away. The dampness made my cheeks sting with the winter cold, sucking the heat from our bones even within the thick-walled tents. I turned toward the firepit, but the coals were long banked and dormant; their faint heat did not warm my face.

Otso-ka did not say anything about Dathlo's death, other than that Dathlo should have been more careful. There was no grief to be spared for a boy; too many men were dead for a boy to have any importance. Dathlo's father Pashlo and most of the rest of the men saddled up the next day and went south again, while we continued northward, fighting into the icy wind that swept from the edge of the world.

We'd killed most of the sheep already, and this far north, we would not be able to graze them most of the year. It was better to kill them now while they were fat and we could eat or dry the meat rather than wait for them to starve. Even so, we had little food, and the little we had stored was diminishing every day.

I heard no one say it out loud, but we all knew the end was coming. Either the Erdemen soldiers would kill us all, or we would freeze like the *carabaa* do in a hard winter, huddled together for warmth that whips away in the ever-present wind. For generations, we had lived in the southern tundra, with our few sheep and our shaggy little horses, barely more than overgrown ponies, content to fight the wolves and the Erdemen soldiers when necessary but otherwise avoiding trouble. There was plenty to worry about with winter storms, cold, and hunger without antagonizing the great army to the south. The tundra was our protection; the barren land did not tempt Erdem, and it was enough for us.

Now the army was coming north, and this time, they did not stop.

One night about a month after Dathlo was killed, Mother used the last of our flour to make flat cakes, which we topped with a puddle of horsemilk and crumbled bits of cheese. We also used the last dried lamb and some dried herbs to make a thin stew; without the thick fat of a good mutton or even a carabaa, it wasn't as flavorful as Mother had hoped. The highest-ranking chiefs had a few sips of *alamaa*, but even that gesture didn't brighten the mood much. Father and Otso-ka murmured to each other in the corner of Otso-ka's tent while we ate. I brought them *imea*, just the way Otso-ka liked it, but Father waved me away before I could hear much of what they said. The next morning, Father and some of the others went on another foray south against the Erdemen.

None of them returned.

I DID NOT CRY for my father. I did not like him, and his absence was, in many ways, a relief. Perhaps I loved him, because the hole he left in our tent was an uncomfortable ache, and the thought of him dying on some snowy, blood-soaked hillside made my gut twist. But tears did not fit the feelings that rose at night when I thought about him. During the day we were occupied with travel, and I was too busy to think about who and what we had lost.

We had no other battles for nearly a month. We kept moving, and they followed, a little slower but relentless, holding every inch of ground they took. Otso-ka sent scouts northward, fearing we would fall off the edge of the world. Perhaps he was wrong; I learned later that Erdemen scholars believed the world to be round, so perhaps there are no true edges after all. But the scouts returned with news that even if the world did not end, they had found a barrier we could not pass. Only six days' journey to the north, the land became a jumbled mass of rocks, chunks of ice, and bottomless depths of water so cold they did not understand why it was not frozen. One scout had fallen through a section of ice already; he succumbed to the cold and sank within minutes, unable to pull himself back onto the ice shelf he'd been attempting to traverse.

Perhaps the men and older boys like me could have managed to cross it. Perhaps, given time, we might have adapted ourselves to the terrain and managed to build lives there. Mother said that far in the past, some of our people had lived in that land, hunting some sort of furred water creatures and living on meat, fat, and little else. But we had no time to figure it out, and no food to last while we scrabbled a new living in a new land. Besides, our clan was now composed of thirty-three women, ages sixteen to seventy, eighteen men between the same ages, and nineteen children below the age of sixteen. Three of the eighteen men with us were crippled, and another two were in ill health and could not be expected to haul the loads up the steep ice the scouts described. Women, of course, could not be relied upon to do the work of men.

Starving, freezing, and trapped, we had little choice but to plead for a parley.

Pashlo, acting as scout, returned with news that the Erdemen general agreed to speak with us. I'd heard of the Erdemen general already, of course, but we knew little about him. Father had said he was a demon or a god, one of the old ones who walked the earth like a man but could not be killed or defeated. He had the strength of a hundred men, the cunning and patience of an alpha wolf, and, perhaps most terrifying of all, the glowing green eyes of a demon. Tirta's father believed the rumors the general could turn men to stone with his eyes, but Father had said that was absurd. Whatever the truth, we knew he was the reason the war had turned against us. The men had been proud and confident for months, capturing women and livestock. Then suddenly the general arrived, and everything turned.

I watched the Erdemen soldiers arrive, and even from a safe distance, they terrified me. There were ten of them, plus the general, and even the shortest of them was half a head taller than Otso-ka. The general himself towered over even his own men. We must have looked like insects to them. Otso-ka did not show his fear much, but I could read it in the stiffness of his shoulders. His fear made my heart stutter with terror. Otso-ka was never afraid of anything, and now he was afraid of the Erdemen general.

I couldn't blame him though; his fear reinforced my own. The man's eyes were green as grass in summer, his complexion a deep olive brown with an undertone of greyish green, an unnatural tone never seen in the great and beautiful north. His hair was the black of coal. The other Erdemen soldiers were Tuyets, fair-haired and fair-skinned, and he looked a foreigner among his own men.

He slid from his horse and bowed to Otso-ka, the movement graceful and confident. His expression might have been set in stone, his mouth tight and unforgiving. I felt his eyes on me for a split second and then they flicked around the camp, taking in everything and discarding it as unworthy of his Erdemen boots.

Perhaps we were. I'd never seen Erdemen soldiers before, and now I could see why the men were frightened of them. Tall, broad-shouldered, muscular, even in the dead of winter and far from their own lands, they looked like they ate better than we did. Stone-faced and grim, they glared at us as Otso-ka ushered them into his largest and best tent. We had called in all the clans within a day's journey for the parley, and so Otso-ka was able to muster ten warriors, local chiefs and their deputies, to stand behind him. The others bustled outside, trying to make our little camp not look quite so desolate as it really was.

The general and a younger soldier sat in the low stools that Otso-ka had set for them on one side of the table, and the rest of the Erdemen soldiers lined up behind them in an imposing display. I wondered if I was disloyal for thinking that their discipline was intimidating, even beautiful, while our men looked like ragged children playing at war.

I was allowed to wait in the corner of the tent for Otso-ka's nod, at which point I would bring the alamaa. Alamaa is used only for great victories and important celebrations, and only the guests of honor may drink it. The Erdemen general would be honored in this way, and perhaps he would be inclined to be merciful to us.

Because, despite Otso-ka's attempts to show our strength, we pled for mercy.

When he sat, the Erdemen general tensed, just a little; I might have been the only one who saw it. A twinge of pain, perhaps, or annoyance. The words between him and Otso-ka were quiet, but I heard the general demand that the treaty be in his king's name, not his own. I did not understand the demand, and neither did Otso-ka or any of the other Tarvil warriors. They debated for a while among themselves, considering whether the unknown king could be trusted and why the Erdemen general would make such a strange demand.

My eyes kept returning to the general. The soldier beside him murmured in his ear, and he answered with an edge of irritation in his voice. A moment later, he glanced at the soldier with a softer expression and put a hand on his shoulder, as if in apology. That action baffled me; I had never seen my Father or Otso-ka apologize for anything, to anyone. Children apologize. Men settle their disagreements with cold silence, screaming rage, or knives, if necessary. A fight is won or lost. The winner wins, and the loser loses. When a boy becomes a man, he is no longer expected or required to apologize for anything. Ever.

I heard the rest of the discussions, but nothing surprised me until the Erdemen general signed the agreement. I couldn't help my smile of relief, but Otso-ka's reaction was more subdued. The general stood, the movement quick and graceful, but then he blinked and wavered a moment. The soldier beside him steadied his right elbow, and he nodded, then bowed again to Otsoka. He mounted his horse, and only then did I realize he had scarcely moved his left arm the entire time. He did not need it on the reins, he was a skilled rider, but the motion of mounting his horse made it more obvious that he kept his left arm close by his body, deliberately relaxed as if he wished to pretend the injury did not exist.

Otso-ka stood beside me as we watched them leave. He blew out his breath and scowled after them.

"What's wrong?" I asked. We had achieved what we wanted, everything we could have hoped from an initial peace agreement. Anything else would have to come later, after the Erdemen king had been consulted.

Otso-ka's frown deepened. "It would be better if he were not wounded. If he dies, the Erdemen king will kill us all."

Pashlo asked from his other side, "Do you think so? Where shall we run, then? West?"

"East. Over the mountains. Make ready. Not yet, but be ready."

Otso-ka was in a talkative mood that night, despite his fear. The relief of even a temporary peace treaty was enough to let him relax enough to explain to me.

"Did you see how he held his arm? He's hurt, and it's not recent, because we haven't had a skirmish in weeks. There's a good chance it's infected, and even Erdemen healers can't heal everything. He's our greatest threat, but all the Erdemen women we've captured say he's the king's friend, the one who helped him regain his throne last year. The king will throw the entire army at us if he dies. Perhaps it would have been convenient if he died earlier, a quick death in some skirmish. But now… no. It is too dangerous. We'd best hope he lives."

WE HEARD NOTHING for almost four months. We moved our camp, trying to find the few stretches of frozen grass laid bare by the wind for the sheep to crunch on while we waited to hear if the king would grant us mercy. We butchered another two sheep, but still the animals ate better than we did. We ate the remaining tubers from the last trip south, and boiled the bones of the sheep to make broth. Mother wanted to kill another sheep, but Otso-ka forbade it; he said we might be able to go south if we could wait a bit longer.

For three weeks we subsisted on bone broth, old imea, dried sheep's milk, and hot water. The sheep produced no more milk; they were far too thin for that. Even so, Otso-ka did not let us kill them. I went to sleep with hunger growling in my stomach every night, but I did not complain. I felt myself getting weaker, and I could see the same despair in everyone else's faces. The hunger was ever-present, sometimes a gnawing anger in my belly, sometimes only a vague unpleasant emptiness. My limbs felt heavy, and I drew my pants tighter around my waist. I've never been skinny; we are not a tall and thin race of people. We are stocky and short, but even so, my stomach grew flatter than I'd seen it in years. We all grew dizzy at times, standing slowly from our pallets in the morning so we did not fall over.

Otso-ka sent scouts north again, to see if the northern reaches became more habitable in the summer, but we had no such luck. The ice melted a little, but that only made it clear that little of the ground was actually ground. The scouts trod on ice over water, the ice cracking and groaning beneath their feet. We could flee no further north, and Otso-ka planned instead to flee east into the mountains if the peace with Erdem did not hold. Perhaps even over the mountains. There are other branches of Tarvil on the eastern side of the mountains; we were not often in contact with them, but we hoped we could push our way into some tiny area sufficient to support our dwindling numbers. The journey over the mountains would be difficult at best, but if we had to undertake it, at least it would be during summer.

Somehow we would live. Otso-ka was still grimly determined to keep us alive, but I had lost hope. We would leave the horses as they fell, because they would not survive the mountain crossing. The dogs we would keep, but the sheep might not make it. We would kill them and at least have a little meat and wool for parkas. If we went west, we might find seals, rock achas, and carabaa if we were lucky. East to the mountains, there might be mountain goats, hares, pika, and the mountain relatives of carabaa, even smaller and leaner but still edible. We would live, as we always live, beset on all sides, hungry, lonely, and proud.

At last, the snow began to melt. Spring was late, but it came suddenly, and the ground turned from snow to slush to a carpet of grass and flowers within a week. The sheep ate constantly, and we waited for new lambs so we could afford to eat meat again. In the meantime, the mice and voles and rock achas of the tundra emerged from their holes deep beneath the frozen ground. We set snares everywhere. The small rodents weren't a preferred food and they were difficult to catch, but they added shreds of meat and a sheen of fat to the thin stews we had been eating for months. Their little bones turned soft in the broth, and we chewed them, grateful for the feel of something solid between our teeth.

FINALLY, AN ERDEMEN RIDER appeared with a parley flag, and Otso-ka set the parley for the following day. Again we drew the nearby clans together as a show of strength. As Otso-ka had commanded, we cheered the soldiers as they arrived, to show our support for the treaty we hoped the general brought. The Erdemen general leapt off his horse with more energy this time. I swallowed my fear of the Erdemen soldiers as I slipped into the back of the tent. The general stalked into the tent like a living sword, sharp and dangerous. He kept his voice low, but that didn't disguise the threat in his words.

I didn't understand. Why would he threaten to prolong the war for the sake of some few farm women he'd undoubtedly never met? Otso-ka and the other chiefs did not understand either, and their fury was obvious. The Erdemen general watched their discussions with cold green eyes that seemed to miss nothing. Otso-ka threatened, pleaded, and argued with everyone for long, tense minutes. But in the end, it wasn't his words that convinced them. Tarek glanced over his shoulder and studied the Erdemen general for a moment when the general was looking at someone else. Tarek turned back to the huddled group and muttered, "You think they won't kill us all? I'm surprised he hasn't yet. It's not much of a choice."

The others grumbled, but they knew he was right. The Erdemen general smiled and nodded when Otso-ka finally relayed their agreement. We had three weeks to find the women and return them all to Erdemen custody or we would again be at war.

The Erdemen general and his soldiers departed with a thundering of hooves, leaving Otso-ka and the chiefs grumbling in their wake, trying to determine whether it was even possible to live up to the promise they had made. Riders spread in all directions to relay the agreement and the conditions of our treaty. Otso-ka said the chiefs would obey his command.

I wasn't so sure, and in fact Otso-ka wasn't sure either. He'd bet his life on it, but he wasn't confident. He had promised all his treasure and his title as high chief to gain the clan chiefs' cooperation. If the general broke his word, Otso-ka would not be likely to survive long enough to fulfill those promises; Jaasku or one of the others would put a knife between his ribs before we fled again. Otso-ka never mentioned that, of course, but Mother and I could guess, and so we tried to keep out of his way. Tension made Otso-ka even more irritable than usual.

Otso-ka ate in our tent the night before the treaty signing. Mother always prepared his food; as the wife of his son, it was her duty. But he preferred to eat alone, and most days I delivered his meals to his tent and returned to eat with my mother. That night, with Otso-ka with us and the treaty signing looming, we ate in silence, the tension thicker than the steam from our thin soup wafting over the battered table.

"Wear your best clothes tomorrow, Elathlo. I will ask Sendoa to take you as his aloka, if the rest of the meeting goes well."

I squeaked in surprise, and Mother stared at him.

"Why would you do that to your only grandson?" she whispered.

"My son is dead. Elathlo is my heir but he has no standing among the men. He hasn't fought in a single battle, and if I sent him to one, he would die. He is a worthless cub who is too weak to take the position that awaits him. A prestigious sponsor is his only chance."

"Sendoa will..." her voice faded and she glanced at me. Her lips trembled, and she picked up her cup and took a drink, using the opportunity to steady her voice. "Are you not concerned that it is dangerous for him?" she enunciated carefully, her eyes on his face.

Otso-ka said, "Any aloka placement is dangerous. Sendoa's reputation will give Elathlo standing, if he survives. I will ask only for a year, not three."

That did not reassure me. I could not imagine surviving a week, much less a year.

Then Otso-ka looked at me, holding my gaze with his own. "You have never met a man like him, Elathlo. When you saw him that first time, he was so close to death he could taste it. Did you see his eyes? He could have fought alone against half the men in our camp and won. He will demand more of you than you have. Do not disappoint him. Remember you could lead our people, if you survive his training. If anyone can make you a man, it is him.

"Keep your mouth shut and don't say anything stupid. Do exactly as he says, or you won't survive a week. Do whatever you must to earn your training. Cook, clean, tend to his horse, make his imea, shine his boots, wash his clothes. Whatever he asks, do it without complaining. Do not slow when you're tired. And keep your whining and crying to yourself. Don't ever let him see you cry.

"Don't shame me, boy."

I nodded, my lips pressed together to keep them from trembling. The intensity of Otso-ka's voice made tears spring to my eyes; Otso-ka had never liked me, and yet he sounded afraid for me now. If he was afraid, it was no wonder I was terrified.

I cried that night, wrapped in my blanket with the folds pressed to my face so I didn't make a sound. My mother was awake for long hours too, but we did not speak to each other. If we did, it would make the fear rise to choke us. If we pretended we were not afraid, perhaps it would be almost like being brave.

TO MY SURPRISE, all but one of the Erdemen women arrived the day of the final parley and the signing of the treaty. I think even Otso-ka was surprised the chiefs had cooperated. Perhaps he guessed, as I did, that it was not love or fear of Otso-ka that ensured their cooperation, but rather fear of the Erdemen general and the army he commanded.

The Erdemen general waited while the women arrived, his cold green eyes playing over our camp with disinterested disdain. I felt he must scorn everything about us. He stood even taller than I remembered, and his eyes blazed brighter. When the last of the Erdemen women arrived, he and Otso-ka entered the tent to sign the agreement. Otso-ka pressed the alamaa on him, unwilling to be dissuaded by the general's offer of wine instead.

Then Otso-ka asked him if he would take me as his aloka. I'd been hidden in the back of the tent, where the general could not see me but I would be available if Otso-ka called for imea or anything else. Someone motioned me in so the general could inspect me.

I tried to stand tall, but when his eyes caught mine, my eyes dropped to the floor.

"Look at me," he said.

Holding his gaze made my trembling worse. I could feel his disapproval, both of me and of Otso-ka's request. All night, I'd held desperately to the hope that he would refuse me. Then the worst I could expect was a beating from Otso-ka for being inadequate. Suddenly, as his eyes held mine, I realized that Otso-ka had put him in the uncomfortable position of refusing a direct request and possibly jeopardizing the treaty.

"How long?" he asked.

"I would ask you to take him a year, though if he disappoints you, you could, of course, send him back earlier." Otso-ka's words were clipped with tension.

My breath caught in my throat as I realized the general was actually considering it! The most feared soldier the Tarvil had ever faced would have me at his mercy for an entire year.

I would be lucky to survive a week. I would be lucky if, when I disappointed him, he killed me himself. Quickly, without the deliberate cruelty my people use to punish alokas who disappoint their sponsors. I tried to gauge his face while we waited for his answer, and what I saw gave me a forlorn bit of hope. His mouth did not twist in a cruel smile, and he'd spoken with the returned Erdemen women gently, from the few interactions I'd seen. Instead, I saw a hard, clean efficiency, and I imagined I could expect beheading rather than a slow, bloody death dragged out over days. I hoped for beheading, if he took me.

But I hoped even more than he would say no, because Otso-ka would not kill me; he would beat me and I would avoid him for a month and then perhaps things might be a little better.

"Agreed. I'll take him."

I sucked in my breath, my heart thundering in my chest.

"What price will you take for his food and lodging?" Otso-ka asked.

I hadn't noticed that they had not discussed it yet, and I couldn't guess what that might mean. I knew Otso-ka would spend everything he had and everything he could borrow to get the general to agree.

"You asked it as a personal favor. I will take nothing. He will be my guest."

I blinked. I couldn't see the expression on Otso-ka's face, but I knew he must be as surprised as I was. More grateful than I, certainly. I was dismissed, and I slipped out, though I heard the general agree to Otso-ka's request to deliver me to the Erdemen camp the next day, so that I would have time to say goodbye to my family.

I didn't go back to Mother's tent immediately. Her gentle sympathy and her fear would have made me weep, and I didn't want to weep yet. I wanted to pretend I was brave, pretend that somehow I would survive, or at least that I would die quickly and with courage. So I went to walk among the dogs, trying to focus my mind on how they curled with their tails over their paws against the still-icy spring breeze. I stood at the edge of camp and stared across the open tundra until the sky fell into the hillside.

Tirta spoke from beside me as the sun went down before us. "He agreed, didn't he?"

I nodded.

He put a tentative hand on my shoulder and we stared at the orange-streaked sky. I was trembling, and I'm sure he could feel it, but he didn't say anything. Too much sympathy would only make it worse.

Finally I turned back toward Mother's tent. Tirta didn't say anything as he paced beside me, until finally, just at the door, he pulled on my shoulder again.

"You'll be alright." He gave me a tentative smile, and we both laughed, although it wasn't funny.

"It'll be over fast, at least."

He shrugged one shoulder. "You can do it. You're smart, Elathlo. You can make it." His eyes held mine, barely visible in the twilight.

"I'll try." I couldn't make my voice sound as brave as I wanted it to.

He didn't turn away until after the tent flap closed.

Mother was waiting, and when she saw me, she ladled soup into a bowl for me. "I'm sorry I'm late, Mother."

She shook her head and brushed at the tears on her cheeks.

"Otso-ka told me the general agreed to take you," she said.

"Yes."

We said little else while we cleaned the dishes and packed my things for the next morning. One pair of pants, a pair of winter overpants, an undershirt, a winter tunic, my parka, and a pair of woolen socks. I'd roll up my blanket in the morning. Mother cut a piece of parchment into three pieces and poured a bit of imea into the largest piece. She folded it up into a tight little packet, then filled the other pieces with dried powdered milk and a bit of sosta, a sweet spice made of dried leaves. She put the packets into her best little iron pot, wrapped two metal tea cups in a bit of cloth, tucked them inside, then wrapped the whole thing in a shawl and put the bundle on the table.

I stared at it a moment then looked at her.

"You'll want a taste of home." Her smile crumpled, and she pulled me close to her. She cried into my hair, her embrace so tight I could scarcely breathe. I wept too, the tears spilling without my permission.

"You'll come back ready to lead. You'll wear Otso-ka's blue sash with the golden ends." She pulled back and cupped my face in her hands. "You'll be High Chief. You'll see. I'll make you lamb skewers, just the way you like them. Otso-ka will drink alamaa with you!"

I snorted, and she pulled me close again. The idea of actually surviving the year was too absurd. Mother's idea of encouraging me with the impossible vision of wearing my grandfather's sash was beyond outrageous. My fear bubbled into hysterical giggles, and I kept my face down, so she wouldn't see. My shoulders shook.

I mastered my face before I looked up at her again. "Yes, Mother. I'll make you proud."

She stroked my hair. "I'm always proud, Elathlo. You're not like Jerenth-ko was, nor like Otso-ka. But you're a good boy, and you'll be a good man. Do your best, and come back to me."

"Yes, Mother."

I tried to imagine what it might mean that the general had refused even a token payment from Otso-ka. Otso-ka took at an expression of generosity, and it pleased him. I thought instead it meant that he intended to get enough work out of me that he didn't feel payment necessary, or perhaps an expression of Erdemen contempt for us as a people, that we had nothing worth taking even when offered.

Pashlo and my uncle Loretso would accompany me to the Erdemen camp. I dreaded departing, but the next morning I found myself so anxious and jittery that my stomach churned and I just wanted it to be over. But Pashlo and Loretso intended to leave just before noon, so I had to hide my nerves for hours. Several men came by Otso-ka's tent to congratulate him on such a prestigious aloka placement for me. Otso-ka nodded his acceptance, and I felt a sudden rush of fury that he could be so calm as I went to my death. My anger burned quickly and died into resignation, but even resignation could not entirely overcome my fear.

The flat cakes Mother made me for my last meal at home tasted like dust, even spread with precious crumbles of fresh sheep's milk cheese. I stared at the plate and finally pushed it toward her. "Thank you. But I'm not very hungry."

She twisted her hands together and started to say something, but then stopped. There was nothing else to say.

When I rode away, she didn't look after me. Maybe it was too hard for her to watch me go to my death, but I wished she had. It might have been comforting to feel friendly eyes on me as I tried to be brave.

THE ERDEMEN CAMP was an hour away, and my fear rose with every step. Pashlo and Loretso said little until we were half a league from the camp, the tents distant but growing closer.

"You'll be alright, Elathlo. You're smart. You'll be fine." Pashlo didn't sound confident, but I appreciated the attempt to be comforting.

Loretso raised his hand and acknowledged the sentries. When we reached the edge of the Erdemen camp, General Sendoa was waiting for me, flanked by a few younger soldiers.

"Thank you for bringing him. Give my regards to his family."

I didn't know what "regards" were, and I doubted Pashlo or Loretso did either. They nodded and rode away without a backward glance or a word to me. One of the soldiers took the reins of my horse, and I understood that I was to dismount.

"Come. You'll stay in my tent." The general turned and strode through the camp without hesitation. As he passed, the soldiers bowed towards him, even when he did not notice them. Some of them glared at me, and I kept close on the general's heels, my pack tight in my hand. My eyes kept returning to the long scabbard that hung at his left hip and the shorter one on his right. I knew the blades would taste my blood soon.

His tent was not the largest in the camp. He pointed out the largest to me as the mess tent, whatever that was, and other larger tents as belonging to the women and squads of soldiers. His tent was, however, the most luxurious, with deep green and bright white fabric accented by glittering gold cloth at the tent flap, the corners, and across the top of each wall.

Inside, he turned to me, the movement quick enough to make me jump. "Make yourself comfortable. We will stay here tonight. Let me know if anyone troubles you."

I nodded, not sure if it would be rude to answer him directly. I didn't know Erdemen customs, and I'd heard many things were different there. In Tarvil culture, it is considered a challenge for a young man or boy to hold an elder's eyes for more than a second or two. Would he be offended if I spoke to him for a reason other than to answer a direct question? He hadn't questioned me, only given me an instruction.

"Look at me."

I was trembling when I looked up to meet his eyes, and his faint frown deepened.

"You are my guest, and I command these men. You will inform me if anyone bothers you."

I nodded hurriedly.

"Excuse me." He spun on his heel and the tent flap closed behind him, leaving me standing in the middle of the tent. I heard a sound outside, an almost silent retching that made me cringe. Perhaps one of the soldiers had indulged himself too much.

A moment later, the general's voice startled me again. "Don't you have blankets and such?"

"Yes, sir." I pulled my blanket from my pack and held it up.

"It's a bit cold for one blanket. Is that all you have?"

"Yes, sir."

"Fine. You'll take my bed. It's over there. We'll head south tomorrow morning." His eyes flicked up and down me, and I felt myself being measured. Found wanting, no doubt. "Are you hungry? Thirsty?"

"No, sir."

"Call me Kemen. We'll be spending a lot of time together. I'd prefer to do it as friends." He smiled at me and took a sip of water from a canteen.

The smile took me by surprise, and I blinked as I tried to interpret the sudden flash of white teeth. A true smile, or the smile of a wolf about to devour a hapless carabaa?

The general stepped outside again, the movement a little jerky, and I followed. He retched, a bit of water coming up while he leaned over, hands on his knees, breathing heavily. He heaved again, but nothing else came up, and and he remained bent over for a moment. His hair was caught in a leather thong, and it flopped over his shoulder, shining black. The position pulled his uniform tight across his shoulders and back, and it startled me to realize I could see the sharp lines of his ribs through the thick fabric. He rinsed his mouth and spat.

"Are you ill, sir?" I asked. Stupid. Of course he's ill. But I didn't think demons got ill. None of the stories mentioned that.

"Aye, a bit. Come, I'll introduce you to some of the men." He straightened to tower over me again, and led me off through the camp. He pointed out some of the young officers, who stared at me with cool eyes. At the mess tent, he stopped by a stocky man stirring thick stew in six pots above cook fires. Sweat glistened on his face from the heat of the fires, and he bowed deeply to the general as we approached.

"This is Toivo. He cooks for the officers. Stay on his good side and you'll have a more pleasant journey."

My tongue had a will of its own, and I said, "Did you offend him, sir?"

Toivo guffawed, and the general glanced down at me.

"What?"

I dropped my head, my heart pounding. I hadn't even made it an entire day before offending my sponsor. Would I die now, or would he merely beat me?

"What did you say?"

"I asked if you offended him, sir." I tried to keep my voice steady.

He smiled and clapped on hand on my shoulder. "I did not. No, it isn't his doing. When's dinner?" he asked.

"Not long. Will you be eating any?" Toivo raised his eyebrows skeptically.

"I think not tonight." The general's hand left my shoulder and he bent over again, hands on his knees. He breathed in and let the air out slowly. Another deep breath. I watched him out of the corner of my eye. He heaved again, almost silently, but nothing came up. Toivo watched him with a worried expression, though he didn't say anything. "You can send Elathlo's dinner to my tent though."

Toivo nodded. "Aye, sir." He turned away, though I could feel his eyes still on us.

"Why are you ill, sir?"

He answered with his eyes still closed. "Kemen."

"Kemen, sir."

"It seems your chief's idea of a good drink is a bit different than mine."

I wondered what he meant by that. Alamaa was the only drink he'd shared with Otso-ka; had it truly made him so sick? Otso-ka would not be pleased to know that his attempt to honor the much-feared general had resulted in such misery. Although he would have been pleased to kill the general early in the war, at this point it was more to our benefit to have him live.

My sponsor straightened slowly, with a deep, steadying breath. He led me back to his tent, where he set up a low table and a pallet on which I would sit for dinner. He sat with his legs crossed a few feet away and took a sip of water. A young soldier came only a few moments later.

"General Sendoa? The boy's dinner." The soldier bowed to him, entered the tent, placed the bowl on the table in front of me, and bowed again toward my sponsor.

"Thank you, Kyosti." The general nodded to him and he slipped out of the tent.

I poked at the stew, examining it before tasting it. They wouldn't poison me, would they? No, it wouldn't be so hard to kill me that they'd need to poison me. The smell was rich and meaty, and there was a thin sheen of fat on top of the thick broth. There were carrots and some sort of tuber as well as a stringy green substance I couldn't identify.

"You're not going to eat at all?" I asked, risking a glance at my sponsor. He had leaned forward, elbows on his knees, with his head hanging down between broad shoulders. His hair fell forward so I couldn't see his face.

"No. I doubt you have to fear the same reaction to our food though. It's cooked well enough." His voice was low and a little rough. I imagined his throat was raw if he'd been vomiting all day.

I took a tentative bite, then had all I could do not to devour the rest in an embarrassing display of gluttony. "What is it?"

"Venison. Maybe some mutton, if there was any left."

"It's good." I would have said delicious, if I'd known the Common word for it, but I was finding that my vocabulary was more limited than I'd realized. I chewed each bite of meat slowly, savoring the texture of each fiber between my teeth. I used the spoon to eat every morsel, and then glanced up. My sponsor had covered his face with his hands and had made no sound while I ate. I used a finger to wipe the inside of the bowl clean and then licked every trace of flavor from my skin.

"Sir? I mean Kemen. Should I take back the bowl?"

"Aye." He stood and walked with me through the growing darkness to the mess tent.

When we returned, another young soldier was waiting at the tent flap. He bowed to my sponsor and followed us inside.

"Are you ready, sir?" He ducked his head in another slight bow as he asked the question, and he glanced at me.

"Yes. The boy can stay." My sponsor stripped off his thick tunic and shirt and sat on the floor with his legs crossed. The soldier knelt behind him and opened a bag. He withdrew a packet of what appeared to be powdered herbs and a piece of white cloth folded into a square. He lit the lantern at the end of the table and pulled it closer.

My sponsor had his elbows on his knees, and he leaned forward a little farther with his head hanging down. A white bandage crossed his chest just under his armpits and crossed over the top of his left shoulder. The lantern light played across the lines of his ribs and the hard muscles of his arms and shoulders. He was even thinner than I'd thought, gaunt, as if he hadn't eaten enough in a very long time. The soldier carefully untied the bandage and peeled it away.

I stepped closer without a thought, my curiosity getting the better of me.

The soldier said, almost under his breath, "If you touch him, I'll cut your hand off."

I froze, my heart in my throat.

My sponsor spoke sharply in a language I did not understand, and the soldier murmured something with a bow to my sponsor's back. My sponsor said something else, this time more quietly, and the tension abated a little. The soldier kept a wary eye on me, and I tried to look as inoffensive as possible.

I learned later the soldier was named Captain Kudret Askano. My sponsor addressed him as Kudret, but I was to call him Captain Askano. My sponsor must have trusted him, because he was allowed to dress my sponsor's wound. It was not new, but it was still healing, the edges white with scar tissue that had not yet filled in the long gash. It was not oozing much, but it was not yet ready to be open to the air. Captain Askano cleaned the wound, dusted it with the powdered herbs, then held the thin square of cloth over it while he wound a long piece of cloth back around my sponsor's ribs and over the top of his shoulder to hold it in place. He tied the cloth with a different knot than the one my people used, and I tried to remember how he did it. While Captain Askano worked, my sponsor waited, his ribs moving with each slow breath.

I decided then that he was a patient man, because I'd seen many of the men in our tribes hurt and injured in various ways through the years. We don't lack for courage, but few people bear pain without complaining. The wound must have been painful; even a demon would feel pain, wouldn't it? But my sponsor did not show his pain except in a slight tightening of his voice as he spoke with the soldier and in one twitch of his left arm, which he then deliberately relaxed.

His patience with his own pain and the soldier who treated him did not mean that I was safe. Far from it. But it did mean that when he killed me, it was unlikely to be in a fit of rage. That was some slight reassurance, because it was more than I could expect from many of the other warriors Otso-ka might have chosen.

When Captain Askano finished, my sponsor pulled his shirt back on and stood. He staggered, and the captain caught his arm in a well-practiced grip that slid directly into the Erdemen soldier's greeting and farewell. Tarvil warriors grip their own hands in front of their body, really more like gripping wrists, so that the arms are parallel to each other. Erdemen soldiers reach out their right arms and clasp each other's elbows, forearms twisted together. It was disconcerting to me, because I saw too much opportunity for a man to use a knife in his left hand against an enemy whose arm was not able to guard against the sneak attack. Our greeting, in which both hands are empty and visible, is meant to show that we are unarmed. Perhaps the Erdemen gesture is meant to demonstrate the opposite, trust in the man you are greeting, even a measure of support. My sponsor flashed Captain Askano a quick, wry smile.

"Do you need anything?" the captain asked, his voice low.

"No. Thank you." My sponsor bowed to him, and the captain returned the bow more deeply before he slipped out of the tent.

My sponsor pulled the top blanket from his pallet near the back wall of the tent and flipped my blanket over the thick pads.

"We'll leave tomorrow morning. I hope you'll forgive me if I turn in early." He spread his blanket on the ground a few feet away. "Do you need anything? There's water in the canteen there if you get thirsty." He sat down on his blanket and pulled off his boots. He removed the belt that held his swords, folded it, and placed it within easy reach.

"Thank you, sir. Kemen."

"Blow out the lamp whenever you want." He scrubbed his hands across his face, sighed, then lay down and rolled over, right arm curled under his head and blanket pulled up to his hair.

I stared at him a moment, thoughts whirling. Was he really going to sleep? I could reach his weapons easily, not to mention my own boot knife. He hadn't taken it from me, perhaps didn't know I had it. I shouldn't have brought it; I had forgotten to remove it that morning.

Did he not fear me because he trusted me, or because it was some sort of trap? Alokas are not given weapons for many months, even under the kindest of sponsors, for many reasons. Many would attempt to kill their sponsors in retribution for cruelties both large and small that add up to festering resentment and hatred. Other times, it is to protect the alokas; there is nearly always a time in an aloka's service when he considers ending his own life. The work is too difficult and too unending, the punishments too harsh, the criticism too cutting. For years, we boys feared our time as alokas, and from what I had heard from the men, we had every reason to be afraid.

My sponsor did not move, and finally I turned to the pallet he had left me. It was made of cloth pads stitched together to fold over itself, then covered in several thick blankets that masked the seams between the sections. I removed my own boots and lay down on the it, keeping one eye always on my sponsor. Would he punish me for sleeping there? What kind of warrior gives an aloka the more comfortable accommodation?

I lay awake, tense and suspicious. After some time I stood and walked outside to relieve myself. My sponsor's tent was not far from the edge of camp, and I slipped through the tents without being noticed. The murmur of soldiers' voices continued around the fires, and I finally remembered that my father had once said the warrior tongue was called Kumar.

I almost threw my boot knife into the night. Keeping it was risking a brutal death. But I was afraid the sound would alert one of the sentries and make my demise worse. I put it on the ground and walked a few steps away, then went back to retrieve it. As dangerous as it was, I feared being without it more. Among an entire camp of Erdemen soldiers, perhaps having it would ensure that my death was quick. If they decided to kill me, they would cut me down immediately, rather than enjoy the slow demonstration of discipline through torture.

I returned to my sponsor's tent only a few moments later, grateful that no one had seen me, or at least no one had seen fit to question me. My sponsor moved when I crept through the tent flap again, but in the shadow I could not see his face. My heart was in my throat as I tiptoed back to the pallet. He did not move again or berate me, and so I lay down, feeling as if I were doing something wrong.

The pallet was not exactly soft, but it was softer than I was accustomed to, and the thick blankets beneath me held my warmth. I pulled my own blanket up to my ears and covered my face with it, inhaling the scent of my mother's tent. I had to sit up again to blow out the lantern, then settled back down.

The tent was made of dense fabric, but when the moon emerged from behind the clouds, its cold light filtered dimly through the tent walls. As my eyes adjusted, I made out the dark figure of my sponsor against the wall of the tent. Sleep came slowly, and as long as I could, I kept my eyes on that figure. I didn't yet trust that it was not some kind of trick, and I wanted to be ready. I dared not touch his weapons; I would be defenseless against his demon strength. But at least I wanted to know when my death was coming.

He rolled onto his back at some point, then gave a soft grunt and rolled back. A few minutes later, he rose and went outside, perhaps to retch, though I heard nothing. When he came back inside, the tent flap opened to let in the bright, cold moonlight, and I kept my eyes mostly closed, pretending to be asleep. He knelt for a moment, his shoulders bowed a little, then lay down again. Despite my fear, I felt a twinge of pity at the effort in his movements. He tipped the canteen up and sipped a little, then set it to the side and rubbed his hands over his face and through his hair. He moved his left arm around, then settled down again into silence, facing away from me.

I dozed, despite my wariness.

WHEN I WOKE AGAIN, the tent was lighter and my sponsor was gone, as was his belt with his weapons. I heard the faint noise of horses and murmured voices outside. A moment later, boots on and shoulders squared, I peered cautiously out the tent flap into a chilly morning. My sponsor stood some distance away, talking to a young soldier who wore what I assumed to be officer's stripes on the sleeves and breast of his uniform. A moment later, he saw me and beckoned me over. I followed him to the mess tent, where we received thick slices of hot bread with a melting pat of butter in the middle and a piece of roasted meat on a slim stick. We stood to the side and watched the soldiers line up for their breakfast.

I wanted to eat, but I wasn't sure if I was allowed to touch the food before my sponsor did, so I waited. His eyes flicked to the line of soldiers and back to the steaming meat. He sighed, then moved to the line.

"Here. I can't eat it." He handed the meat to a soldier in line.

"Sir?" The young man raised his eyebrows.

My sponsor only shook his head and turned back toward me. "Do you want this?" He held out the bread.

"Yes, sir!" I began to eat, trying to eat as quickly as possible without being rude enough to merit punishment.

"Slow down. We're not leaving yet." He glanced down at me and quirked up one eyebrow with wry amusement.

"Yes, sir." I cast about for what to do with the stick and he took it from me. I finished the bread as I followed him past a pile of sticks, on which he tossed mine, and then toward the larger tent where the women had slept. He stopped and spoke to a soldier who stood at the front of the tent. I didn't understand all the words, but I guessed that it had to do with the women inside, as the soldier glanced back at them several times as he nodded at my sponsor's commands.

Soon after, we were riding south. My sponsor helped me saddle my horse, because I was not yet tall enough to lift the saddle high easily. I could have done it, but he saw me struggling and reached over my shoulder to heft it up without a word. He watched me cinch the girth tight and check the bit and bridle before I mounted. Then he mounted his own horse, a magnificent grey mare that pranced beneath him, tall and proud.

We rode for hours, most of the convoy behind us. My sponsor dozed in the saddle at times, and I glanced sideways at him. Aside from the fact that his eyes were closed, I might not have been able to tell that he drifted off; his back was still straight, the horse perfectly controlled. He took sips of water at long intervals. Perhaps he grew overconfident and drank too much, because once he leaned to the side to heave up the water he'd just drunk. The sound made me a little sick myself.

Near noon, when my stomach was growling again, someone rode up beside my sponsor and offered him something.

"Not yet, thank you. Maybe tonight."

The soldier kicked his horse forward and around in front of us, then offered me a handful of dried meat, a bit of bread, and a packet of something I couldn't identify. He watched, trying vainly to suppress a smile, while I tried to figure out how to hold everything.

Finally he tucked the meat into the packet with the other things and said, "Hold this with your left hand along with the reins. Eat with your right."

"Thank you, sir." I felt my face flush.

I glanced at my sponsor as I ate. It might have been my imagination, but I thought he looked a little more pale, his eyes more tired. Perhaps it shouldn't have surprised me, but since I wasn't entirely sure he was human, any sign of humanity was unexpected. The dried things I could not identify tasted like some sort of fruit, perhaps a tart apple. So far in the north, we ate fruit rarely and I was unable to decide whether it was an apple or something new.

Some hours after lunch, after he'd leaned over the side of his horse to vomit a bit of water again, I asked, "Was it really the alamaa that made you so sick?"

"The drink your grandfather gave me?"

I nodded.

"Aye." His voice was mild, not showing any hint of irritation or anger.

"Why did you drink it? Didn't you have it last time, when you signed the truce?" I could not explain this to myself. If it made him sick now, it must have made him sick then, and probably even worse, because he'd been wounded, perhaps ill already when he came first to parley with us. At least Otso-ka had thought he was ill, and I could believe it. Why subject himself to the misery twice? The first time may have been a surprise, but this time he must have known it would happen.

"Aye. I didn't wish to insult your grandfather. The treaty benefits us both too much to cause needless offense." He glanced at me and one corner of his mouth rose in a faint smile. I could hear the rasp of his sore throat.

I hesitated, but finally said, "You might have told him it would make you ill."

He raised his eyebrows. "Would he have believed me?" He looked amused at the thought.

"Probably not." I tried to smile. "A high price for a treaty, isn't it? Was it worth it?" His calm manner had lulled me, and the boldness of my words was a surprise even to me. I braced myself for a rebuke or a blow for voicing such doubts, for questioning his decisions.

"We'll see. I hope so." He said nothing else, but he smiled a little as he looked ahead again.

He took only a piece of bread for dinner. He ripped off a corner of it and handed the rest to me.

"You don't want it, sir?"

"It wouldn't be wise." His smile was so quick I almost missed it, as I barely raised my eyes to his face. He sat beside me outside his tent while I ate both our thick pieces of bread, the centers melting away under rich pats of butter, then the roasted venison. The luxury of meat three times in one day nearly took my breath away, and I wanted to thank him for feeding me as if I were one of his soldiers. The first hour after I ate, the food always felt heavy in my stomach, but soon the feeling passed and instead I felt strong for the first time in months, my muscles no longer starving.

That night I couldn't keep my eyes open, despite my caution. I woke only once in the night, and stared across at his empty blanket. A moment later, his tall, dark figure slipped in the tent flap and knelt. He tipped up the canteen, poured a little water in his hand, and scrubbed it over his face, then wiped his face on the corner of his blanket. He lay down again, and this time the weariness in his movements was more obvious. He turned away from me and muffled a cough.

If he'd been my own father, as much as I disliked him, I might have offered him some sympathy. Even a hard man, like my father was, appreciates a bit of coddling, if you offer it with the appropriate amount of respect. But I didn't know if or how to offer sympathy without offending my sponsor. I did note that however terrible he might be feeling, he had not betrayed a temper with me, or with any of his men. From my father, I would have known to expect an ill temper, and I would have been prepared. My sponsor was more frightening because I could not predict him.

I WOKE AGAIN with sunlight streaming through the tent flap, which had been tied back. My sponsor's blanket was folded and waiting to be packed on his horse, and my sponsor was gone. A piece of bread was waiting for me with a thick smear of some sticky red substance over the top and a thin piece of crispy meat laid beside it. I stared at it for a moment. Had my sponsor brought me breakfast while I slept? Was he now recovered himself?

The red substance was shockingly sweet, and the meat was crispy and salty. The combination was delicious, and although my stomach was satisfied, I wished for more. I stepped outside to see my sponsor saddling his horse, my horse's reins looped over his shoulder. I hurriedly folded my blanket and packed my bag to reemerge as he spoke with a young woman. She had a green bruise over one eye, and she twisted her hands together nervously as she addressed him. She barely came up to his chest.

He said something to her, then bent over with his hands on knees, the posture now familiar as he tried to control his nausea. A few moments later he straightened again and said something to her that made her smile. He turned back to his horse and tightened the girth. I wasn't close enough to hear what they said, and I wasn't sure whether I should approach or not, so I hung back. She seemed to ask a question that surprised him, and they exchanged a few more words. She was older than I was, but she looked so shy and nervous that I couldn't help feeling sorry for her. A moment later, my sponsor boosted her up onto his own horse.

I approached then. My horse was not yet ready, and the general helped me lift the saddle. The men were already packing the tent behind us. I was grateful, for perhaps the first time, for my sponsor's standing, because I had no idea how to break down such a complicated and luxurious tent. The soldiers did it for him, and I bene-fited. I had been so terrified the first day that I didn't even realize how great this benefit was.

My sponsor dozed off and on throughout the morn-ing, eyes drifting closed as he rode. The girl wrapped her arms around his narrow waist and rested her head be-tween his shoulders. Sometimes they spoke to each other, the words too quiet for me to hear. I could tell he was kind to her, his voice gentle despite his discomfort. At noon, he dismounted and helped her down. She ate with the women. My sponsor went a little way from the rest of the men, lay down, and pulled the hood of his cloak over his face. One hand rested on his stomach and the other lay across his eyes. The sharp points of his hip bones jutted upward. The twinge of pity I'd felt earlier made me brave.

"Do you want me to bring you something, sir?"

"No, thank you." He sounded like he was half asleep.

I ate beside him, wondering when I would be in-structed to do something. Perhaps that was why he had been willing to take me as his aloka. He had no idea what the position entailed, and no expectations of me. He was still a warrior though, and he breathed *kestan* like I breathed air. Despite his illness, he was the alpha wolf in this pack, and I imagined in the whole of Erdem. Every-one shifted around him, never forgetting where he was, never forgetting to offer him respect, even when he was asleep.

Just because he didn't intend to work me to death didn't mean that I was safe, nor that he might not erupt in fury at any moment. It just meant that I was unable to predict what might make him angry.

The afternoon sun slanted across our faces as we rode south, the light like a caress after the long, bitter winter. We camped again before nightfall, and I realized the men were setting an easy pace to accommodate the women who traveled with us. My sponsor ate a few bites of bread for dinner and gave the rest to me. The young woman ate with us, though she didn't say much. My sponsor helped her to her feet and walked her to the women's tent.

Inside our tent, with the last rays of sunset lighting the west wall, he stood swaying a moment, and blinked as if he was dizzy. He flipped his blanket open and removed his belt. Even from a few feet away, I could see his hands shaking as he worked the buckle.

"I'm going to bed. Wake me if you need anything," he said.

A moment later, Captain Askano opened the tent flap and bowed. "Sir, are you ready?"

My sponsor sighed, then sat up. The captain changed his bandage in silence, and my sponsor thanked him with a voice so low I barely heard it. The captain left with another respectful bow, and my sponsor rolled up in his blanket without a word.

The camp was not entirely quiet; many of the soldiers were still awake, sharpening swords or talking in low voices around the fires. The silence in my sponsor's tent felt restful, and for the first time since the war began, I felt a thread of peace steadying my fearful heart.

I WOKE to the quiet snick of my sponsor sharpening his bootknife on a stone. He sat cross-legged with the tent flap barely pulled open to let in a stripe of light. I didn't move at first, afraid to bring attention to myself. Then he murmured, "Morning," over his shoulder, and I knew he'd heard me wake.

"Morning, sir."

In the bright, cold light, the grey tint of illness beneath my sponsor's olive skin was more pronounced, and I eyed him cautiously as I edged closer.

"Will you eat today?" I ventured.

"I'll try." He gave me a quick glance and slipped the knife into its sheath. "Come." He stood, quick and graceful, then staggered a step before he caught himself. "Sorry," he muttered, as if his unsteadiness was something to apologize for. I followed him to the mess tent. Breakfast was a soft, flat cake rolled into a tube, with three pieces of crispy, salty meat inside. I devoured mine in moments. My sponsor ate cautiously, and he stopped at half.

"Do you want the rest?" he asked.

I hesitated, then said, "If you're not going to eat it."

He licked his lips, then shook his head and handed it to me. I bit cautiously, half-expecting to taste a faint hint of demon saliva on the end he'd bitten from. The meat and flatcake tasted only like delicious meat and flatcake, and I felt a bit guilty as I finished it. My sponsor's eyes swept across the camp, watching the men pack their things and get ready to move out again.

It took five more days to reach the Erdemen military base that my sponsor called Fort Kuzeyler. We found a path down from the high tundra to the lower hills of the Erdemen north. My sponsor said that in practice, the border was marked by the sharp-edged delineation between tundra and hillside, a natural shelf that marked out their land as separate. It was easy to see why; the tundra offered little to them, and the shelf, varying in height from thirty to perhaps two hundred feet, kept their rich lands relatively safe from marauding barbarians like us. On Erdemen maps, the border was some short distance onto the tundra, a straight, arbitrary line, but it mattered little because no Erdemen lived there.

Perhaps the old kings of Erdem thought a straight line made more sense than a natural boundary. We Tarvil never knew nor cared where they said the border was; the shelf marked our safety.

Picking our way down the path, the specter of Stonehaven rose before me. I was going, I was being *taken*, to the Erdemen capital, and even if my sponsor had not yet killed me, everything I had ever known was receding behind me.

We descended into a land of green, evergreen trees a dozen times taller than a man, bright late spring growth on shorter trees, bushes covered in vibrant green leaves, and green moss by the side of the path. The richness and color assaulted my eyes, and the scents of a thousand growing things startled me with every breath.

By the time we reached the grand fort, my sponsor was no longer violently ill, but he was still cautious with food. What startled me more than his illness was his even temper about it. Any man I'd ever known, even the other boys of my own age, would have vented his misery upon others.

We stayed one night at the fort, and my sponsor was given the commander's room, the largest and best-furnished among the officer's quarters. There was only one bed, but there was a low couch against one wall. It was much too short for my sponsor, and besides, it wasn't fitting for me to sleep in the commander's bed while my sponsor slept on a couch. I put my pack and blanket on the couch while my sponsor was talking to the commander. When he noticed, he gave me a quick smile and said nothing. I was proud of myself; for once, I had done something that an aloka should do.

We rode out early the next morning. I jolted awake to my sponsor shaking my shoulder, my heart pounding, knowing that somehow I had done something wrong, but he said, "Come. We'll eat before we leave."

The women were left at Fort Kuzeyler, with the commander having received strict instructions from my sponsor on how they were to be escorted back to their families.

Now that the women were no longer with us, the men set a brisker pace. The first night after we departed Fort Kuzeyler, I fell onto my pallet exhausted and sore. I woke the next morning to find my sponsor already awake and speaking with someone outside. I bowed and went a little way into the woods to relieve myself before breakfast. When my pants were down around my ankles, I heard murmured voices close by. I tried to hurry, but a moment later, a tall, blond Erdemen soldier grinned down at me.

"Ah, the Tarvil brat." He looked delighted.

I heard a crunch behind me, and then something slapped my bare buttocks hard enough to make me cry out. The blow knocked me onto my knees, and the sting brought surprised tears to my eyes. I jumped up, pulling my pants up as quickly as I could while drawing my boot knife.

A moment later, my sponsor was there. He disciplined the men, and I was afraid he would also discipline me for having my boot knife. I cursed myself for not having left my knife behind when we moved camp, and tried to steel myself for my coming death. He told me to put my knife away. Perhaps he forgot about it, because he did not confiscate it from me, then or in the following days. Nor did he punish me for having it.

It did not entirely surprise me that my sponsor defended me against his men. An aloka belongs, in every sense of the word, to his sponsor. A sponsor may use, discipline, or kill his aloka in any way he chooses; an aloka is property. Perhaps by disciplining the men so harshly, he was asserting his own status; showing that despite his injury, he had not ceded his leadership position.

I was mortified, and my tears, barely concealed in the tent when my sponsor left me alone for some minutes, were tears of shame and frustration rather than pain. I wished I were stronger, better able to bear the humiliations that I knew were due to me as an aloka, and a Tarvil among Erdemen.

Part of the men's punishment was that they had to run alongside the horses for the next three days. We dismounted and ate our lunch in a long break, and I wondered if my sponsor extended the break out of consideration for the men who were running. After lunch, he rode while the men walked for an hour. When we began trotting again, he dismounted and ran with them. This perplexed me for hours, and I watched him whenever I could. I asked him about it later, whether he was tired, and whether he was human. He seemed confused by my questions, and said he was both human and tired.

Then I made the mistake I thought would cost me my life. We were talking about kestan, and I was trying to determine whether he truly did not understand or whether I was being tested in some way. He said that he knew the king Hakan Ithel would be a good king when he realized Hakan Ithel would give up the crown if he thought another man would be better for the people of Erdem.

I blurted, "That's stupid!" before I realized verbalizing that particular thought might have been the most foolish, dangerous thing I'd ever done.

My sponsor did not punish me, either then or later. He seemed confused by me, rather than angered or disappointed. He assured me that he would neither kill me, nor even beat me, and seemed puzzled, perhaps even a little troubled, by my fear.

I wasn't sure how to interpret that. I was relieved, certainly, but I was reminded again that I could not predict what would anger him, and thus I could earn punishment or death without even realizing it. His assertion that I would not be physically punished seemed far too generous to be possible. He was a warrior after all, feared by my people and accorded every possible respect among his own men. Even I, unfamiliar as I was with Erdemen custom, could see that the men looked at General Sendoa as a hero, waited for his every quiet word, and sprang to obey his every command.

The next day he questioned me about what I was meant to do as an aloka. Anything he wanted, of course. I mentioned the menial tasks that an aloka always performs, but I did not mention the services an aloka is sometimes required to perform. Things a warrior might do to a young boy alone in his tent, as part of the "toughening regimen" that my father had alluded to only rarely. If my sponsor didn't think of such things, I did not want to give him ideas.

I prepared him imea the next morning, the way Otso-ka liked it, with the addition of sosta. Not many men drink imea with sosta, which makes the drink sweeter and lighter. But I thought if my sponsor had never drunk imea before, it might make the spicy drink more palatable to him. I wanted him to enjoy something of my culture, to see that despite our poverty, we were not without pride.

He smiled and said he liked the drink, and we talked. I felt more comfortable with him than I had yet, but I did not let down my guard entirely. He gave me few tasks, only to water the horses and brush them down each night. Otherwise, I acted as his shadow, speaking only when spoken to.

My sponsor said, about Stonehaven, that "things would no doubt be very different" than I was accustomed to. I thought that he could not possibly imagine how different things already were from what I had imagined. Despite the ever-present tension in my belly, I knew myself to be fortunate. I had been an aloka for almost three weeks and had not yet been punished at all.

AS WE DREW CLOSER to Stonehaven, the land fell away before us, lower in elevation as we rode south. The air grew hot, though the Erdemen soldiers did not seem troubled by the heat. My sponsor said it was early summer. The men around me enjoyed the golden sunlight and the thousand shades of green that covered everything.

We crossed the Greentongue and Silvertongue Rivers over great stone bridges, and the Purling River over a ford, a wide shallow area where the horses splashed through up to their knees in cold, clear water. Pastures full of lush grass fed fat black and white cows and flocks of sheep. Fields of grain lined the road too, of half a dozen types I'd never seen. I wanted to ask my sponsor what they were, but I didn't want to display my ignorance. Most were not yet ready for harvesting, but some looked ready; perhaps they were winter crops.

Beside the roads and in some of the pastures, wild flowers bloomed with colorful abandon. Their hues of blue, white, yellow, pink, and red seemed too fantastic to be real. What must a nation be like, to have such flowers growing without effort or cultivation? We passed many towns too, though we camped in the woods. My sponsor seemed to think little of their bustle and wealth, but to me they were cities. I'd never seen a gathering of more than a few hundred people before, and some of these cities held several thousand.

My sponsor paused a moment at the top of a hill and we looked out over the valley in which Stonehaven nestled in a curve of the Purling River. I knew the city was old, the well-fortified center of an ancient, prosperous empire. Even so, looking on it amazed me. A wall circled the city center, dating from the early part of the Second Age. The city had long since spilled out of those restraints and was surrounded by a patchwork of newer walls, the youngest of which was five hundred years old. The stone buildings and paved streets spread out in a jumble along the riverbank and away from the water. I wondered whether the Purling River was large enough to provide water for such a great city, and I learned later that the city boasted many wells that supplemented the river's supply.

"This is Hyoski's Ridge. General Hyoski made his stand here in 456, Second Age, against the Eastern Tuyet tribes under Surakama." He glanced at me, and I tried to look as if I knew of that war. I don't think it worked.

He said, "When we ride into the city, stay close to me."

"Yes, sir." I wondered whether he thought the crowds would be hostile.

Beside my sponsor's mount, my horse looked small and scrubby, and I felt like its human equivalent riding with the Erdemen soldiers. They were all so tall and grand, and my sponsor was the greatest of all. Despite my fear, I felt a surge of pride as we trotted down the last hill toward the city. My grandfather had secured for me a truly magnificent position as aloka for such a warrior. Somehow, I had survived so far; perhaps I would live out the year after all.

Crowds in the streets cheered us. Well, not me, of course, but the Erdemen soldiers. I was glad to stay close by my sponsor's side. The city was overwhelming as we entered, full of stone buildings two and even three stories tall. There were wooden buildings too, of fine finished wood, much grander than the towns and villages we had seen on our journey. Some of them even had slate roofs rather than the more common wooden shingles or thatch I'd seen thus far.

Trees lined the main avenues, and the wide roads were of stone with a fine packed dirt surface, which was better for the horses. Other broad avenues intersected the one we rode on, and smaller alleys and streets too, paved with old flagstones or cobblestones. The smells and sounds of a city assaulted my senses. I was still accustomed to the barren north, clean and cold, and the busy prosperity of the city, full of people and animals, was very strange to me.

The palace rose up behind a great wall, a massive structure of white marble that gleamed in the sunlight. The gate was of dark wood and iron, and it opened for us as we approached. My sponsor waved a quick salute to the gateman as we entered.

We circled around the palace to enter a courtyard at the rear, some distance from a large stable. The soldiers had mostly dispersed, sent by my sponsor to wherever they were to be quartered, and there was only a small honor guard with us. Around us rose the gleaming walls of the palace, with many windows. I learned later, from my history tutor, that the city had been more or less at peace for many centuries, and that the royal palace had been built after the last war that surged through the capital. If I'd known what to look for, it would have been obvious; the palace was not built for defense, but for comfortable living, with windows to catch the light on even the first and second floors. Even the stable was grander than any house I'd ever seen, a spacious structure with white marble walls and a dark slate roof.

The king Hakan Ithel himself met us in the court-yard. I knew him by the thin gold circlet on his head, and by the way the soldiers and palace servants spread out behind him, but he was not as I'd imagined. I'd expected him to be like a god, a great and awesome warrior-king to command such devoted and fearsome soldiers. He was tall and handsome enough, but hardly a god. In-stead, he was young and slim. He looked intelligent and perceptive, only a few years older than I, though with confidence I could only dream of. Not at all frightening in his person.

It shocked me to see my sponsor, the great warrior General Kemen Sendoa, drop to one knee and bow his head to him with such obvious and deliberate respect. Then he stood, and they clasped each other's elbows in the Erdemen soldier's gesture of respect and friendship. The king nodded at me, and I ducked my head.

A servant woman took me to a room. She said her name was Sinta, and she would help me if I needed any-thing. The room would be mine, and I could leave my things there. There was a pitcher of water to drink, some Erdemen tea, and some pastries and cheese sitting on a tray on a little table by the window, which looked out on the courtyard. She said someone would come to help me prepare, because there would be a banquet that night.

I'd never been to a banquet before. We had festi-vals, certainly, but my grandfather did not have a palace. I didn't think a festival in even the grandest tent could compare to a king's banquet. She asked me if I had any other clothes, but I didn't. She said I would be measured for clothes the next day, but for now she would try to find some close to my size. I should rest, and someone would come for me later.

I explored the room. It was six steps by nine, a little larger than my mother's tent, and it had a great flat soft thing that I assumed was a sort of bed, though not like the pallets I had seen before. It was a little higher than my knees, covered in layers of rich fabric and pillows.

A man came and heated a bath for me in a small room attached to my sleeping room. Someone had already drawn the water into a tall metal basin, but he heated it with a small brazier. At first, I didn't know what it was for. The man barely blinked at my ignorance, and he explained that I was to undress and wash myself with soap to be clean for the banquet. The sensation of bathing in warm water was perhaps the most entrancing thing I had ever experienced, and I wondered whether all the rooms in the palace had this unimaginable luxury. The man waited while I washed and presented me with a thick towel when I finished.

He gave me new clothes to wear instead of my old ones. The pants were a little long, but more disconcerting was the difference in the fit. Tarvil clothes are worn in many layers because of the cold, and though I'd stripped my outermost layers off in the Erdemen heat, I felt naked and strange to be wearing only one pair of pants. They were close-fitting but not tight, cinched with a narrow tie around my waist. The bottoms tucked easily into my boots.

The shirt was also strange. We wear our inner shirts close-fitting to keep in the warmth of your body and outer shirts are larger, so as to be worn in many layers. This was a single layer, but it fit more loosely, with a triangular neckline and wide sleeves, though it did have cuffs at the wrists. The fabrics were excellent quality, far better than I'd ever seen even Otso-ka wear, and it all felt smooth and soft. Expensive. There was also a tunic went over it and fitted more closely. Over the tunic went a belt of dark, supple leather. When I looked in the mirror, it was strange to see myself in Erdemen clothes, and I wondered whether I was disloyal to wear them.

THE BANQUET was overwhelming. The food came in several courses, with wine to match each one. I couldn't even name all the things we ate. My wine was watered, because I was young, but by the end I felt slightly dizzy with the wine, the music, and the many voices speaking in Common and Kumar.

The music was very different than what I knew. Everything was brightly lit and glittering. My sponsor was dressed in splendid clothes, more severe than those of the king and other nobility, but still elaborately embroidered and cut of expensive fabrics. I wondered whether even Otso-ka knew how rich the Erdemen crown was, nor how powerful my sponsor was. If he had known, would he have dared ask for my position?

I sat next to a beautiful woman my sponsor introduced as Riona, and my sponsor sat on her other side, next to the king. My sponsor looked at her most of the night, and the king spoke with her several times. She seemed ill at ease, though she knew nearly everyone. Once, when I fumbled with my utensils, not sure which one I should use, she leaned over and whispered in my ear, "I don't know what I'm doing either."

She had kind eyes and a beautiful smile. I wondered who she was. She seemed like a queen, but the queen was sitting on the king's other side. The queen was younger, only a few years older than I was, but infinitely more poised and confident. She had a rippling laugh that seemed to make the air sparkle, and it was obvious the king and queen were very much in love.

I was very tired by the end of the banquet, especially since I was so nervous that I would make a mistake. I watched my sponsor and Riona to see what I should do. The day had been long, and I was glad when afterward Sinta took me back to my room.

I would probably never have found it by myself. The palace was unimaginably grand, beautiful hallways of rich white marble and dark wood and gilt, with beautiful tapestries everywhere. Alone, I would have become hopelessly lost. There were new clothes for me to sleep in, and Sinta said my sponsor would come for me the next morning.

I didn't sleep especially well. The bed was much softer than my pallet at home, and it felt strange and unfamiliar. Quiet sounds came from the hallway and the courtyard outside. There was nothing to complain of, but everything was new and different. I woke several times and looked around in the dim reflected moonlight. Even the ceiling was decorated, subtle carved floral designs lining the walls and in a great seal in the center of the room.

I WOKE to a quiet knock. It was dawn, the early light streaming in the window. I padded over to the door, unsure whether I'd really heard a knock at all, but when I opened it I gasped.

It was the great warrior himself. "Get dressed. I'd like to see what you already know before we begin your training."

I bowed. He sat at the table while I dressed hurriedly. I couldn't believe I had begun so poorly; an aloka should never make his sponsor wait for anything. I tried to apologize, but he shook his head. "No matter. I'd let you sleep later, but I need to be finished early this morning."

He mostly watched me that day. I showed him what I knew with the scimitar and the bow. He had me demonstrate punches, but I knew no kicks at all. He asked me to show how I would fall without hurting myself, and I did not know that either. Nor did I know how to throw him to the ground using his hand or wrist, or how to choke him if we were grappling.

I felt very inadequate as he asked me more and more things that I did not know. He showed no displeasure, and at the end he smiled.

"Good. You have few bad habits at least. Today we will do strengthening exercises and run, and your training will begin tomorrow."

He did all the exercises with me, demonstrating proper form and helping me when I could not do them correctly. He was very patient, but I was terribly afraid of disappointing him. Until that day, he'd barely spoken to me; I'd been a shadow as he went about his duties on the way back from the north. Now, I was the focus of his attention. I expected him to strike me any moment for an offense I might not realize I'd committed, or simply for my weakness and clumsiness.

He didn't raise his voice, and he even encouraged me at times, but my image of him then was more informed by what my grandfather had told me than by what I could see. After the strengthening exercises, my arms and legs were shaking with the strain. He told me to sit and rest for a bit before we ran.

The well was close by, and he drew water for us both and brought it to me before I realized what he was doing. An aloka should never be served by his sponsor; it is the aloka's place to serve. I was shocked, but he did not seem to notice my confusion and dismay.

After that we ran. He took us up a long hill and around a pasture with some beautiful horses grazing. It seemed like leagues and leagues, and I was stumbling by the end, although I tried desperately to keep pace with him. At last he slowed to a walk, and I nearly wept with relief.

He clapped a hand to my shoulder. "Put your hands above your head. Breathe. Keep walking to cool down." He was not even breathing hard, but he walked with me. "You did well today. Go get a bath and Tanith will bring you to breakfast."

I collapsed into my bath. It was strange and luxurious to bathe again so soon. Rarely in my life had I sweated. I had exerted myself, certainly, but never had I felt beads of sweat forming on my forehead and trickling down the sides of my face. The slick sweat left me feeling sticky and rank, and the bath made me feel human again.

Once I was dressed, Tanith, a young, pretty servant woman, met me at my door and led me through the halls to a small room overlooking a garden outside.

My sponsor was already there, speaking with a silver-haired lady I guessed to be a servant. We don't have servants in the north, of course, but I had already gathered that there was a great difference in station between servants and nobility. Nobility were people of standing, such as my sponsor, the king, queen, and the guests at the banquet the previous night. Servants did things for them, and were mostly ignored. In the north, you could say that women and children were servants, and warriors and chiefs were nobility. So I was surprised when my sponsor bowed to her so courteously. She blushed, smiled, and ducked her head, and he watched her leave with a faint smile still on his lips.

"Sit. Breakfast will be here in a moment." He stood in the doorway as if he were waiting for someone, and a moment later he smiled more broadly.

Quick footsteps echoed in the hall, and he opened the door wider to let a girl of about my age slip under his arm, carrying a tray with both hands. She set the tray on the table as quickly as she could, then spun to jump into his arms. He whirled her around with a grin.

"You're back! How was it? I didn't get to see you before the banquet last night! Are you better? You look better." Her words tumbled over each other in her excitement.

"Much better, thank you." He bowed and kissed her fingertips formally, and she blushed, giggling. She hugged him again, and he wrapped his arms around her.

Then he flinched, and she pulled back. "Sorry. It still hurts. I didn't think." Her lips trembled. It made her look very feminine and pretty, and I realized I was staring.

"It's fine." He smiled back at her, then looked at the tray. "That's enough to feed all of us. Would you like to stay?"

"May I?"

He pulled out a chair for her and then slid into the chair between us. "This is Elathlo. He'll be staying with us for a while. Elathlo, this is Lani, Nalani when she's in trouble."

She blushed again and looked at the table. He reached out to put the plates in front of us. There were three, as if she'd hoped or expected to be asked to join us. She served the food, nimble hands reaching between his to lift the basket of steaming bread toward me, then the lid covering the plate of eggs and meat they called bacon, some sweet, sticky grainy substance that my sponsor called rice, and a bowl of fruit.

My sponsor helped for a moment, until she said, "Please let me, Kemen. I'm supposed to be serving, after all."

"As you wish." He smiled at her, and she grinned impishly. I had the feeling she thought she was getting away with something.

My sponsor ate quickly, though not without courtesy. Lani shot curious glances at me from under long, pale eyelashes, and I sat up even straighter. My muscles ached from the exercise of that morning, but my sponsor looked fresh and energetic, ready to go conquer something.

"How is your father's health?" my sponsor asked, voice quiet.

Lani took a deep breath and let it out slowly. "About the same. Maybe a little worse. He's weaker."

My sponsor reached out to touch her hand for a moment, his long fingers curling around her smaller ones. She smiled, and even to me it looked a little forced.

"Thank you for breakfast. I have a meeting in a few minutes. Would you escort Elathlo to his room? His tutor will be there in an hour or so. I should be there around the same time."

"Yes, sir. I need to take the tray back too."

"You have some time." He bowed to her again.

"I'm glad you're back, Kemen." She blushed and scuffed one foot on the floor.

He smiled, his green eyes warm. "So am I."

Then he was gone, striding off down the hall, steps fading in the distance. Lani and I stared at each other across the remains of our breakfast.

"So, you're a Tarvil."

I nodded.

"You know your people..." she stopped, her voice tight. "Never mind." She glared at me and twisted the napkin in her hands. "Anyway, he's back now. Don't get any ideas."

Two

D espite my well-intentioned words to Hakan, I asked Riona to marry me on the second of Loiste, only a week after I returned from the north. I asked her while we danced during a small dinner party with some of the Stonehaven nobility. I could bear to wait no longer, and I resolved to continue courting her long after the wedding. She deserved that.

I'd thought on Hakan's words though. *You must be blind. She's only waiting for you to ask.*

I've never pretended to know women well, nor to guess what they are thinking or feeling, and I wondered if I had been blind to Riona's feelings in a misguided attempt to respect her. She had been so kind, had blushed and smiled when I kissed her fingers. She had... I could scarcely imagine it! She had told me she loved me, when I confessed to her my deepest shame. Even then, when she made it so clear, I doubted.

So I was bold when I asked her. I imagined that if Hakan was wrong, and she wasn't ready, I would take it with good grace. I would court her longer, with more kindness and consideration. I would be stronger and wiser in this rejection than in the last. I would not give up my suit.

But she accepted!

I was… shocked does not convey the joy I felt, but no other word begins to convey my surprise.

We scheduled the wedding for the beginning of Sato, four weeks away in midsummer. We didn't want to wait even that long, but Hakan suggested gently that we might delay a little so that preparations would be less frenzied.

"What preparations, Hakan? This isn't a royal wedding."

He almost rolled his eyes. "You're a royal minister now, Kemen. There are preparations which must be made."

"Such as what?"

"Preparations." He smiled slightly at my puzzled look. "Riona needs dresses, for one thing."

"Plural dresses?" I raised my eyebrows.

"Yes. Didn't you pay attention during my wedding?" He smiled a little more. "White and gold for the ceremony. Green and gold for the banquet. And presumably night things. She'll have to talk to someone else about those." He grinned at my embarrassment. "You're older than I am, Kemen. You do know how babies are made, don't you?"

He laughed aloud at my attempt to scowl at him even as I was biting back laughter.

That night over an intimate dinner with Riona, I asked her if she minded the delay.

She blushed most becomingly. "It's fine. I…" she hesitated. "I'm actually a little nervous. Are a lot of people going to come?"

"I have no idea. I think Hakan is plotting something." I wrapped my arms around her. "It's our wedding, Riona. I want it to be what *you* want."

"What do you want it to be like?" She looked up at me.

"Small. Preferably today." I smiled. "But if you'll be my wife, I don't care about the details."

My joy consumed me.

IN THE MORNINGS I woke early to train Elathlo. He was a good student, not overly talented, but he made up for it with hard work and the humble, eager attitude that is a student's greatest asset. He listened well, and it was obvious he wanted to please me. When we began to spar the third week I discovered our first real difficulty.

He was afraid of being hit. It wasn't the caution I might have expected of a new student though, for when I did hit him, he didn't complain. He didn't fear the normal bruises of training; instead, it was as if he expected me to attack him with my full strength at any time. I worked with him gradually to build his confidence and trust, but I also wondered what he'd experienced to make him so cautious.

I encouraged him to strike back, to kick and punch me. A student does not learn how to strike a person by striking air; he learns by striking a person.

I didn't question him about it. I wasn't sure I had the right to yet, but I tried to demonstrate by my actions that he didn't need to fear me. I must have seemed terrifying, but I liked the boy. He was always respectful and quick to obey. He worked hard, sweating and blinking back tears of frustration at times, but he didn't complain. He was embarrassed by his tears, but I pushed him and he was young, so occasional tears didn't surprise me. He was the kind of student every teacher desires, and I discovered again the joy of teaching.

After his training, I trained myself. I was cautious at first because my shoulder was still weak and sore, and it was some time before I could really exert myself. But that time too was good. The sweat, the pounding of the blood in my veins, the exquisite perfection of the moves done well. It had been too long since I'd tested myself in training. I was slow and far from fit, but the work was glorious. I did all the training sequences with open hands and with every weapon, the staff, the scimitar, the longsword, the short swords, the boot knife, even the sequences using a horse bridle, a boat oar, a scythe, an axe, and other unusual weapons.

Those hours were incredibly self-indulgent, because afterwards I was no good to anyone for some time. I would stagger inside and bathe away the sweat and dirt, and only then could I present myself to Hakan or Riona.

A few days after I asked Ria to marry me, I pushed myself a bit too hard in my morning exercises. I'd been cautious for over a week after returning to Stonehaven, and perhaps I grew overconfident. I missed the effort and pleasant exhaustion, the pounding of my blood in my ears, the feel of moves executed to perfection. The morning was also hotter than previous days. I had already sent Elathlo in to bathe before breakfast, and so I did not have him to slow me down. Sweat slid down my back as I leaned against the edge of the well, suddenly light-headed, my shoulder throbbing again. Even my ribs ached after the stretching we'd done. I lay on the ground with my arm over my eyes to block the sun. Flat on my back, the dizziness passed, but I let myself rest for several minutes, my breath growing slow and steady.

"Would you like some water?"

The question startled me. When I opened my eyes, I saw Lani smiling down at me and already drawing a bucket of water.

"Please." I sat up and almost groaned. I smiled my thanks when she handed me the full dipper of water.

"Are you okay?" She looked at me, biting her lip.

"Just a bit tired."

"You work too hard." She looked down at her hands twisting in her lap.

"Sometimes." I watched her face, trying to discern what was worrying her. "I haven't spoken to your father yet. I'm sorry."

She shrugged one shoulder. "It's fine."

"I'm sorry, Lani. I should have before now. I promised."

She shrugged again. "You've had a lot on your mind."

"May I speak to your parents tonight?" I asked.

She glanced up, finally meeting my eyes. "You really mean it?"

"I told you I would."

"Yes. You did." She gave me a shaky smile. "Any time. Father doesn't go out anymore. He'll be in all night. Mother and I are finished after washing the dinner dishes."

"I'll come by after dinner, then."

I KNOCKED on their door with a peculiar sense of trepidation. Ena opened it immediately and curtseyed to me, looking as nervous as I felt. When I stepped inside, she introduced me to Joka, her husband. He could not have been much older than I, not more than forty, but he looked older, as if the years had been long and difficult. Grey streaked his hair, and his eyes were tired. He coughed when he rose to bow to me. Lani curtseyed politely from beside him.

I licked my lips, wishing I'd rehearsed my words. "I don't know if Lani told you what I meant to say."

Lani shook her head hurriedly, and Joka glanced at her, a hint of irritation in his eyes.

"I know you're worried about her and you want to provide for her in case... your health declines." I tried to phrase things as gently as possible, but Joka still frowned.

"She should not have complained to you. I'm sorry to have bothered you, sir," he said.

I shook my head. "She didn't complain. She understands why you're worried. But I wanted to give you my assurance that she won't be without protection. She will always have a place in our house, with Ria and me. As will you, if you want it." I smiled at their startled looks. "She'll have a dowry if she needs it."

Joka narrowed his eyes. "What exactly do you mean?"

Ena put a restraining hand on his arm. "Thank you, sir. But our daughter's marriage is our affair." Her voice was gentler than her husband's, and I could see she understood me better than he did.

Joka's frown deepened. "What exactly do you want from her?"

Lani twitched, then failed at her effort to keep silent. "Father, that's just it! Do you think Ria would love him so much if he was like that?"

"May I sit?" I asked. Perhaps Joka would be more friendly if I did not tower above him.

80

They nodded belatedly, and I sat at the table, leaning forward to rest my arms on the edge. I held Joka's gaze and made my voice as gentle as I could. "Your daughter is a friend, nothing more. I never expected her friendship, I never asked for it, but I cherish it. As long as Ria and I have a roof over our heads, Lani will have a home."

Ena smiled a little, and even Joka softened at my words. Then, filled with the thought of Ria in my life, I said, "I'm happier with Ria than I've ever been. Inexplicably, she seems happy with me too. I want that joy for Lani."

Joka and Ena glanced at each other, and he slipped his hand over hers. He nodded, and in a gruff voice he said, "I understand."

Ena smiled at me, her eyes showing her gratitude. "Thank you, General."

"Soon enough we'll be almost family, won't we? Call me Kemen."

Joka smiled reluctantly. "As you wish, sir. Kemen."

A few moments later, I left. Lani stood at the door, and I bowed to her because it made her smile.

"Kemen?"

I looked at her with raised eyebrows.

"Thank you." She almost whispered it, her eyes brimming with sudden tears. She brushed at them. "Sorry."

"Thank you, Lani." I waited until she met my eyes and smiled back at me.

I'D ENGAGED KAEDE BEKENDI as a tutor for Elathlo. Bekendi had been one of my history instructors as a young student in training, and I remembered him as demanding but fair, kinder than some of the other instructors.

Elathlo was already frightened enough, and I didn't want a tutor who would be harsh with him. Bekendi worked with him after his training until lunch. Sometimes I ate with him, sometimes with Riona, and sometimes with Hakan and Kveta. After lunch, Bekendi often worked with Elathlo again for a few hours, and then Elathlo had additional studying to do for the next day. Bekendi and I were not close, but it was good to see him again after so many years.

I worked for Hakan during those hours after my training. I advised him on the military posts that needed to be strengthened, and a few that required repairs before they could be manned. I recommended young officers for additional training, and then I was faced with the challenge of how to provide it. That too, required planning.

Beginning in Sensaasti in the fall, they would be recalled to Stonehaven in small groups and I would lead them in discussions of strategy, of military policy, and theory. I interviewed scholars whom Hakan recommended, men who could lecture on psychology, history, theories of culture and human motivation, and economics. Organizing the officers' rotations, finding lecturers, and planning discussion topics took weeks, and that did not even begin to cover the work once the sessions began.

I also planned the curriculum for the Tarvil-Erdemen school that we would open in Ironcrest as part of the treaty. That was a new challenge too, one that took a great deal of thought. Our purpose was to create some level of trust and unity between the Tarvil and Erdemen students. But trust and understanding cannot be created by fiat; they must grow organically. I didn't want to test the students as soldiers are tested, yet some level of challenge that they could conquer together would be beneficial. Duplicating the experiences of the Erdemen military schools, which was my only reference point, would not be ideal. It would be neither wise nor appropriate to reveal that much of Erdemen military strategy and training to foreign children.

I wanted to let them teach each other, to show that despite their differences, each side had something to offer. I wondered whether perhaps I was giving the Tarvil children too much credit; did they truly have anything to offer aside from the ability to survive on the cold tundra? What was that worth?

Hakan had begun work on the curriculum for the school he wanted to start for Common children, and we discussed that at length as well. The Tarvil-Erdemen school curriculum we planned was fairly similar, with more emphasis on cultural exchange and less on Erdemen history.

I also met the other ministers, who presided over the justice system, the currency, and the trade guilds, as well as many of the noblemen and gentry who held property for Hakan under various arrangements with the crown. I regretted my inadequate understanding of the nobility and all the ways that Hakan's father had held them in check; I found myself less prepared to give Hakan advice than either of us would have wished. Many of the nobility held land under inheritance arrangements, although they owed taxes to the crown in order to maintain ownership of their holdings. Others, Hakan told me, did not own the land but only leased it from the crown, though it was impossible to tell from their title or standing in society. A few held titles bequeathed by inheritance but owned little property, and seemed to live on the perpetual credit that merchants felt obligated to extend to nobility. I wondered whether such merchants ever recouped the costs of such patronage. Hakan didn't think it fair either, but he said that often such men, noblemen by title but in my estimation nothing but well-dressed rogues, paid their bills through gambling winnings. At least they sometimes paid.

Ria retired early because she rose early to work. I often put off my work for Hakan so I could spend my afternoons with her. I did whatever work she was doing, laundry or preparations for meals or cleaning. The servants said I didn't need to, and I could tell it made them a little uncomfortable. Not me, not anymore, but my status, which still seemed strange to me, as if I didn't quite merit the titles I had been given. I knew how to command, and how to accept respect from soldiers, but not how to accept deference simply for walking into a room. Not from civilians.

To be honest, I didn't do it out of some magnanimous attempt to show my opinion of social status. I did it because I wanted to spend every possible moment with Riona. While we worked, sometimes she would sing, but even when she didn't, I could steal glances at her face as she concentrated, at her skillful hands forming ornate pastries, at the graceful sway of her hips as she walked. When I helped, she might be done faster, and then we could slip out to the gardens for an hour to walk hand in hand, or lay on a blanket in the sunlight and listen to her read, listen to the leaves in the summer breeze.

Late at night I turned to my work for Hakan. I wished again that I could write, because I had to keep it all in my head. Finally I requested a scribe to attend me every evening after dinner. That made my work much easier, for I could dictate my plans and questions and let them go from my mind until I presented them to Hakan the next day.

I THOUGHT LITTLE of the tiring schedule since I was so unashamedly happy, until I fell asleep in the garden while Ria was reading to me. She had one hand entangled in my hair, the gentle movement of her fingers against my scalp soothing me inexorably to sleep. I faded sometime in the story of the Third Battle of Highden's Gap. I don't remember what I dreamed of, but I woke to her hand on my cheek.

"Dearest, wake up."

It took me a minute to realize where I was. I imagine the dream was of some battle in the north, because I remember that I was cold in it and I was startled by the warmth when I woke.

Ria's eyes were worried. "What did you dream of?"

"I don't know." I sat up and ran my hands over my face and through my hair. "I'm sorry. I didn't mean to doze."

Still she looked at me as if she were concerned. "You cried out, Kemen. What was it?"

"I don't remember. I'm sorry." I lay back down with my head in her lap and resolved to listen to the end of the story.

The next afternoon I fell asleep again, this time in the middle of an account of the battle of Whiteson. I loved the sound of her voice reading anything at all, but the histories made me think of parallels that might be useful for Hakan to remember. I knew history well, but he was even better versed than I and had a quick mind to analyze what he read. Nevertheless, sometimes I had something to offer.

The sun was on my face, so my eyes were closed anyway, and in my dream I was in the battle of Whiteson. I don't remember much of the dream itself, only that Yasu and Yori were both there, and Yuudai. Kudret fought by my side. I dreamed of a great tree in

85

the middle of the battlefield, and we were defending it, Erdemen soldiers dying to keep the space around the tree clear. My dream conjured this; the battle of Whiteson was between the Rikutans and the Tarvil, there were no Erdemen soldiers there at all. On the tree hung the bodies of Erdemen soldiers. I remember putting a noose about Hakan's neck, and he asked me why I did it. I woke then, and it took me a few moments to steady my breathing.

Riona caressed my cheek, ran her fingers through my hair, but I could not shake the memory of Hakan's eyes when he asked me why. I felt ill at the thought, and finally I had to get up. I exercised again in the heat of the day, using the exhaustion to push away the image.

I don't mean it to sound as though I always had unpleasant dreams; surely I had pleasant ones too, and often I slept without dreams at all. But it is the unpleasant ones I remember most clearly.

I worked with Hakan for the next few afternoons and saw Riona at lunch and in the evenings. But when we next went to the garden to read, I couldn't stay awake even for the first children's story. Her voice was so soothing and I was so tired that I dozed almost immediately, waking with a sudden jolt to the sound of my own voice. I don't remember that dream either; it's funny how dreams can be so real and immediate, yet fade so quickly. Ria was worried and questioned me several times, as if she thought I was being stoic, but I truly didn't remember much of it.

"You're so tired, love. Are you not sleeping at night?"

Before, I would have brushed aside her concern. I was happy; I worked each day with joy and love for my dear Ria and for Hakan. This time I thought better of it because she deserved honesty.

"Probably not enough." A few hours a night, but I didn't mind. I smiled because she looked worried and I wanted to soothe her. "Ria, don't worry. I'm sorry I fell asleep. I'm fine."

"Must the work be done now?"

"It must be done."

"But now? Not in a day or two?"

I raised my eyebrows at her. "Are you really that worried? Every old soldier has unpleasant dreams." I sat up so that I could see her better.

She bit her lip and hesitated before she said softly, "I don't like to see you unhappy."

I kissed her fingers one by one. I love her hands. They're strong and yet so delicately beautiful, so gentle. "Sweet Ria, I have never been happier."

"Will you work so hard even after we're married?"

It was a fair question, but one I hadn't really stopped to consider. I'd planned for Hakan, for the school, for the officers' training, but I had not planned for our life together. What would she do? Certainly she should no longer scrub floors.

In fact, I hadn't even inquired about whether and how much Hakan was paying me. I hadn't thought about it. Officially I had a title, several titles, so I supposed I must be earning some money. At the palace everything was provided for me, and when I'd gone north, I'd requisitioned everything I needed. Riona would want a house of her own; it wouldn't be a palace, certainly, but even border women have their small houses to tend.

"I'm sorry," she whispered.

I was thinking so hard that her apology startled me. "Don't apologize. I suppose I won't. You're right, Ria. Not all the work must be done now. It won't be much longer."

"Hakan, the wedding should be small."

"Agreed. Only a few dozen people."

I glared at him. "No! Not a few dozen. Only people Riona wants."

He sighed. "Kemen, a certain level of ceremony is required for someone of your status. It would only be the other top-level ministers, their wives, and your personal friends. That's all."

"It will be who Riona wants. No more and no less."

He met my eyes for a long moment and finally sighed. "As you wish. You know the other Ministers will feel slighted."

"That is none of my concern." My voice was cool, and I felt a little guilty for it, since he'd given in to my request.

"But it should be, Kemen. Kveta says the nobility in Rikuto are fickle and subtle and dangerous as vipers. Ours can be much the same. It isn't wise to antagonize them needlessly."

I sighed as well, no longer irritated. "Riona has been more than patient with me. If I can make this day what she wants, I will."

Besides, I told myself, what would they care? It wasn't as if they liked me anyway. They barely knew me.

I spoke to Ria that evening over dinner to see what she wanted. She hesitated, then said, "It would be un-wise to limit it only to the people I want, Kemen."

"I want you to be happy."

She licked her lips. "The king is right, and I think you know it."

I almost groaned. She had waited for me to cease be-ing so stupid, she had been gentle when I needed gentle-ness, she had been kind, she had been brave, and she had given me hope and strength when I had none of my own. Now she was wise, and though I knew she was right, it frustrated me to concede to the demands of my new status. As a soldier, I could have had as small a wedding as I wished, or as large a wedding as I could afford, without worrying about political repercussions.

"What do *you* want, Ria?" I asked again.

"I wish for you to be wise." She smiled up at me, clear blue eyes gentle and understanding. "Have the wedding a Minister and Ambassador should have. We'll have time to ourselves later."

I let my forehead rest against hers and closed my eyes. "As you wish, Ria." *I love you, Ria.*

I told Hakan the next morning that he should invite whomever he thought was appropriate.

In the end, the Ministers were all invited, as were most of the higher nobility and some of the lower nobility within easy traveling distance of Stonehaven. I didn't even know many of their names. Of course Riona's friends from among the servants, Kepa, Hayato, Kudret, Eneko, Akio, and Kyosti were also invited.

THREE

My tutor was named Kaede Bekendi, a retired army officer with a shock of unruly white hair. My sponsor had known him before and written so that he would be ready when we arrived.

The first morning, after breakfast with Lani, I sat nervously in my room waiting for my sponsor or my tutor to arrive. My sponsor arrived first, which relieved me, and a few moments later Tanith brought my tutor to the door.

My sponsor ushered him into the room and bowed to Bekendi, who returned the bow so deeply it was obvious even to me that he revered my sponsor. They gave each other the soldier's greeting, then they sat at a table to discuss my sponsor's expectations.

"Thank you for agreeing to tutor Elathlo on such short notice," my sponsor said. The door opened a crack and my sponsor nodded that Lani could enter with a tray of tea.

"I was pleased to hear from you, General. I'm honored that you remembered me after all this time." Bekendi bowed again. He was obviously a man of standing, well-dressed, who kept the erect bearing of a long-time soldier.

My sponsor smiled. "I remember also that you were an excellent instructor." He turned to me. "Excuse us a moment, Elathlo." Then he switched into Kumar. I wondered what he wanted to say without me understanding him.

Bekendi glanced at me several times, nodding at intervals. I imagined my sponsor telling him that he was permitted to beat me when I did not study hard enough, or perhaps warning him of my woefully inadequate education. My sponsor had not yet been cruel to me, but I did not imagine that others were as kind.

Only a few minutes later, my sponsor said, in Common, "Elathlo, I have work I must do for Hakan now. You may address your tutor as Colonel Bekendi or Sir. He will supervise and instruct you in your academic studies. Obey him as you obey me."

"Yes, sir." I tried to keep my voice from shaking but a tiny quaver betrayed my fear.

My sponsor glanced at me again. Though his expression didn't change, his voice softened a little. "You'll have your lessons in your room or in one of the studies, as Colonel Bekendi prefers. Someone will come and fetch you for lunch in a few hours, and I'll see you at dinner, if not before." He bowed to us both and then strode out.

I wished I could feel as confident as he did. Colonel Bekendi gave me a faint frown, though I thought it might be more of consternation than irritation.

That first day, as my sponsor had, he seemed to conduct a sort of survey of my knowledge. I believe he found it sadly lacking, and after an hour or so, he suggested that I begin taking notes. He had to explain what that meant, and he provided me paper and a quill pen with which to write.

Paper was a luxury I'd rarely seen before, and writing merely for the sake of remembering ideas made me feel as if I were committing some sort of crime. I was barely literate, and could not keep up with the flow of his words. He was more patient than I'd expected. Once he said something under his breath that I did not understand, an exclamation of frustration or annoyance. But he did not raise his voice, nor strike me, and I was grateful.

Sinta came to retrieve me and took me to the kitchen for my lunch. I ate surrounded by the bustle of work, but I was apart from it. No one spoke to me, but I felt their eyes on me while I ate. I had the feeling I was there so that I could be supervised.

I WAS USED to waking early; our nomadic life in the north didn't permit anyone to be lazy. But although I was accustomed to rising while the sky was still dark, the sun rose later in the north, and my sponsor's exercises were exhausting in a way I had never experienced before. Every morning, as the courtyard turned from dim grey to sunlit gold, my sponsor and I trained for two hours. He taught me techniques for fighting without weapons for the first two months. After training, we would run and do strengthening exercises.

My sponsor was patient with my clumsiness and didn't mock me when I blinked away tears of frustration. He didn't raise his voice at me, and he never hit me in anger. He told me how and why each technique should be done the way he said. I'd never thought of fighting as so technically complex, so precise, but I couldn't deny that it seemed effective. He desired perfection, but he was not cruel when I failed to live up to his standards. For a week we did only drills, hitting and blocking imaginary opponents. The next week we began partner drills, where he would punch or kick at me and I would attempt to block his attack. He did hit me, but not hard, not as my father or Otso-ka often had.

After we'd been in Stonehaven about three weeks, he told me we would begin sparring the next morning. I barely slept because of my fear.

I should have known, even by then, that he was not a cruel man. Busy, focused, stern, but never cruel. He wouldn't kill me simply for being a boy, for being weaker and slower than he was. But I'd been trained by a lifetime with Father and Otso-ka to expect cruelty from the strong.

Perhaps he saw my fear, because although he hit me when we sparred, I ended the day with no more bruises than I'd started with. His attacks were slow and easy to block, and he encouraged me to hit him back, to counter-attack as we had practiced. When we finished, I bowed to him with more gratitude than he could have imagined.

I ATE BREAKFAST with my sponsor a few days later. Our tray arrived with an envelope on it. An envelope of creamy paper edged in gold, sealed with green wax stamped with the sign of my sponsor's title as Minister of Military Affairs. The front had an impressive swirl of calligraphy on it.

My sponsor picked up the envelope and held it out to me.

"Me, sir?"

He nodded and waited for me to take it, eyes sparkling. *Elathlo, son of Jerenth, son of Otso.* I stared at the elaborate lettering, so ornate that at first I had not recognized my own name.

"What is it?" I asked.

"Open it and see." He was smiling a little, amused by my confusion.

I broke the seal, careful not to destroy the little emblem of my sponsor's office. Inside was a sheet of smooth, pale paper, also edged in gold, with calligraphy flowing down it like water. It took me long minutes to sound out the words; I spoke Common, but reading it was a challenge I had not yet mastered.

I, General Kemen Sendoa, Minister of Military Affairs and Ambassador to Rikuto, do invite you to witness my wedding to Riona of Stonehaven, on 1 Sato, in the southern ballroom of Stonehaven Royal Palace.

I looked up at him. "Me?" My voice squeaked.

"Yes, you." He smiled. "There won't be many others of your age there, but I hope you find it enjoyable."

I stared at him, trying to find words for the honor I felt. "I... thank you, sir."

Four

Kemen

Perhaps two weeks after I'd returned, I sat off to the side while Hakan, Kveta, and Riona sang one evening. Hakan played the mardosin. I'd never heard him play before, but it didn't surprise me to find that he was talented.

I held little Kemen, the new heir to the Erdemen throne. He was almost eight weeks old, tiny and fragile in my big hands. He'd taken to me immediately, and I felt his infant trust as balm on my heart. Their voices rose around me and I stared at the child's face, brushing my hand over the top of his fuzzy head. I watched Ria too, the smooth pale skin of her neck and the soft line of her jaw as she glanced at the music over Kveta's shoulder.

I let my eyes close, listening. Breathing. The warmth of the little body resting on my chest made me smile.

I woke to Riona's whisper in my ear. "Come, my love. You're tired."

I smiled sleepily, brushing a kiss over the baby's head before I let Kveta lift him from my arms. "Perhaps a little."

I walked Ria to her room. We lingered outside a moment, my hands around hers. "Sleep well, Riona."

She blushed, and lifted one of my hands so the back of my fingers brushed her cheek. I smiled and bent to kiss her hand, my heart full.

FIVE

ELATHLO

My sponsor taught me first every morning, and then we ran together. Sometimes the king came to train as well. My sponsor sparred with the king as he sparred with me, as a teacher. When the king kicked him in the ribs, he smiled, and I guessed he had probably given the king the opening. He was pleased when the king hit him, as if that's what he'd been hoping for all along.

After he trained the king, he trained himself. It was only then that we saw his true speed and power. His skill was breathtaking. He made the moves look easy, but I've never seen anyone before or since who was his equal. He trained to exhaustion, hours of work that ended only when he was drenched in sweat, muscles shaking with fatigue. He earned his skill, there was no doubt of that, but still I was left amazed. It helped me realize that if I thought he pushed me hard, he demanded much more of himself.

From the dawn of the world, there have been legends. Erdemen history records things differently, but in our legends, gods and demons walk the earth much like men. They are long gone, or perhaps in hiding, and have been for uncounted generations. All the same, I could see how my sponsor inspired the fear of their return in our warriors.

But gods and demons do not feel as we humans do, and at last I had to conclude that he was human after all. He'd been sick from the alamaa, he'd been wounded, and now I saw him happy. When he was with Riona, I saw warmth and love in his eyes that made him seem totally vulnerable. I could not have imagined it, but there it was. Passionate, hopeless love such as everyone dreams of but very few find. It surprised me that one so honored should find it in a servant, but that he found it could not be denied.

My studies challenged me as I had never been challenged before. Perhaps I was better prepared for the physical training, despite my fear. I knew what it was like to force myself past exhaustion, and despite his high expectations, my sponsor was never cruel. The exercises were different than I had done before, but the idea of pushing my body past its limits was not new.

My tutor, Colonel Bekendi, taught me arithmetic and grammar and history and penmanship. My vocabulary in Common was more limited than I'd realized. I knew enough to carry on many basic conversations but I didn't know the names of the months, or the names of any of the foods that we ate, or many other useful words and phrases. I'd barely learned enough math to count on my fingers the days of a journey or the days until a feast, to calculate the number of men lost in a skirmish with the

Erdemen army. Colonel Bekendi now wanted me to understand how to multiply and divide numbers, how to use fractions, how to calculate the area of a circle and other things I had never imagined the need for.

Colonel Bekendi taught me for a few hours every day. Sometimes we ended the lessons at lunchtime, and sometimes he continued for an hour or two afterwards. He gave me work to do after he left, readings and practice work, arithmetic problems or questions about the history readings. I worked alone in my room until dinner.

I ate most dinners alone. When I'd first arrived in Stonehaven, I was so terrified that being left alone was reassuring. Now enough time had passed to understand that my sponsor was unlikely to kill me in a sudden, unpredictable fit of rage. The solitude turned to loneliness as I realized how very long a year in Erdem would be.

ONE MORNING, I saw Lani off to the side of the courtyard, imitating our movements as we did a technique drill. My sponsor noticed her too, but he did not say anything immediately.

After some time, he called to her. "Lani, what are you doing?" Affectionate amusement tinged his voice.

"Practicing."

He left me and spoke with her quietly, though I could still hear most of their words.

"Why, Lani?"

"It looks fun."

"Elathlo needs to learn because he may be the next Tarvil chief someday. You have no such need. It's hard work, and not always fun."

"I know how to work hard." Even from a distance, I could hear the plea in her voice.

"For what purpose?"

"For the joy you have in it. I'm sure it's hard, but you can't deny you find joy in it. I want to try, Kemen. Please."

There was a long silence. "You'll need breeches. You can't kick in your dresses. You can't let your chores suffer, either."

She nodded, wide-eyed.

"I ask a lot, Lani. You don't have to do everything, but I won't slow Elathlo's training for you. It wouldn't be fair to him."

She nodded again before throwing her arms around him.

That day we worked on hand techniques and he did not expect her to run in her dress. She was a quick student, more coordinated and faster than I was, but my experience was greater. She was strong for a girl, I think. Maybe scrubbing floors and carrying buckets of water was good exercise too. My technique was better, but soon I had a sinking feeling that with some time she could surpass my skill.

After that she trained with us every morning. She tried gamely to keep up and gritted her teeth in frustration when she didn't know what to do. My sponsor had us practice blocks and strikes with each other, which was terribly awkward at first. It did make things easier, because she was close to my height, but it felt odd to practice such things with a girl.

She was slim, just beginning to curve like a woman. She had wide blue eyes that always seemed filled with laughter.

It was only another week before I realized that I liked her. Perhaps it was inevitable; she was the only girl close to my age that I'd seen in months. The girls in my grandfather's tribe were younger than I was, still children. Otso-ka would arrange a girl for me from one of the other tribes. I'd thought about it before; it would most likely be someone from one of the Red Tarvil tribes to the west. He had fewer ties with them, and a marriage would strengthen the failing bonds. That would be especially important if the peace held with Erdem. The Red Tarvil could be enticed to hold their peace as well, and then we wouldn't pay the price for their aggression.

I tried to squash any feelings for Lani. My marriage was something Otso-ka would figure out, and I had no choice in the matter. It would be better not to imagine otherwise.

Six

After a month back in Stonehaven, in Loiste only a week and a half before the wedding, I could finally do pushups in a handstand again. I was glad, because I'd been starting to think I'd never be strong enough. It hurt though; the deep ache in the bone persisted for hours afterward. I tried again the next morning, and the next, and then I tested myself on one hand. My right wasn't too difficult, although I was out of practice in balancing. The left was a failure. Again the next day, and the next, and again. Finally I managed three left-handed vertical pushups the day before our wedding.

The accomplishment was proof that my recovery was almost complete. Between that and the thought of marrying Ria, I was hard-pressed not to grin like a fool the entire day.

One of those first mornings, after I'd tried unsuccessfully for the fourth time in a row, Hakan met me in the courtyard. I was drenched in sweat from the summer heat and the long hours of practice. He drew a bucket of water while I caught my breath and leaned against the edge of the well beside me as I drank. He looked very satisfied with himself.

"It's only a week now until your wedding, isn't it?"

"Yes."

"You haven't asked about your pay. Don't you want to know what you're paid?"

I smiled. "I suppose."

"How much do you want?" he asked.

I shrugged. "That's for you to say. You're the king."

He grinned then. "Good. Taisto was paid eleven hundred golden eagles a month and had the free use of the second estate." He gestured toward the manor house on the other side of the stables, which I had never entered. "Your assistance is far more valuable than his was to my father, and I would like to recognize that in your pay."

I believe my mouth actually dropped open. When I was retired, I drew ninety-five golden eagles a month. Sixty golden eagles was regular pay for my rank, plus ten for valor at Dorvale, ten for the Iron Shield award, and fifteen for the twice-weekly hand to hand combat training sessions I taught at the request of my commanding officer. My food and lodging while on duty were provided, of course, so my expenses were minimal.

"Do you think fifteen hundred is fair?"

"Hakan, that's absurd. What would I do with it all?"

He raised his eyebrows. "Whatever you want. It's not entirely out of line with what the other ministers are paid, and you've done quite a bit more for me than they have. You'll get back pay, of course, from the date of the coronation."

I shook my head. "No, it's too much. I have no need for that much." My head hurt just thinking about it. "One *hundred* is more than enough. What expenses will I have anyway?"

"I can't pay you less than Taisto was paid. As for expenses, there is the staff of the estate. I can check the records, but that probably cost him some five or six hundred a month. Food. Clothes. Horses. Whatever you like, Kemen. The Minister of Military Affairs should not live like a pauper."

It was awkward. Hakan had always been generous, but I didn't know how to accept this. I had to think. "Can I tell Riona she doesn't need to work anymore? Or do you need time to find someone else?"

"Tell her whenever you like."

Perhaps she would like some things then. I could buy her a necklace or something. I didn't know what men were supposed to buy for women. "Could I have some of my back pay now?"

He laughed. "It's yours. You can have it whenever you like. I waited so long to tell you because I had the estate cleaned and readied. Noriso didn't trust Taisto's servants, so he's found others he likes better for you. My father had Taisto's pay delivered at the end of each month."

That afternoon I took two hundred golden eagles and went out into the city alone. I'd rarely held that much gold in my life, and the weight of it on my belt made me feel awkward and conspicuous. Not that I feared anyone would try to take it; it was more that I felt like a pompous, arrogant nobleman for carrying that much at once.

I hadn't spent much time in Stonehaven, and when I'd been there, I'd either been in the palace or traveling with a destination in mind. I certainly hadn't spent much time in the markets.

I visited the central market and wandered among the stalls. The crowds were stifling. I should have brought Elathlo; he'd seen almost nothing of ordinary Erdemen life. Most people don't enjoy the quiet, privileged life he experienced in the palace. Perhaps I was not the best guide to ordinary Erdemen life either.

The following morning, after training, bathing, and breakfast, I spoke with Bekendi and excused Elathlo from his lessons. Elathlo followed me without question. He no longer appeared terrified of me, but he was still skittish, like a puppy that had been kicked too often. He'd changed since he'd arrived though. He stood a little taller, his shoulders not quite so hunched, his chin just a little higher. He'd gained both height and muscle already; our food and the hard work agreed with him. His clothes were much better than he'd come with, and he might have passed for Erdemen unless he opened his mouth. His Common was good but he had a noticeable accent. I hoped it wouldn't be a problem in the market.

We rode out about an hour or so before noon, with one of the stablehands following to handle the horses while we walked the stalls. Elathlo drew closer to me as we approached the market. We left the horses with the stablehand and began our exploration.

Elathlo stuck close by my side as we entered the teeming market, but I was almost as overwhelmed as he was. The press of a crowd is always disconcerting to me, and I imagine it would be worse if I had a view level with everyone's elbows or shoulders rather than the tops of their heads. A few people might have recognized me; I may not have been out much, but I was a Dari wearing expensive clothes, and perhaps that was enough. No one spoke to me directly, but they gave us a little space to breathe. Perhaps they were only shy because I was Dari.

The air was filled with sounds and smells, shouted prices and greetings, laughter and arguments. Everything was covered with smoke from grills cooking lamb, beef, chicken, doves, tomatoes, peppers, tubers, and dozens of kinds of fruit. Fresh fruit and vegetables were available too, and fresh meat a few rows over. You could buy nearly anything. Tools. Knives. Swords. Clothes. Cloth of all sorts. Jewelry and loose jewels. Spices. Paintings. Carvings. Trinkets. Livestock. You could have letters written or read to you, if you couldn't do it yourself. You could have papers translated. I think Elathlo was a little frightened, and I couldn't blame him. I've never been entirely comfortable amid so much noise and so many people.

For some time, we simply walked around, and Elathlo stared about with wide eyes. I bought us grilled lamb and peppers for lunch. Elathlo grinned at me as he ate, the excitement of our excursion breaking through his nervous reserve.

I did see two other Dari, a man selling wood carvings and an older Dari woman selling silk shawls. I looked at her cloth, and after a little searching I chose one for Riona that matched the deep blue of her eyes and one for Lani of a lighter blue edged with silver.

"What is your name?" The woman was staring at me. Her eyes had probably once been dark, but now they were mostly clouded. She must have been quite tall, but she sat slightly hunched with age.

"Kemen."

"General Kemen Sendoa?" Her voice was soft.

"Yes." I bowed slightly.

She smiled and motioned me closer. "My name is Jassanalir. I am so glad to meet you at last." She clasped my hand between her two dry, bony hands. She was older than I'd thought at first. "You have made my life better. Please, sit with me a while, if you have the time. You are so important." She stood to give me her one rickety chair, but when I protested, she sat again.

I knelt beside her with a glance at Elathlo. He was staring at her curiously.

"I thank you," she said. Then she shifted into Dari.

"I'm sorry. I don't understand. I only speak Common and Kumar."

"You don't speak our language?" She sounded very sad.

"I never learned it well. I was raised in the army. I spoke Kumar first."

She patted my shoulder as if consoling me. "Poor boy. It must have been so hard."

I smiled and let her wrap her hands around mine again.

"You are so good to an old woman. I used to have trouble here sometimes. People don't like us. They say we brought the plague. Maybe it's true, I don't know. But I didn't do it. I remember the fear of it like everyone else. I lost a daughter to it, and my husband. They sometimes dirtied my shawls, threw dirt or rocks. Not too often, but often enough. You changed that."

She patted my hair, and I smiled. She was nearly blind; she touched me partly so she knew where to direct her gaze. "When you became known as Erdem's hero, no one bothered me anymore. We are respected now. Thank you."

I swallowed. "I'm glad things are better for you." My words sounded awkward in my own ears.

I started to stand, and she patted my shoulder again, holding onto my elbow for a moment as she stood. She was tall, and must have been quite beautiful when she was young, despite the dark skin. I'd never seen a young Dari woman; I'd seen only a few Dari in my life, and most of those few were soldiers.

Riona was my love, is my love, but I confess I wondered for a moment what might have been different if I'd known other Dari. Perhaps not much. Perhaps everything.

I would not trade my life for anything, but I did wonder.

"Take those as my thanks. It is too little for what you have done, but I don't have much to offer."

"I cannot take them for nothing. What is the price?"

"It is not for nothing. You have already helped more than you know." She smiled proudly and patted at my shoulders again, as if I were a well-loved son. "Remember me when you serve your king. Remember us."

I bent to kiss her fingertips and slipped twenty golden eagles into her purse. I imagined the shawls would have cost no more than six golden eagles each, and a little extra wouldn't be amiss. But I would not deny her the pride and generosity of her gift.

We made our way to the rows of jewelers. Elathlo stared about in amazement. Stonehaven's Grand Market is the greatest in all of Erdem, where the best of everything can be found. I'd never in my life bought a piece of jewelry, and I was cautious. I knew little about what makes good workmanship and what makes a fair price. Though I had more money than I'd ever had before, I was hardly accustomed to throwing gold around without a care.

I must have looked at a thousand things. Necklaces, earrings, bracelets, collars, anklets, circlets for a woman's head, hairpieces. I finally found something for Riona, a delicate golden collar made in the shape of a vine, with sparkling emerald leaves and flowers with ruby petals. I'd never seen her wear any jewelry, but I wondered if perhaps that was because she didn't have any. I'd have to remedy that. My eyes widened at the price, but the piece was beautiful. I bought it.

Then I thought perhaps Elathlo would like something. I led him to the weapons section of the market and we looked at hundreds of knives. I selected three knives for him to try, all relatively plain but excellently made.

"Which of these do you like best?"

He looked up at me in surprise, then held them each, one by one. The hilt of one was a bit long for him, and he debated for a moment between the other two.

"They are both good, sir."

"But which do you like better?"

"This one, sir." He was nervous, as if he thought I were testing him somehow.

I bought it. It was overpriced, but that was to be expected. Everything was more expensive in Stonehaven. I gave it to him as we left.

"Here. It's for you."

His eyes widened. "Me, sir?"

"A gift. Every boy needs a knife." I smiled at his confused expression. "Your father would have given you one, wouldn't he?"

"Yes, sir. But..." he hesitated, then whispered, "Alokas are not trusted with weapons until their service is complete. Or almost complete. Their sponsors do not wish them armed."

I put one hand on his shoulder and steered him out into the market and toward the wide avenue back toward the palace. "Should I worry you'll use it on me?" I asked the question lightly, but he looked up at me with a serious expression.

"No, sir. You are not like those sponsors." Even in the warm air, his shoulder trembled beneath my hand as he shivered.

"Then it's yours."

THREE DAYS BEFORE the wedding, I was delirious with joy, barely able to believe my life could be so perfect. I packed a picnic lunch and surprised Riona by sweeping her away for the afternoon. We crossed the Purling River to go a little farther north to the Silverfall, the great waterfall of the Silvertongue River. We left the carriage at the base of the footpath with Drokan, who would watch it for us, and stepped into the lush coolness of the forest. Just the two of us. I carried the basket slung over my shoulder, and she slipped her hand into mine.

The path was not long, and in less than an hour we reached the waterfall. For some moments we stood, fingers intertwined, watching the play of sunlight on the thundering water.

"I had no idea this was so close to Stonehaven. I feel I've missed so much, being in the palace for years." Her voice was barely audible over the water as it crashed into the river below.

"We'll have to remedy that. There is beauty in Erdem you should see."

She smiled up at me. I thought of many things I wanted to show her. Bluebells in the northern woods in early spring. Irises along the Purling River. The western shore, some parts sandy beaches, other parts stark granite cliffs beaten by crashing salty waves. The rice fields in the southeast, all waving green stalks and hazy humid air. The graceful, dignified ruins that dotted the country, each with their wonderful stories.

I carried her into the grotto behind the falls, the rock walls lined with quartz and mica, all dancing shadow and light. She laughed and pressed her head against me, sweet smelling and golden, and I smiled into her hair.

"Three days. Can I wait that long?" she murmured.

I spread a blanket on the ground and we sat across from each other, both smiling so much we could barely eat. Afterward she leaned back against me and we watched the water crash down, the light filtering through the water to make everything glisten.

"You're getting better." She twisted to smile up at me, her eyelashes wet with spray. Her warm breath brushed my cheek.

I bent to kiss her. "For you." My voice shook with sudden emotion, and I murmured, "I love you, Ria. I love you." I tightened my arms around her.

She spoke into my chest. "I love you." I could feel her smiling. "Everything is more beautiful with you."

I MET HAKAN for lunch the following day as he finished a meeting.

"Come in," he called, and I bowed as I entered. Not because Hakan demanded such courtesy, he never had and did not expect such formality from me now, but because flaunting our friendship in front of other nobility would only antagonize them. I did not want to cause problems for Hakan, especially when his crown was still so new.

"Kemen, have you met Captain Baretz Sirkhar yet? He served my father faithfully for many years." Hakan stood as he introduced me to the man across from him.

"Captain Sirkhar, this is Ambassador and General Kemen Sendoa."

I bowed and reached out to give him the soldier's greeting. He hesitated, then gave me an uncomfortable smile, hands still at his sides.

"Your pardon, General. The title Captain is honorary, not a military rank. I don't wish to presume." He bowed again.

"The fault is mine. I thank you for your service to our former king."

He gave me a thin smile, this one less uncomfortable and more cold, as if he wanted me to understand that he knew something I did not know. He stared at me for just long enough to feel impolite, then bowed to Hakan. "Thank you for your time, Your Royal Highness."

"Of course, Captain. Thank you." Hakan's smile didn't quite reach his eyes, and he watched Sirkhar step around me and out the door, closing it with a quiet click behind himself.

We talked of our plans for the schools over lunch, but mostly we enjoyed a few moments of rest and quiet jokes before immersing ourselves in work again that afternoon.

"What exactly did Sirkhar do for your father?" I asked, near the end of the meal.

Hakan sighed and leaned forward to rub his hands over his face. "I don't know all the details. My father never told me and Sirkhar says everything was in the official records. I haven't even found all the records. They were kept in separate places, one set for his training and another for the actions he undertook on my father's behalf. I think he knows the official records contain gaps, but he won't tell me what's in those gaps. The records weren't his responsibility and I think he means that if it wasn't recorded, my father didn't want anyone to know.

Maybe he's being loyal to my father. Maybe he's protecting himself."

He sighed and toyed with his roll, then said, "Basically, he was my father's solution to messy problems. Nobles who were intractable. Merchants who refused to lend the crown money. Army leaders who got too independent. Except for Taisto, obviously. I don't think he was cooperating with Taisto; I think he did exactly what my father told him. And my father trusted Taisto."

"He was an assassin?" I asked.

"Only when necessary. He probably did more intimidation. Blackmail. Information gathering. Betrayal of confidences to the wrong people. That sort of thing."

I pondered the quick impression I'd gotten. Tall, though not excessively so, reasonably fit but not as if his profession depended on it. Quick, blue-grey eyes that gave an impression of cold analysis. An attractive but forgettable face. Blond hair liberally sprinkled with grey. Perhaps forty or forty five. Forgettable clothes, neither fashionable nor unfashionable enough to attract notice.

"You still have work for him?" I tried to keep my face neutral. I didn't exactly dislike the man, not on the basis of one meeting, but I didn't think his profession suited Hakan's reign. Not the assassination part, anyway. But of course, even a king like Hakan could not afford to naively assume that all nobles were trustworthy and supported him. Something about Sirkhar made me uncomfortable, but I could not place it into words, even within my own mind.

Hakan's frown deepened. "A little." He looked away from me, and I watched expressions flick across his face, fear, shame, anger, and finally resignation. I waited, knowing he would tell me if I were patient.

He took a deep breath, then a sip of of his tea. "While you were gone the last time, there was a possible attempt on my life."

"Possible?"

"I haven't told Kveta." He glanced up to catch my eye. "I was on a quick ride, just out to get some air. Early in the morning, just past dawn. Someone shot a couple of arrows toward me. I hotfooted it back to the palace. There was no pursuit, and my escort didn't find anything conclusive. Perhaps some footprints at a good vantage point, but they weren't sure that's where the arrows came from."

"You weren't injured?"

"No." He sighed. "I don't know who it was, don't know why, and don't know if it will happen again. I don't even know if it was a serious attempt."

I let my breath out slowly, trying to sooth the tension that made my shoulders ache.

"Don't worry about it, Kemen." He looked up and smiled, putting it behind him. "I'm careful. Sirkhar is investigating, and I'm escorted whenever I leave the palace."

I nodded. "Let me know if he finds anything."

"Of course."

I asked Ria that evening about Sirkhar.

She shuddered, then gave me a rueful smile. "No one knows anything about him. He just showed up one day, long before I was here, and somebody trained him to do... tasks. We never knew what those tasks were. I heard he used to have a temper when he was young, but I never saw it."

I studied her face. She was always gentle and kind, trying hard not to say anything unpleasant about anyone. "And…" I prompted.

She looked down. "I don't know anything for certain. Just that we all knew not to make him angry. We just heard things, rumors. You know. The king found him useful so he had the run of the palace. He always frightened me; if you look in his eyes, it's like he's calculating whether it's useful or not to stab you. We all avoided him."

"Did he ever hurt any of the servants?" I frowned.

She hesitated. "I don't know. There's a story that once he broke some kitchen boy's arm because the boy tripped and spilled something on him. But I'm not sure if it's true. No one who saw it was still in the palace by the time my mother and I arrived."

I pondered that. Would Sirkhar target Hakan? If he considered it, that was another threat, because I had no illusions the man I'd met would be so inept as to miss an arrow shot. He had better opportunities to strike at Hakan from within the palace.

THE DAY OF THE WEDDING dawned bright and clear, the early morning air already warmed by the summer sun. The wedding was held in the southern ballroom.

I waited with Hakan at the front of the room. Ria would enter from the back, escorted by Joran the cook and Ena, her aunt. The guests sat in chairs brought in from one of the banquet rooms.

One of the men opened the door for her. Ria stepped into the room and my breath caught in my throat. She smiled at me across the room, and I smiled back, my heart near beating out of my chest. I saw no one else. Her hair was caught up with pearls and emeralds, and she wore the golden collar I'd given her. The white and gold of her dress sparkled in the sunlight streaming through the windows.

We knelt together before Hakan, hand in hand.

"Love has brought these two hearts together. Love binds them. Love keeps them. But love is a decision, not a feeling. This vow they make is a vow for life. Let no man break this sacred trust.

"In illness, in health. In poverty, in wealth. In anger, in pain, in sorrow, in rejoicing, this vow holds. In everything under the sun, this vow holds.

"Kemen, do you take Riona as your wife?"

"I do." I looked into her beautiful blue eyes as I said it. We were both blinking back tears.

"Riona, do you take Kemen as your husband?"

"I do." Her voice was sweet and pure.

He raised the wedding cloth and flicked it out to the side, then swung it around and over our heads. Ria and I grinned at each other in the green darkness, the light filtering through the silk.

"This cloth covers Kemen and Riona like the blessing of their love. They are two people, but they are one. This cloth symbolizes that from now until death, they are one in the eyes of the crown, and one in the eyes of the world."

Hakan's voice changed, and I could tell he was smiling more broadly now. "And it gives them privacy for their first kiss as man and wife. I'm sure there will be more for you to cheer, but this kiss is for them to share alone with each other. You may kiss your bride."

For a moment we only gazed at each other before I leaned forward to touch my lips to hers. Gently, to honor her with tenderness, then I pulled back to smile at her before I kissed her more thoroughly.

Hakan raised the cloth and beamed down at us. "Now rise. I present Ambassador and General Kemen Sendoa and his wife, Lady Riona Sendoa."

We stood, and I clasped her hand as we stood before these people who cared for us. Everyone was smiling, and I pulled Ria close to kiss her again. I lifted her off her feet and spun her around, and everyone laughed and cheered.

Seven

T he wedding was even larger than I had expected, full of noblemen and women wearing extravagant clothes. The women all had decorations in their hair, feathers or pearls or flowers the size of my hand. There were also servants I recognized, as well as a few army officers in dress uniform. I was surprised that such an important event included so many servants, but Riona had been a servant. My sponsor treated them as equals, but the nobles did not speak much with the servants who attended as guests.

My sponsor wore his full dress uniform, and when I saw him the first time, my eyes widened. Erdemen uniforms aren't full of ostentatious gold and glitter everywhere. Instead, the crisp severity of the uniform makes its own statement of discipline and purpose. Brown trousers, a white shirt beneath a green jacket, a brown leather belt and boots, and a sword. It was simple, but the effect was imposing, to say the least. Officer's stripes covered the left breast of his jacket, the colors noting different engagements. Small gold and silver medals were sewn in a line above the stripes. A matching set of stripes sat high on my sponsor's left sleeve.

Riona looked not at all like a servant. Her dress was made of some fancy fabric, perhaps silk, all white and gold. I hadn't seen her much, but she was beautiful. She was glowing with happiness. My sponsor's eyes were fixed on her, as if the rest of the room had ceased to exist. He was barely breathing, the smile on his face full of such joy that he might have simply forgotten that he needed air.

The ceremony was simple, despite the richness of the setting and the sumptuous banquet that would follow. The joy in my sponsor and Riona was wholly unique in my experience, and I found myself unable to look away from them for the rest of the afternoon. After fearing him as a demon, to see him so gentle and so happy was beyond strange. Not only because my perception of him was changing, but because my idea of Erdem, and Erdemen people, was changing.

My sponsor, and indeed everyone, had been kind to me since I'd arrived. I'd been terrified, both of him and of being so far from everything I'd ever known. Terrified of being in the Erdemen capital. Erdemen did not like Tarvil, I knew that. I knew also that perhaps they had good reason; I'd heard enough about what my father and other warriors did on raids. Their stories hadn't horrified me because they weren't real to me. Those people who were killed, the girls who were raped, weren't truly human like I was.

I'd never met an Erdemen before my sponsor had come to negotiate with my grandfather, and my idea of them was something between demons and dogs. Intelligent enough to be dangerous, but not worthy of the consideration due to a human. Being sent to Erdem was like being thrown to wolves; I couldn't afford to be arrogant in my superiority, because they had all the power, but I didn't see them as true equals.

Now, looking around at the wedding celebration, filled with people who were just like me, only perhaps more cultured, wealthier, taller, and kinder, I was ashamed. Ashamed of my thoughts. Ashamed of my people.

After the ceremony, we went out to the western garden while the banquet was made ready indoors. We snacked on pastries and cheeses, expensive cured meats and wines. There was music and dancing in the small pavilion in the center of the garden.

I liked Erdemen music. It was very different than ours, but I liked it. For a wedding, it was all joyful music, of course, sweet love ballads and merry little dancing songs. I didn't dance, but I wished I knew how. Everyone enjoyed it. My sponsor danced with Riona, and then later with the queen Kveta, who leaned in to whisper something that made him choke back laughter. He glanced at the king and shook his head, smiling, as if he'd caught the king in some prank. Then he saw me.

"Elathlo, come dance." He motioned me to the dance floor, but I shook my head. He glanced across the room and smiled at someone, and a few moments later, Lani stood before me.

"You should dance. It's polite to dance at a wedding." She smiled at me triumphantly, as if I wouldn't dare argue with her. "It shows you are happy for the newlyweds." She put out her hand. "Dance with me." It was a command, not a request.

I looked down at my feet, feeling stupid and unsophisticated, like the barbarian I suddenly knew I was. "I don't know how," I muttered.

Lani shrugged. "Just follow me." She grabbed my hand in hers and pulled me onto the pavilion floor. Our dance was awkward and off time with the music, but I did my best and she didn't seem to mind. I only stepped on her toes twice.

She was beautifully dressed. I'd never seen her in fancy clothes before, and her flashing smile made me feel fluttery inside. Her hand was strong in mine, and I liked that she smiled at everyone. Everyone smiled back, too. You couldn't help it.

EIGHT

KEMEN

After the banquet and more dancing, Riona and I were shooed away to our new estate. I had not yet entered it, and had little idea what to expect. It was large and luxurious. It didn't feel like mine.

We strolled through the warm summer night, the stars rising above us. Music filtered through the garden, and a soft breeze caressed our faces. The moonlight lit the front entrance at an angle, casting deep shadows over the stone patio. Several windows showed the warm light of lamps inside. I knocked, and then felt that perhaps that was foolish, since it was my estate now, and started to turn the knob.

The door opened suddenly and a young man, barely out of his teens, bowed deeply to me. "My apologies, sir."

"So I am at the right house?"

He bowed again, looking a little nervous. "Yes, sir."

I swept Ria up in my arms and carried her through the doorway. She nestled her head against my shoulder, and I felt her soft chuckle against my chest.

"Where is our room?"

"Follow me, sir."

Ria murmured, "Are you going to carry me the whole way?"

"May I?"

She giggled quietly. "You don't have to."

"I like you in my arms." I wondered if the boy ahead of us could hear. I thought his ears were turning a bit pink, but it might have been only the bobbing lamplight.

"Do you?" She reached up and traced my jaw with one finger.

The boy opened a door and bowed as I stepped inside. He closed it behind us and I heard the latch click.

The bed stood in the center of the room, covered in soft, white linens for summer. A bunch of roses nestled between the pillows at the head, and another stood in a white porcelain vase on a table in front of the open window. There was a fireplace, though it was not filled with logs but with an array of candles. Candles stood on the nightstands and beside the vase too.

"It's beautiful," Ria said softly.

I looked down at her and our eyes met. The moment stretched out as I gazed at her beautiful blue eyes, the candlelight on her cheek, the curve of her lips as she smiled at me.

The night was perfect.

HAKAN HAD TOLD ME that he did not want to see me for at least a week after the wedding. I was not to do work. I was not to train in the courtyard, either with Elathlo or alone. I was not to visit the kitchens and do servants' work.

He was right.

I woke early by force of long habit, but I did not get up. I watched Ria's face as she slept, the tiny movements of her eyes beneath their lids as she dreamed, the soft rise and fall of her chest as she breathed. She sighed and nestled her head into the pillow, and I heard her breathing change as she began to drift into wakefulness. I brushed the back of my hand across her cheek, and she smiled, leaned in to me.

We picnicked in the garden, then explored the grounds. A little gazebo was nearly hidden by the willows at the edge of a little pond filled with fat goldfish. In the heavy warmth, the breeze barely rustling the leaves above us, we walked with fingers entwined. We sat on a stone bench for a while, admiring the way the water glittered in the sunlight.

We returned to our picnic blanket and found the remains of lunch vanished, and a stack of books beside a pitcher of cool water with raspberries floating in it. We took the hint, and I silently thanked Hakan for finding such excellent servants. I would not have asked for such luxury, even for Riona, because it would not have occurred to me. But we enjoyed the gift.

Riona did not read for long. We lay beside each other, still holding hands, eyes closed against the brilliant sun. We drifted to sleep and, for once, I remember that the dreams I had were sweet.

The days with Ria were long and slow and perfect, full of laughter as we discovered little quirks and mannerisms we hadn't known about each other. Ria was disconcerted that she had no tasks, no chores, no work to do, and I felt at loose ends in the morning, when I was accustomed to training. We filled the time with questions for each other, learning how to be friends without the distraction of work, training, and other people. We explored each other, bodies and hearts and memories.

We were shy, and those first days were filled with awkward moments, when neither of us quite knew what to do. But even those awkward moments were wonderful, because we gave each other grace and forgiveness, in ways we hadn't known we even needed to.

NINE

ELATHLO

N o one knocked on my door the morning after my sponsor's wedding, but I woke a short time after dawn, blinking at the ceiling in the morning light and wondering what I was supposed to do with myself. I dressed and wandered out to the courtyard. I did some exercises and ran for a while, but without my sponsor, the effort felt aimless. After an hour I went back inside, bathed, and drifted down to the kitchen for breakfast.

"Good morning," Sinta said.

"Can I help?" I asked. Everyone was scurrying around, preparing lunch and a mid-morning tea tray for the king and queen.

"Just stay out of the way. I'll have yours in a minute," Tanith said as she brushed by me.

I stood by the wall, feeling out of place. At least I wasn't sitting in my room alone. I tried to be grateful, because I knew it was kind of them to let me stay, but the cheerful chaos seemed to only point out how solitary my days were.

TEN

KEMEN

Ria traced a finger over the scars on my chest and back, asking how I'd gotten each one.

"And this?" She spread her hand across the long, faint scar on my ribs, her palm warm against my skin.

I'd forgotten about that one until she noticed; it was old and I had not thought about it for years.

"A sword during a skirmish when I was in the south. It wasn't bad. I was..." I tried to remember. "Nineteen? Twenty? It was a long time ago."

"That's younger than I am now." I felt her tremble slightly. "It must have been terrible."

I smiled and pressed my lips to her hair. "It's what I trained for. I don't know what else I would do."

She pulled back and looked at me, her head cocked to one side. "Really? You're brilliant. You know that, don't you? You could teach. You could do anything."

I studied her face. "You think so? Would you want me to do something else? Would you want me to not be a soldier?"

"I just…" she swallowed and looked down, then pressed her head close again. She shuddered, and I wrapped my arm around her more tightly. She whispered, "I don't want to lose you, Kemen."

I sighed, breathed in the sweet scent of Ria, soap and sunlight and warm skin. "I don't plan on doing anything foolish, Ria. I have too much to live for now." I smiled as I said it, knowing she would hear my love in the words and in my voice.

She ran her fingers across my chest again, her featherlight touch sending tingles down my entire body. "You're beautiful, too. You should know that."

I couldn't help my snort of laughter. "Men aren't beautiful. Least of all me."

She giggled, snuggled closer. "It's true!"

"As long as you're happy." I could scarcely believe that we were married, much less that she seemed to still be pleased with the decision. "You, Riona, outshine the stars."

I felt her soft, surprised intake of breath, and knew that I did not say what I thought often enough. "Do you feel my heart thudding?" I drew her hand up to press flat against my chest, so she could feel the steady beat beneath her palm. "It's for you. Always for you, Ria."

ELEVEN

ELATHLO

When my sponsor knocked a week after his wedding, I leapt up to open the door. "Good morning, sir."

"Morning." He gave me a slight bow. "You're ready?"

"Yes, sir." I'd woken early and was already dressed, although the sky was still grey, the sun not yet risen above the trees.

He smiled, and I hurried to keep up with him as we made our way to the courtyard.

Training that morning was even longer and harder than usual, but I didn't mind. My sponsor was just as he had been, quiet and meticulous as he corrected my form. He congratulated me on being able to do more pushups than when he'd last seen me. We ran together, my short legs straining to keep up with his long, easy strides. For the first time, I understood some of what he saw in the training, the chance to push my body, perhaps to enjoy another person's company without speaking, simply to exist beside each other.

I saw a little more of my sponsor in the following afternoons. He continued his work for the king, advising him on military matters and helping with the development of the classes for a new military school. I listened to many of his meetings, and afterwards he would ask me if I had any questions. He told me about the Erdemen military, how it trains, how it promotes officers, major theories of leadership, of strategy, tactics, and logistics. He listened to Colonel Bekendi's report of my progress so far and nodded his approval.

Still, I found my loneliness growing. My sponsor was not my friend; he was kind to me, but he had many things on his mind. He was a warrior, and I was his aloka. An aloka is meant to serve in order to earn his training. I did nothing for my sponsor. I did not clean his weapons or tend his horse. I did not fix his meals. I only benefited from his generosity, and I felt this as a constant, gnawing guilt. His kindness to me only increased my guilt.

As awkward as it was when Lani joined our morning training sessions, I was thankful for her. Thankful for the way her initial caution and mostly-concealed dislike of me turned to friendly joking and smiles. She didn't like me the way I liked her, that was obvious, but I didn't mind. At least she noticed me.

My sponsor didn't let us spar each other for quite some time, but we did partner drills together, practicing punching, kicking, and blocking. I was very careful, because she was a girl and I wanted her to like me. She glared at me when my punches were too slow and my kicks too careful, and said that I wasn't doing her any favors. She was right, although it felt wrong to punch at her with all my speed.

For several days, everything went well. But then I hit her, really hit her, my kick snapping up into her stomach at full strength. I was used to hitting my sponsor, and I'd been less careful with her than I should have. Under his tunic, my sponsor might have been made of stone, but she was softer, and I felt her body give as the breath whooshed out of her. She bent over, tearful and gasping. It was the one time during training that I saw a truly dangerous light in my sponsor's eyes.

"Turn around. Kneel."

I did, and waited for my death.

It did not come. I heard him speaking softly to her.

"Put your hands up over your head. Breathe. You're fine. Keep breathing. Deep breaths. Slowly. Good. Deep breath. In. Hold it. Out." I heard her sniffle. "Do you want to continue?" She must have nodded. "Elathlo, stand up. The same thing. Again."

This time she blocked better, and I was more careful. I apologized to her later, when we stood next to each other and watched him train alone. She raised her chin proudly. "I don't want special treatment."

All the same, I was cautious with her for the next month. By then she was already nearly as good as I was, despite my greater experience. She was faster, though I was stronger. Every time we fought she ended with bruises all over her arms, but she grinned with glee at the fun of it all.

Watching her spar with my sponsor was odd. He was so much taller and stronger, but he took great care with her. He pushed her, as he pushed me, but his love for her was obvious. I wondered how they had come to be friends, and I gained respect for her to face such a man with her confidence. Her trust made her fearless, and I wished I could be so brave. I still half-expected the fury that my grandfather had warned me about, though it never came.

Once the king questioned my sponsor about Lani. I didn't hear much of it, only the questioning glance, some quiet words, and a shrug. Lani obviously expected to be in trouble, but the great warrior's name covered her and she continued to train with us.

LANI'S FATHER DIED on the thirteenth of Runsaasti. Her mother presided over the preparations, and even Lady Riona helped.

Tarvil dead are stripped and oiled, wrapped in a beautiful shroud, and left for the wolves. It is civilized to let the bodies provide food for the wolves. We fear the wolves, yes, but we also respect them as fellow survivors, clinging to life at the edge of the world like us. I didn't really believe in the spirits. Many of us didn't. But the old women and some of the old men did. They thought a person's spirit was freed when the body was destroyed. Burning a body, as the Erdemen did, was a harsh way to free a man's spirit, providing food for no man or animal. Our way, of giving the body as food to the wolves, was a kinder way, and the freed spirit would be happier in its generosity.

I'd always thought that was odd, because only in death were my people generous. In life, there was no place for generosity; the warriors scorned it as weakness. Perhaps death inspires us all to greater virtues.

After a Tarvil death, there is wild mourning, passionate and loud, to let the sorrow out and to honor the dead. Then it is over. After that, grief is private, not to be shared even with the closest friends and family.

The Erdemen traditions set my teeth on edge. There was mourning, but it was quiet and uncontrolled. Tears at unexpected times. Silent, warm sympathy.

The body was wrapped in oiled cloth and covered with flowers, and then they burned it. The funeral pyre was built on a flat stone pavilion at the top of a small hill, inside the palace grounds but a little distance from any of the buildings.

Lani and her mother stood to one side, their hands clasped quietly between them. Lady Riona leaned against my sponsor, her eyes dry and red, and he kept one arm around her. I stood uneasily beside him, the other servants ranged out around the pyre. The smells of burning oil, burning flesh, burning flowers and wood all together made me sick, the throat-searing acrid scent an almost visible reminder of their sorrow.

It made me sad that I couldn't grieve. I hadn't known Lani's father, barely met him once when I ate dinner in their little room. He'd been terse and watchful, his eyes on every movement I made. But Lani loved him, and seeing her pain made my heart twist in sympathy. I wanted to show her I cared, if not for him, than for her.

I did what Tarvil do when we grieve, but more quietly, because I was frightened and uncomfortable, afraid Lani wouldn't appreciate the gesture. I sank to my knees and raised my hands to the sky, murmuring words I should have shouted. "Gods and spirits, take this spirit and make him joyous. Give him the joys of the spirit world. Show him the good hunting grounds and good pastures, and…"

My sponsor hauled me to my feet, his hand hard on my arm, and I stuttered to a stop.

"Silence. Now is not the time." His voice in my ear was quiet and stern, and I nodded hurriedly.

We stood and watched the fire roar, the wood crumbling in the flames. After a long while, my sponsor went to Lani's mother and spoke to her quietly. She nodded, and thanked him, a courteous bob of her head accompanying it. Then he spoke to Lani, his words inaudible but his expression of kindness quite clear. He put his hands on her shoulders, bent to speak in her ear, and when she threw her arms around him, he held her close, one hand stroking the back of her hair as she wept.

TWELVE

KEMEN

My namesake was tiny, with feathery blond hair and huge blue eyes. I loved to make him laugh. At first he was very quiet, except for when he screamed, and Riona said that most babies start that way. They don't laugh much at first; they smile sometimes but mostly just lay there. They're not as cute at first as I'd expected; I'd never seen a baby so young, and I thought they came cute.

As he grew month by month, he showed more personality. He liked when I made faces at him, and he liked to grip my fingers or my hair with his tiny hands. He'd pull my hair, and Kveta would gently try to extricate me, but I thought it funny. He smelled of milk and Kveta's rosewater and sometimes shockingly unpleasant odors reminiscent of a barnyard. I wasn't entirely sure how such a tiny creature could produce such a variety of smells.

I had much work to do, and I spent most of my free time with Ria, of course. But when we were together with Hakan and Kveta, I took every opportunity to hold little Kem. His soft, warm body, so helpless, contained so much potential. Who knew what sort of man the child would be?

Neither Hakan nor Kveta could have imagined how much I enjoyed those moments with the boy snuggled into my chest. Nor could I have explained, even to myself, how the longing for a child of my own clamored within me. I wasn't jealous; I was too happy for Hakan for my longing to turn to jealousy.

But I hoped.

Thirteen

Elathlo

When I had been in Erdem almost five months, my sponsor took me to the market with him again. I was excited; the palace was beautiful and peaceful, but the market was fascinating, filled with exotic sights and smells. After my bath, the crisp late fall air made me feel fresh and alive as we entered the crowded marketplace.

My sponsor was so tall and authoritative, people naturally parted before him, though he never raised his voice. I had no such luck, and found myself constantly elbowed and jostled as people moved in behind him without noticing me. My sponsor went first to the Dari silk scarf seller he had met before. She smiled at him, and he bought another shawl for Riona. He meant to buy her other gifts too, and we headed toward the jewelry section of the market.

I fell a little behind and pushed forward, trying to catch up to my sponsor, as someone elbowed me again. Then I tripped and fell full length in the dust. I tried to scramble to my feet immediately, but before I was even upright, I was knocked flat again by a heavy blow on my head and shoulder.

A man yelled and started kicking me. I began to roll away, but there were so many people standing around that I couldn't protect myself well. He buried the toe of his boot into my stomach, and I curled up, gasping for air and trying not to cry. I expected another blow, but suddenly there was a tense silence.

I looked up to see my sponsor standing over me, his sword at the man's throat. He extended his hand and helped me up without taking his eyes off the man.

"Elathlo, are you hurt?"

My mouth felt dry and gritty. "No, sir."

The man was still speaking angrily despite his obvious fear. "The boy is a thief! He took rings from my table, see if he didn't. Check his pockets! Thieving Tarvil brat."

There were many eyes on me and I edged closer to my sponsor, my breath coming short with fear. I didn't steal anything, but I was suddenly terrified my sponsor would believe him.

"He is no thief. See for yourself. Elathlo, empty your pockets."

I dug my hands into my pockets and pulled out everything. My heart nearly stopped when I drew my right hand into the light. Among a strip of leather, a pebble from my tribe's last campsite, and a half-crushed feather I'd found that morning, the sunlight caught the gleam of gold.

Three gold rings and one silver earring. I dared raise my eyes to my sponsor's face for only a brief instant; he looked grim and quietly furious.

He picked the jewelry from my palm and handed it back to the man without a word. Then he sheathed his sword and turned on his heel. The crowd let me pass this time, but the scornful angry stares burned my back. I had to jog to keep up with my sponsor.

The kick in my stomach and ache in my head made me feel sick and dizzy, and the blinding sunlight only made things worse. I was terrified, but only much later did it occur to me that I might have run away. My sponsor didn't look back for me until we reached the gate in the wall surrounding the palace. I followed him into the courtyard where he turned to face me.

I fell to my knees and pressed my face to the ground. Surely this time his patience was exhausted. I had dishonored him before everyone in the market. He should have disciplined me there immediately. My public shaming and death would have cleared his name. To spare me that shaming was a great mercy, but death was inevitable.

"Stand up, Elathlo." There was an edge in his voice I had never heard before and I jumped to my feet, my eyes lowered in respect. I staggered a little from the dizziness, and he caught my shoulder with a firm hand. It wasn't harsh, but I was already so frightened it made little difference.

"Look at me."

I could scarcely do it, I was so terrified, but I raised my eyes to his face. His mouth was tight, his eyes bright on my face. I tried to slow my breathing and face my death with courage.

"Tell me exactly what happened." Every word was carefully enunciated, his voice clipped. He kept one hand firmly on my shoulder.

"I tripped and fell when I was walking behind you, sir. I tried to get up but he hit me and kicked me."

"Did you take the rings from his table?"

I nearly wept. I did not do it, but the evidence was so clear. He could not believe me. For honor I would tell the truth, but I expected my punishment to be increased because I did not acknowledge my supposed crime.

"No, sir." My voice was only a whisper.

He stared at me for one long moment. "Let me see your shoulder."

I pulled off my shirt.

"Can you move your arm?"

"Yes, sir." He watched me rotate my arm, eyes sharp on my face as I winced.

"Where is this from?" He pointed to a spot of blood on my shirt sleeve.

"Probably my head, sir." I bowed my head and he pushed my hair aside with careful fingers. I still expected to die, but now I was a bit calmer. It was not in his nature to be cruel about it; he would make my death fast and relatively painless.

"Come."

I pulled my shirt back over my head and followed him into the palace and through the halls.

"Saraid, please see to Elathlo." He turned to me. "If you don't feel strong enough for class with Colonel Bekendi this afternoon, tell Saraid and she'll excuse you."

Then he was gone.

Saraid was very kind. She examined my shoulder carefully, asking if it hurt when I moved it in all different directions. She asked where else I was hurt and checked my stomach and head. She washed the cut on the back of my head, but the bruise hurt more.

Once my fear subsided a bit, I was shaking a little. Saraid patted me like my mother would have done and took me to the kitchen for some watered wine, bread, cheese, and a delicious honeyed pastry.

When I finished, she asked me how I felt.

"Better, thank you."

"I'll tell Colonel Bekendi you can rest today."

"I can study. Please."

She looked at me doubtfully, but at my pleading she finally nodded. I wanted to face my death as an aloka should, with courage and perseverance. When my sponsor came to punish me, he would find me studying as I should, not resting. I wouldn't take advantage of his generosity in giving me those last hours and the comfort of Saraid's care. Even if I was not to be tested on the material, at least I would be obedient. Also, perhaps he would see my effort and grant me an easier death.

I tried very hard, but I must have been disappointing to Colonel Bekendi. I felt dizzy and sick, and I kept forgetting what he had just said to me. When he asked me to explain the factors important in the Steeling, my answer was so disjointed that he shook his head and told me that class was over. I was to go rest.

I imagined he was going to speak to my sponsor about my unsatisfactory performance. That fear was more than I could bear. One unsatisfactory class would hardly matter against the great dishonor of that morning, but still I was terrified. Ashamed too. My last bit of pride had been that my final hours would not disappoint my sponsor. I stood to beg Colonel Bekendi's forgiveness. My head spun and I staggered against the table. I didn't faint completely, but everything became fuzzy and distant. I sat on the floor half-leaning against the table leg, murmured voices above me fading in and out. Colonel Bekendi. My sponsor. Saraid.

My sponsor picked me up, one arm behind my knees and the other behind my shoulders, then I was laying on top of my bed. Saraid's voice was the one I heard most, and I remember her hushing me several times as I tried to get up. I did not see my sponsor for the rest of the day, but Saraid stayed with me all day and only left until when I promised I felt better.

Though my head still hurt, I felt much better the next morning. I woke to the sun already up and realized my sponsor must be in the courtyard already. I dressed, still feeling shaky and weak, and made my way out into the frosty morning. My sponsor was in the middle of a complicated sequence of moves. He must have been up for hours; his shirt was off, and even in the cool air, sweat dampened his hair and slid down his torso.

I knelt and pressed my face to the ground, waiting for my death. His footsteps approached, quiet on the packed earth of the courtyard, and stopped in front of me. I did not raise my eyes.

"Stand up, Elathlo." His voice was quiet, and he didn't sound furious. I drew hope from that.

I stood, my hands clasped in the Erdemen waiting posture. I couldn't bring myself to meet his eyes, as I knew he preferred, so my gaze settled on his chin.

"Did you or did you not steal from the man in the marketplace?"

"I did not, sir." I was very proud that I kept my voice from trembling, though it was only a whisper.

"Then you will not be punished. Do not go creeping about as if you are guilty if you are innocent."

I blinked. "You are not angry, sir?" I might have kicked myself for it, too.

"With you? Why would I be angry with you, if you're telling the truth?"

I frowned. Such logic had never entered into my father's punishments, nor Otso-ka's. Nor those of most sponsors who punished their alokas. Alokas are punished because their sponsors are angry, regardless of the cause.

"I..." I raised my eyes to his and found him frowning down at me thoughtfully, as if I were a particularly perplexing puzzle to be solved. "I thank you for your mercy, sir." I bowed hastily, in the Erdemen style as he had taught me.

"Go back to bed, Elathlo. I'll see you at breakfast."

"Yes, sir."

FOURTEEN

KEMEN

While Saraid treated Elathlo that afternoon, I went back to the market and questioned the merchant. He had a table there every week; the other vendors vouched for that.

"Did you actually see the boy steal anything?" I asked.

The man shrugged noncommittally. "Not exactly. I saw his hand brush by my table, though. Someone told me he'd stolen the rings."

"Someone told you? Who?"

"I didn't see him. It was crowded. He was right though. I've caught enough scamps trying to steal things off my tables. I don't have much patience for it anymore." He glared at me.

I frowned. "I'm sorry for the inconvenience."

The incident concerned me, but I had no way to know what it meant. I believed Elathlo was telling the truth. Mostly believed it. I hadn't seen any evidence of lying before, and he had no particular reason to steal. He lived in the palace, surrounded by riches, and had been excruciatingly careful not to touch anything without permission. Besides his obvious fear of punishment, I saw no reason why he would have committed the crime.

Which left the possibility that someone had tried to frame him. That also made little sense. For what purpose? Revenge on him for being Tarvil? When he spoke it was clear from his accent, but nothing in his appearance made it obvious.

Was it somehow connected to the attack on Hakan? Nothing had happened in months.

It perplexed me, and I had no answers.

A FEW DAYS LATER, the first group of ten officers arrived for their advanced training sessions. Kudret and Eneko were among them, and it was good to see them again.

On most topics we reached no consensus, but the debate was more valuable than any lesson I might have devised alone. The men were reluctant at first to debate at all, preferring instead to defer to me, but I insisted that they challenge each other, to defend their views and to consider others' views as well.

After the first discussion went so well, I required a scribe to take notes of the men's comments. Some of it would be useful for Hakan as he thought about these issues as well. He had many changes to make from his father's policies, but he was being cautious, and wisely so, in how he pursued the changes. The nobility, who owned the land and much of the wealth, were already irritated with him about his changes in the tax laws, and he couldn't push them too far or too fast.

He asked me about the first session when we met for lunch the next day, and I told him some of the best points. He nodded thoughtfully and said he would sit in on some of them, if I didn't mind. He slipped in some minutes after the second discussion had begun, and the men all stopped, rose, and bowed to him formally. Then silence reigned for a long moment.

"Iretzi, you were saying…" I prompted.

"Sir?" He looked at me with wide eyes, and I realized he was nervous. The topic was on the role of the military in Erdem, but I wasn't sure exactly where he was going with his comment.

I nodded to him to continue.

He licked his lips and said carefully, "I was going to say, sir, that I wonder if," he stopped and glanced around the room again, then swallowed. "I wonder what the role of the military should be. Rather than what it is."

"In what respect?"

He glanced at the king. "Well, for example. If there was a disaster of some sort. Say a large storm that destroyed many people's houses near a fort. What would be the response?"

I glanced at Hakan too, but his face was neutral. I answered, "Currently, the policy would be to do nothing. Rebuilding private citizens' homes is not a military responsibility."

"Should it be, though?"

Hakan shifted but said nothing.

"What are you suggesting?" I asked.

"Well, it *is* in Erdem's interest for people not to be devastated by freak tragedies."

Kudret spoke up. "It's not that I mind the work, but we don't take an oath that supports helping some citizens over others. And that would clearly be the result. Who would prioritize the work? Who would direct it? It isn't appropriate for soldiers to be under the command of civilians."

Hakan glanced at me but remained silent.

"The king is a civilian. We are all under the authority of the king," I said.

"Yes, sir, but beyond His Royal Highness, we take orders only from our commanding officers," Kudret said.

"Who prioritizes investigation of crimes? The governor, isn't it? But soldiers do the work," said Iretzi.

Hakan corrected him quietly. "Soldiers provide the physical force to apprehend suspects if necessary. Private citizens do the legal and investigation work. The court pays for it."

Iretzi sat back. "Hm." It was obvious he was thinking, but equally obvious he wasn't ready to say more.

Eneko took it. "You're suggesting that the army take responsibility for disaster response? I assume you'd include rebuilding after skirmishes too."

Iretzi shrugged slightly. "I'm not suggesting it exactly. But it would solve some issues."

Everyone stared at each other thoughtfully. It was an interesting discussion, but it became clear, as the silence lengthened, that no one wanted to take it farther. Perhaps because Hakan was there. Perhaps because I was there. Perhaps because it was a huge idea and we weren't sure how to tackle it.

We moved on to other topics for the rest of the day.

Hakan brought it up during dinner. Riona and I were eating with Kveta and Hakan in the private royal suite.

"What did you think of that idea, Kemen?" He pushed his plate away and spread his hands on the table.

"It's interesting. But no." I'd been pondering it all afternoon.

148

"Why not? He brings up a good point. The people are vulnerable to disasters, including the results of border skirmishes, and there isn't really any alternative solution. Right now, the people just suffer the results with no recourse but to rely on the charity of family and friends. You'd need more money, of course, for building materials and engineers."

I shook my head. "It puts entirely too much power in the hands of the military. Someone like Taisto could rise and use it against you."

He raised his eyebrows. "Taisto is dead. And I trust you."

"That's fine while I serve you, but it wouldn't shift back to the crown when I die. It needs to be an institutional solution, not one that relies on personal loyalty." Not that I knew how to devise that type of solution, but I knew it went beyond giving me more power.

He sat back and sighed. "I know. I agree with you. But I'm not sure where to start. The issue is larger than responding to storms. The current system of the crown paying for private investigations into crimes isn't working especially well. The same investigators do all the work, and they're not always unbiased. Because it's not steady work, they have their own side businesses, and of course they favor their friends and business associates. There are a lot of problems like that. The system functions, but it's not as efficient or effective as I'd hope." He sighed again and rubbed his hands over his face. "And of course it's all new to me too, since Father didn't let me know what was going on in any detail."

I didn't envy him the many decisions he had to make. No matter what he did, someone would be displeased by it, generally someone with money and power.

KUDRET STARTED the evening sparring sessions. He asked me one afternoon as our discussion session finished if he might have the honor of a few minutes of sparring with me. We were about a week into the rotation, and it was early winter.

The others watched from the side. Elathlo was finished with his afternoon lessons by then and watched too. It was a good session that I much enjoyed. My shoulder was almost entirely healed by then, and so Kudret and I grappled as well.

When we finished, the men applauded, as if we had put on a good show, and the sessions became a regular occurrence. I sparred four or five of them every night, and the others preferred to watch rather than fight themselves. Afterwards they would ask my advice on their individual weaknesses and strengths. Kudret was fast but sometimes his precision was lacking, especially on his left side. Shui needed to work on his balance. Miloso was naturally talented but tired quickly. Shevar had limited vision in his left eye and sometimes forgot to guard his blind spot.

Ria watched these sessions sometimes too, though she did so from a palace window. She told me later that she felt awkward standing there near the men but not part of their group. The first time I realized she was watching, it made me nervous. I wanted to do well for her. But soon enough I relaxed and focused again on my opponent.

One night I was sparring Shui. I gave him an opening and his kick split my lip. It was a good kick, the one I'd been trying to get him to do for several minutes. The contact was a slight miscalculation on his part, and on mine, but nothing serious. I stopped to spit out the blood, and of course he apologized profusely, but it was nothing worthy of concern. It stopped bleeding before the bout ended. Such things are inevitable in training, and these men were highly trained already. We'd all had our share of bruises. Only later did I realize it had upset Ria. She'd turned away with tears in her eyes, and Lani comforted her.

That's when it came out that Lani was also training; apparently she hadn't even told Ria. Ria spoke to me about it later. She didn't think it was appropriate. I would have agreed at first, but Lani had proven she had the heart for the hard work and more talent than many boys. She was still more fragile and delicate than a boy her age, and I would never have agreed to send her into battle as a soldier regardless of her skill. She enjoyed the training though, and I enjoyed teaching her.

Fifteen

Elathlo

It was perhaps a month after I was attacked in the market that the loneliness finally overwhelmed me. I had kept it at bay by focusing on my studies with a vengeance. My time in the palace had been productive in terms of my learning, and for a time, that was enough. I struggled in my studies, despite my hard work. Even the idea of stretching my mind was new. I found it exhausting.

My sponsor also began training me in close quarters knife combat, which terrified me. We used dull knives, of course, so it wasn't any more dangerous than the open hand combat we'd been practicing for months, or the scimitar work we'd done, or the training with the wooden staff. Still, I felt my mind constantly straining to remember everything we learned from day to day. Exhaustion and loneliness crept in.

The great warrior was kinder than I'd expected and I'd finally learned not to expect cruelty from him, but this was his world. He excelled. He was respected, already a legend. I was honored to serve him, and he expected little in return for his generosity. But I missed my few friends and the familiar food of home. I missed the sound of my language. I missed my mother, her kindness, the warmth of her tent and cook fire. I missed the tundra, the wind and the frost and the open sky that seemed to stretch forever. I even missed Otso-ka's shouting when I disappointed him. I missed making him imea and his smile of pleasure when I gave him good luck again. Summer had faded into autumn and now into the beginning of winter, but it was not the brutal cold I knew.

After our training session, I went to the stable to be alone before my lessons. I had been more clumsy than usual that day, and I didn't want to cry where anyone might see me. My grandfather would have said I cried all the time. At least this time I could have privacy for it; there is nothing worse than eyes on you when you're already frustrated and embarrassed. I found an empty stall and sat on the floor, staring at the wall.

I don't know what I wanted. To be honest, I did not want to go home, certainly not then and maybe not ever. I didn't want to face Otso-ka's disappointment again. An aloka's training is generally three years, and I didn't want to spend the second and third years of my aloka service under a different sponsor. Despite the bruises of training, I had never been hit by my sponsor the way I had been by Otso or my father. He had not even *said* anything cruel to me. When I wasn't sweating in the courtyard, the Erdemen weather was admittedly much more hospitable than our bitter northern winters.

But I was so tired, and I missed the good parts of home. Mother's smile. Tirta's sympathetic slap on my shoulder when Otso-ka yelled and beat me. Even if I did go back, everything would be different. Besides, if I served well, I could not go home until my service was done. Six or seven more months at least. Not serving well would be infinitely worse. It was not an option.

I tensed when I heard steps. I turned away, hoping it was a stable boy come to get a horse. But the steps stopped near me. "Elathlo? Are you here? Is something wrong?"

It was Lani, and I brushed hastily at my eyes. "I'm fine. Just resting."

She sat down next to me, and I wished she would go away. "Does the hay bother your eyes, too? It does mine." She sniffled and rubbed her nose.

"Yes." We sat in silence. I wondered whether she really believed my eyes were red because of the hay, or whether she was trying to be kind. Knowing her, probably the latter.

"Do you miss your home? It must be hard to be gone so long." She played with a piece of straw.

"A little."

"What's different about it?"

"Everything." I didn't want to say any more. My throat closed up and I took a deep breath, willing myself not to cry.

She sat quietly and tied another piece of straw to the first.

"The food is different. It's too hot here. The clothes are different. I'm tired of thinking in Common." I felt stupid to be telling her this.

She gave a sympathetic sigh.

Louder steps, quick and authoritative. "Lani!" It was my sponsor.

He was there in a moment, looking down at us. "Your mother is looking for you. She was worried." His voice was softer now.

She gave me an apologetic look before jumping up. He followed her out and I hoped he would go too, but in a minute he was back. Much to my surprise he sat in the straw beside me, just where she had been.

"What's wrong?"

"Nothing, sir." I looked at my hands clasped in my lap.

"Is that true?"

"No, sir." I tried to keep my voice from shaking. "I'm just tired, I guess. I miss home." Of all people to blubber to, he should have been last. A sponsor does not need to know or care about his aloka's feelings; they are none of his concern.

"That's understandable," he said quietly. "Do you want to go back?"

I drew in a terrified breath. To send me back now would be unimaginable. My grandfather would kill me, but not before a public shaming. I saw it once before, when an aloka so disappointed his sponsor that he was sent back in disgrace rather than killed immediately. My stomach crawled at the memory. *So much blood!*

"No, sir." I fell on my face before him, nauseated with fear and breathless as I waited for his condemnation.

He cursed softly, and I felt his hands on my shoulders. "What is the matter? What are you afraid of?"

I tried in vain to steady my voice. "If you send me back now, sir..." I couldn't finish. "Please, sir, just take my head yourself. Be merciful and do it yourself." I was too terrified to cry, even to breathe.

His jaw clenched and he kept both hands on my shoulders. "I meant that I would take you for a visit, if Hakan gives his consent."

I fell on my face again, sobbing with relief. He pulled me up to put his arm around my shoulders. I choked on my tears, and he rubbed my back as if I were a child and he was my mother.

I was terribly embarrassed, but I was too tired and too relieved to stop myself from weeping. I was exhausted when I finished, sweaty and covered with the dust of hay and the dirt of training. I sat up, hiding my face in embarrassment.

He tightened his arm around me for a moment before letting me straighten. I choked out some sort of apology, but he shook his head. He stretched out his long legs and leaned back against the wall of the stable with a deep sigh.

"Elathlo, how is your tutor? Has he been harsh with you?"

"No, sir."

"Is the work too much for you?"

"No, sir." I was struggling with arithmetic, but I did not say this. I was too afraid of disappointing him.

"Did I hurt you today?"

"No, sir."

"You're tired?"

"Yes, sir." I could not deny this, since I'd said it myself only minutes before. I wished I wasn't so weak.

"You've been training hard since the end of Hekku. It's nearly the middle of Kylma. Rest the next two days."

"Sir?" I felt as though I had failed him, though his smile seemed kind. "I can train. I'm not too tired."

"I forget you're only thirteen, Elathlo. Take the next two days and rest. You've earned it. Would you like to go hunting after that?"

156

"Yes, sir." I blinked in confusion.

"We can go on Kuudenne, then, if Hakan doesn't need me." He sat in silence for some time, as if he were still thinking, but finally he stood. He pulled me to my feet and brushed the straw from the back of my tunic. He looked me over critically, and I drew in my breath and stood taller.

"Go get a bath. I'll tell Colonel Bekendi you have today off as well."

My eyes widened. Surely he was displeased with me.

Perhaps he saw my expression, for he smiled very kindly. "You've earned the rest. Enjoy it." He put one hand on my shoulder and guided me out into the blinding sunlight.

I DID AS I was told. I took a bath, and after I dressed I stood in the middle of my room for several minutes wondering what to do. I jumped at a knock on the door. It was Lani, and she smiled at me.

"Do you want your breakfast here or with Kemen and the king?"

I had a choice?

"Should I go to the king?" I bit my lip. Probably I should not turn down such an invitation, even though they could not really want me there.

"I would." Lani smiled. "Don't be so serious. You'll be fine."

I followed her through the halls. If I wasn't Tarvil and she Erdemen, I might have hoped for something more than friendship with her. I couldn't imagine what her mother would think of that, though.

I liked her a lot, and not just because she was pretty. It was disconcerting to train with her in the mornings and then to see her in a dress later. She was quick and hardworking. Sometimes she said things without thought, but she was always quick to apologize if something sounded harsh, even when there was no real need for an apology. She was generous and warm-hearted, and I wished I could have her smiling confidence.

"Here." She stopped in front of a door, but turned to me before she opened it. "Don't frown so! What's wrong?"

"Is he angry?" I was really steeling myself more for disappointment, but I was too ashamed to ask about that.

"Of course not. It's just breakfast. Go on." She smiled and patted my shoulder reassuringly.

I bowed when I entered. My sponsor and the king sat at a small table and they both smiled at me when I entered. "Come. Sit, Elathlo." One doesn't normally sit in the presence of the king except at banquets, and I sat nervously.

My sponsor spoke to the king about the school in Ironcrest that was nearly ready to open. He had received word about the preparations being made to receive the Tarvil students. He hoped to integrate the Tarvil students and the Erdemen students in the same classes, and had already arranged for a squad of soldiers to maintain the peace between them if necessary.

I kept my eyes down and my hands folded in my lap as an aloka should when he is not working. I'd done nothing for my sponsor to earn my training. He tended to his own weapons, and other tasks were handled by the servants. I wondered if he would ask the king about the political repercussions of sending me back to my grandfather. He had said he wouldn't, but I did not understand yet how honor is different in Erdem.

Later I learned that his word was his honor, that he always spoke the truth. Later still, when I was much older, I understood that even that was not entirely accurate. He had lied a few times in his life, and suffered no guilt for it. He lied in the service of his king, to keep the king Hakan Ithel safe before he assumed the throne, and a few other times when a higher honor demanded something other than the literal truth. In any case, I suffered much more fear than I needed to, for he had no intent to go back on his promise to me that morning.

Lani brought our lunch in a few minutes, and I waited until they began before I ate myself.

"Hakan, I'd like to take Elathlo to see his family sometime soon. Could we leave next week?"

"On Nelja we receive the Ophrani ambassador. I'd like you to be here for that. But you could leave as early as the next morning if you wanted to." The king smiled at me. "It has been a while, and you've been working hard. Enjoy your visit.

"Thank you, Your Royal Highness." I ducked my head, my voice barely above a whisper.

My sponsor said, "We'll take our time on our way north then. It will be our hunting trip."

SIXTEEN

KEMEN

I spoke to Ria about the trip north that evening after dinner. We were sitting close by the fire in our bedroom, already in our sleeping clothes. Her gown was nearly sheer, and she'd blushed bright red when she first wore it in my presence. Now she was comfortable, and I enjoyed her confidence even more, if that was possible.

I was brushing her hair; sometimes in the evenings I did it for her. She made little moans of pleasure as if I were doing much more than simply running a brush through her hair, and quite often the brushing proved to be only a prelude for other activities. Even when it was only a brush, though, I enjoyed the sleepy contentment on her face, her eyes half-closed as she murmured unnecessary thanks. I breathed the sweet smell of her hair running through my hands like silk, and thought how very lucky I was.

"He's not just tired. He must be lonely too. I should have thought."

"I'm sure he is."

"Do you mind if I take him to visit his family? It shouldn't be more than a month or so."

She sighed, and I could feel her disappointment in the set of her shoulders. "No, I don't mind. I want to be selfish and demand you stay here, but he's only a child. Go, and have a good time."

"We'll hurry back." The words felt inadequate.

"I know." She twisted to wrap her arms around me. "I know you will. Don't feel guilty. I know you do, and you shouldn't. I'll be here when you return." She smiled up at me, clear blue eyes warm and kind.

I pressed a kiss to her forehead, then her nose, then her lips, lingering to taste her, tender and slow. "Thank you, Ria."

I ran my fingers through her hair, then rubbed the base of her neck slowly, letting the palms of my hands move slowly over her smooth skin. She closed her eyes and smiled, and I thought of how I might show her I loved her even while I was gone. Her nightgown was loose around the neck, and I slipped my hands lower to feel the delicate muscles of her shoulders, my thumbs tracing circles against the silk of her skin.

"You don't have to do that. I know you're tired," she murmured.

I was, and it was late. But I smiled at her voice and knelt beside her, leaned in so that our foreheads met. She opened her eyes and smiled at me, blue eyes dark in the dim light.

"Ria, you are my rest."

She almost laughed at me. "Kemen, even you need to sleep. How late were you up last night?" She put her hands on my shoulders and pressed a kiss to my lips, then pulled back to look at me. She cupped one hand on my cheek and ran her thumb under my eye, tickling my eyelashes.

I closed my eyes and pressed my cheek into her hand. "I need you."

Seventeen

Elathlo

The next morning, I woke slowly, the bright winter sunlight slanting across the room and onto the foot of the bed. My sponsor had not knocked on my door, nor had any servants woken me. The hall outside my room was silent. I hadn't slept that late in months, perhaps years. Though I wouldn't have said I felt at home in Erdem, I had grown to enjoy my soft bed, and I snuggled down in the covers for some time, luxuriating in the warmth. In the haze of drowsiness, the day stretched before me in blissful simplicity.

I finally dressed and wandered down to the courtyard, which was empty, and then to the kitchen. Joran, the cook, was working on something for dinner that night. His name was terribly hard for me to pronounce, with a soft *J* at the beginning that was foreign to my tongue. He was kind, though. Sometimes my sponsor and I would eat in the kitchen after our morning exercises, and sometimes I would eat there with Lani and the servants when my sponsor ate with the king or Lady Riona and I wasn't invited.

"Have you had breakfast yet?"

"No, sir." I shook my head, and he nodded me toward a table.

"Help yourself, then. Grapes and moonfruit, fresh olive bread, cheese, meat pie if you want."

I made myself a small plate and watched him work.

"You have the morning off, then?" He smiled at me kindly.

I swallowed before answering. "Yes, sir." Joran's olive bread was a delicacy unlike any I'd ever had before. I preferred it even to the sweetbreads that Lani loved. Rich and filling alone, it was even better topped with goat cheese and drizzled with oil and crushed herbs.

"They're in the garden near the trellis, if you want to go out. It's cold, so wear a cloak."

"Thank you, sir." I ate the rest of the meal in silence, listening to Joran presiding over the kitchen.

When I finished, I washed my dish, and meandered back out to the courtyard before turning toward the garden.

I wasn't entirely sure from Joran's directions whether my sponsor wanted to see me or not. However, he had said I was to rest, and the garden was a beautiful place to do it, even in winter. Warmth like an Erdemen summer doesn't exist on the tundra where my people live. Now, in early winter, the sun was so bright and strong it warmed the air so that it didn't feel as cold as I'd thought at first.

I saw them before they saw me, and the sight so startled me that I stopped in my tracks. The great warrior lay on his back on a blanket spread upon the fading green grass. His head rested Riona's lap. She was reading from a book balanced on one knee.

My sponsor sat up. He must have heard me.

"I'm sorry." I bowed and turned to retreat, but he stopped me.

"Come. Sit with us." He gestured to the space beside him.

I knelt by them, knowing I was intruding although neither of them said it.

He smiled. "Ria was reading to me. You might enjoy it."

Riona smiled at me too. I ducked my head, feeling my cheeks flush. She looked a bit like Lani, though she was older. It was difficult to tell how much of her beauty was in her features and how much was in the kindness of her smile and the softness of her voice.

She opened the book and began to read. I was distracted by watching them. I hadn't seen them together often, except sometimes when I ate with them, and at the wedding of course. I'd never seen my mother and father so relaxed around each other. My father was not an easy man to be around. Much like Otso-ka, but younger and stronger. Less patient.

My sponsor reached over to hold her hand. Their fingers intertwined and they both smiled quietly. After some time my knees began to ache. I was in the waiting posture, kneeling, ready to serve though he almost never asked me to. I tried to shift without being noticed, but Riona saw me.

"Relax. That can't be comfortable." She smiled.

I stiffened when my sponsor glanced over.

He raised his eyebrows at me. "You're not in training today. Relax. Take a nap if you like."

Riona snorted softly. "Take your own advice."

His lips quirked up in a wry smile.

I sat with my legs crossed and Riona continued reading.

This is the story she read.

"In the sixth year of the king's reign, the queen bore him a son. The boy was given the name Ciram, and he was loved by all, for he was beautiful in both body and spirit. When the prince was five years old, the queen bore the king a daughter, who was given the name Dia. The princess too was of surpassing beauty, and as the brother and sister grew, they were fast friends. The prince became skilled in the arts of war, but he was of a peaceful nature and used his strength only when justice demanded it. Though his father the king was well-loved, the people also looked forward to the reign of the young prince, for he showed much promise as a wise and good ruler. Both the prince and princess were talented poets and musicians, and when they sang together, their voices could bring tears from a stone.

"One day they were hunting together with all their retinue. The princess Dia set her hawk to chase a hare, and a short time later it returned with its prey in its talons. But the hawk's eyes were wild and the princess was unable to hood it again. The hawk shrieked and died on her arm, and only then did they see the worm biting the beautiful hawk between the golden feathers of its neck. The worm was golden like the hawk, with flashing golden eyes, and when the hawk died it turned to the princess with an evil hiss. The princess flung the glove away and the hawk's body and the worm with it. The prince struck at the worm as it fell, but his sword gave a crack as though he had struck steel, and he cried out at the pain of the jolt. The worm fled unharmed, but the prince was always weak in that arm.

"Both the prince and princess were plagued by evil dreams even after they returned to the palace. Once the princess awoke screaming in pain. There were two tiny holes on her ankle that might have been a very small bite, but though her

room was searched by many servants, the prince, and her fa-
ther the king himself, nothing was found.

"*The princess grew distraught and finally she traveled
again to the northern forest there they had first seen the worm.
She did not tell her brother, though she took several servants
with her. When he heard that she had gone, the prince went in
search of her.*

"*They found nothing. She and her servants were gone,
and no sign of them was ever found.*

"*Many years later, after the prince was crowned king and
had grown sons of his own, he received word of a strange sight
in the north. He rode to see it and was amazed. There was a
stone in the shape of a hand reaching from the ground, and his
sister's cloak was wrapped around it. The fabric was not aged
or dirty at all, though it had been nearly forty years since she
had disappeared. On each fingertip of the stone hand a tiny
figure of a snake was inlaid in gold. The king ordered that the
stone hand be dug from the ground to discover if it belonged to
a body. The stone hand was broken off at the elbow, and there
was no stone body or statue beneath the earth. No other sign of
what had happened to the beautiful princes was ever found.
The king was distraught, and to the end of his days he believed
that somewhere his sister was alive.*"

"Was she?" I could not hold back the question.

"You don't know this story?" Riona asked.

I shook my head, and my sponsor smiled.

Riona answered, "Some believe that King Ciram
was right, that his sister did not die, at least not when she
disappeared. They say she was the mother of the northern tribes, your people."

I frowned. "Really?"

"Well, no one can know for sure. One of the stories
says that the Tarvil came from the marriage of that princess and an unknown man from one of the older tribes
that are gone now. Another says that the snake was the

father of your people, and others say the father was a wolf. Of course that sounds impossible, but who knows what really happened to her?"

Either way, it would mean that my people and Erdemen Tuyets were siblings, brother and sister separated at some point long past but still bound somehow. I wondered whether it was true. I'd never heard any Tarvil legends that said we were related to Erdemen, at least not more than by common humanity. Even that was somewhat suspect; my father and the other warriors had certainly been content to think of Erdemen as Other, not similar to us in the least. I wondered whether this was why Erdemen were kinder, or whether it was a result of their greater riches or some other aspect of the culture that I did not yet understand.

Eighteen

Kemen

I spoke to Glaw, the head servant of our new estate. His function was something like that of Noriso, the palace administrator, though our estate was much smaller than the palace. Noriso had interviewed him and liked him, and Hakan himself had given final approval for his hiring. Glaw was about my age and had previously served in the house of Lord Oshiro, an old and respected family, though not of the highest rank. Glaw looked a little overawed by the grandeur of the estate, and I couldn't blame him. He looked even more intimidated by me, and I tried to put him at his ease.

"I'll be leaving in a few days for a trip north. It should take about a month. Ensure that Lady Sendoa," the sound of her new name on my lips made me smile, "is accommodated in every regard while I am gone."

"Yes, my lord." He bowed.

I sent him to the market to buy some paints for Ria and some drawing charcoals for me, papers, and a box to carry them in. While he was gone, I worked with one of Hakan's scribes on the plan for the officers' training.

I ended my work early, just before dinner, and found Ria in the garden where she was walking. "Come. I have something for you."

"What is it?"

"Come and see." I smiled at her confused expression. She slipped her hand into mine as we went inside, and I tightened my fingers around hers. Even after months of marriage, her love still surprised me; when she touched me, my skin tingled and my heart beat faster. In our room, I showed her the paints, charcoals, and paper laid out on the breakfast table.

"While I'm gone, paint me something every day. I want to know what you see, what you feel. And I'll draw you something. Paints don't travel as well, so I have charcoals."

She made a funny sound, and I bent to see her face more clearly. She looked at me and burst into giggles.

"What?" I had the sinking feeling that she thought it was a foolish idea. She was laughing at me.

"Oh, no, Kemen, don't look like that!" She wrapped her arms around my waist and gave me a gentle smile that made my hurt melt into warmth. "It's sweet. I've just never drawn anything. I'm no artist. You'll laugh when you see my scratchings."

"You don't mind?" I tried to find the right words. "I thought it would be like doing something together."

She tightened her arms around me. "Darling, I think it's wonderful. *You* are wonderful. I just think you'll find my painting skills less than enchanting. But I'll think of you when I try."

"I'll think of you," I murmured, kissing her lips, then her neck. "I always think of you."

Nineteen

Elathlo

As my sponsor had promised, we departed the day after the Ophrani ambassador arrived. I was excited to see the ambassador, and my sponsor must have realized it. He let me attend the reception dinner, which was small but luxurious. The Ophrani ambassador was darker skinned than the Erdemen Tuyets, though still lighter than my sponsor, and he stared about the palace with pale brown eyes that saw much. His clothes too, were different than Erdemen clothes. He wore tight-fitting black breeches, soft black boots, and a white shirt accented by bold colored embroidery around the neck and down the sleeves. His black vest was similarly embroidered. My sponsor said the patterns signified his family and lineage, and I wondered how he could read the complicated symbolism.

We left at first light, in a cold snap that startled me with its suddenness. My horse Aratso was fat and lazy from the rich pasturage and generous oats of the palace stable, and I pictured my friend Tirta laughing at how spoiled he was when we arrived.

We did not travel too slowly, but we took a whole day to go on a leisurely hunting trip shortly before we reached the northern border. I had some experience with a Tarvil bow; sometimes we shot rock achas and snow hares from horseback. Our bows were small, easily shot while riding. My sponsor taught me to shoot an Erdemen crossbow. He showed me how to shoot the Erdemen longbow as well, sinking six arrows in a row into the center of the tree we selected as our target. I struggled with it for several minutes, but the draw was much too strong for me.

I thought of the scar on my sponsor's back and wondered whether it was strange for him to teach a Tarvil to shoot, but I didn't ask.

He congratulated me when I shot a large buck with the crossbow. We roasted it over a fire and even the men of our small suvari escort congratulated me on providing our dinner. Although it was winter, and suddenly cold enough for it, we had no snow until we reached Fort Kuzeyler. My sponsor said it often snowed only around the new year and afterwards; the first part of winter was cold but dry.

Every night, my sponsor spent an hour after dinner sitting on the ground at a small table, charcoals and paper spread out in front of him. I looked over his shoulder sometimes. I'm sure he must have noticed, but he never mentioned it, nor explained. I didn't think of him as an artist, and perhaps he wasn't trained to be such, but I liked his drawings. They were somehow both lonely and peaceful, and they made me feel as if my sponsor understood how I felt, being so far from everything I had ever known. A man who felt nothing could not draw with feeling.

One night he also dictated a letter to the king, asking if all was well in his absence. There was nothing in the letter or in my sponsor's voice to indicate that he was worried about anything in particular, but it was a little strange to me that he asked at all.

AS WE NEARED the border, I found myself almost sick with nerves. It had been a beautiful trip, but my enjoyment of the journey faded as the meeting with my grandfather drew near. I was afraid his scorn would sting even more since I had not felt it in months. Besides, I desperately wanted to please my sponsor, and although I could not understand why, I felt that so far I had done so, at least for the most part. I was afraid Otso-ka's words would threaten that quiet approval I so valued.

Perhaps my sponsor could see my fear, but he did not say anything until we reached the far northern outpost the Erdemen called Izotz. My grandfather had called it Pezcht, a curse so foul I was never allowed to say it.

He sent several scouts to find where my clan was camped, and we spent a few days waiting for their return. My sponsor inspected the fort and I stayed close by him. It was a small, sturdy place. I knew my grandfather would ask if it had any vulnerabilities, but I could see none, at least none that the Tarvil were equipped to exploit. Nor did I want them to. My loyalty was divided, to say the least.

My sponsor stopped and knelt on the ground. He rested his hand on the icy dirt for a long moment with his eyes closed, then sighed and stood. I did not ask why.

Only a little snow blew about in the gusts of wind, eddying in about in the corners of the walls, dry and powdery. If we had waited any longer to go north, we would not have been so fortunate. But then I remembered that it was my homesickness that had initiated our travel, and I felt my nerves and my gratitude rise in equal measure.

Some of the Erdemen soldiers stationed at Izotz eyed me threateningly, but close by my sponsor I had no trouble. When one of the riders brought word that my grandfather's clan was camped some five leagues northwest, my sponsor said we would leave the next morning.

He spoke to me after dinner. "Elathlo, what do I need to know before I speak with your grandfather?"

"About what, sir?"

"What could I say about you that would disappoint him and what would please him?"

"It would disappoint him to hear that I am disrespectful or lazy. That I am a coward. That I don't work hard. That I am weak or clumsy or slow. That my progress or skill is unsatisfactory."

He nodded. "Anything else?"

I shook my head.

THE NEXT MORNING we rode out to the place the rider had said. It was only my sponsor and me, and we spoke little. I was terribly nervous, but he looked as stern and confident as he always did. He wore simple clothes, just a bright white shirt and green tunic over brown trousers, with a heavy green cloak against the frigid wind. He'd chosen to wear a single straight shortsword rather than his longsword. I wished he'd chosen the longer blade; it was much more impressive. I wondered whether it was wise for him to go alone, but I remembered what Otso-ka had said when he first signed the treaty. Those words were still true. Even now, the Tarvil had too much to lose by his death to kill him.

As we approached, I smelled the familiar scent of burning arsana wood and sheep dung. I wanted to see my mother, but I could not have described my feelings about the meeting with my grandfather. Nervous fear. Desperate hope for his approval. Love of some sort, complicated though it might be. Resentment sometimes.

My mother came running to greet me, and behind her was Tirta. She stopped suddenly when she saw my sponsor, and came more cautiously, but she did come. I dismounted and met her, and she embraced me. It was only then that I realized I was taller than before; I'd grown almost a hands-breadth. She touched my shoulders, brushed her hand over my hair, smiling and speaking all the time. The sound of her voice speaking my language was like music.

My sponsor dismounted and took the reins of my horse, and I barely noticed. Tirta ran up and pounded me on the back, shouting and laughing, and we grinned at each other. I was taller than he was now; I'd always been shorter, but now his eyes were lower than mine. I wondered if I'd finally hit my growth, or whether the Erdemen food had helped.

"How is he? How are you?" He glanced at General Sendoa cautiously.

I smiled. "He is a generous sponsor. Better than I could have wished for. You should be so fortunate."

"Really? He looks..." he hesitated and glanced at my sponsor again with a fear I could easily understand. The general had gained weight in the months since I'd gone south, no longer gaunt but lean and strong, all hard efficient muscle. He looked fiercer than ever. The change had been slow, but Tirta's reaction made me notice.

"Truly." I smiled again.

I spoke to my sponsor in Common. "Sir, this is my mother, Intan, and my friend, Tirta." Then I introduced them in Tarvil. They could not understand each other, but my sponsor bowed solemnly. It was not a deep bow, but now I knew enough to understand that it was a respectful bow to one of common birth.

Then my grandfather arrived, and Tirta led our horses away with a quick, encouraging smile.

"You've grown."

"Yes, sir." I ducked my head respectfully. I was almost as tall as he was, though not nearly so strong. Still my sponsor seemed like a giant in comparison.

Otso-ka took us to his tent to talk before the welcome *hasrana*, a traditional feast. My mother and the other women must have been working all night to prepare it, since they had only heard of our coming the day before. I wished I could speak with her more, but my grandfather would expect me to attend him and my sponsor. I made their *imea* while they sat across from each other on the rug.

"How is he? What has he learned in training?"

"He is an intelligent and hard-working student. I train him every morning myself, and in the afternoons he studies with a tutor." My sponsor spoke formally, and he smiled his thanks when I placed his cup of *imea* before him, and then served Otso-ka. Normally I would have served Otso-ka first, because he was the chief, but an *aloka* always serves his sponsor first.

"His tutor teaches him arithmetic, history, reading and writing in Common, and other subjects. I train him in combat, both unarmed and armed, and military history, strategy, and tactics. He attends many of my meetings with the king Hakan Ithel and is observing our preparations for the school in Ironcrest."

"You have had no problems with him? He is not lazy or disrespectful, is he?"

"He is a pleasure to instruct. He works hard and well, and is always respectful."

"Good." He turned to me, sternly pleased. "Bring us alamaa."

I bowed. In a few minutes I was back, but when I knelt at the low table, I hesitated. "Otso-ka, my sponsor would prefer not to drink the alamaa."

He struck me hard across the face.

I fell back, off balance, though I managed not to spill the pot of alamaa. I saw the blow coming; my sponsor had demonstrated in sparring practice how the weight shifts before a strike, and my grandfather's movement was far from subtle. He was also slow, moving at the speed my sponsor used when we sparred at "half-speed." Perhaps if I had been ready, I could have blocked the blow, but I was not yet skilled enough to block it with no warning. It would also have been disrespectful.

My sponsor's sword was at my grandfather's throat so quickly I had not even heard it drawn. Otso-ka looked at him in baffled anger.

"No one strikes my aloka." The general's voice was low, but every inch of him radiated absolute fury. I swallowed blood, coppery and warm.

"He insulted you! He would have denied you the honor of the alamaa. He said you would prefer not to drink it." My grandfather was angry, but he was also right.

I bowed in apology toward the general. I should have known that an aloka does not speak for his sponsor. In fact I had known; I had spoken without thinking of etiquette.

The four men along the sides of the tent had their hands on the hilts of their scimitars. A thousand thoughts flashed through my mind, and fear was not first. Only later did that surprise me.

With my sponsor's sword at Otso-ka's throat, the men had no hope of defending him. Even Otso-ka must have known that. It was not beyond Otso-ka to order them to attack my sponsor anyway, out of anger and pride. The man across from me would not obey such an order; I could see it in his eyes. The other two I could see would obey, not because they loved Otso-ka, but because they hated the idea of an Erdemen getting away with threatening a Tarvil. I could not see the face of the man who was closest to me, I was nearly sprawled at his feet, not moving for fear of worsening the tension in the tent. But I could kill him with my boot knife if I had to; he would step past me to reach my sponsor, and his back would be toward me. At the very least I could hamstring him, which would delay him enough to remove him from the fight.

That would leave the odds at two or three against my sponsor. A sick realization crept up like bile in my throat as I realized they had no idea how truly dangerous my sponsor was. He did not need my help to defeat four warriors in a tent.

I also realized in that split second that if there was a fight, I would fight with my sponsor, not with my people. I did not hate Otso-ka, nor did I hate my people, but I found my loyalties drawn inexorably toward my sponsor. I could not have fought against him, not in this.

"Do you think he lies?" He did not remove the edge of the sword from my grandfather's throat.

"You don't want the alamaa?"

"I thank you for the honor, but it makes me ill."

That cooled Otso-ka's anger a little. "Nevertheless, he should not have spoken for you. An aloka serves his sponsor with unquestioning obedience and does not presume to speak for him."

My grandfather was right. I bowed my apology again to my sponsor, on one knee as an Erdemen would apologize.

"I understood that he was under my instruction as my aloka. Was I wrong?" My sponsor's voice was icy.

"He is. But such disrespect should not tolerated." Otso-ka hid his fear well, but I could see it in his widened eyes.

"I am quite capable of disciplining him when and if it is necessary. I do not judge it necessary now. I expect him to think before he acts, which he did." My sponsor sheathed his sword deliberately. "You cannot teach a man to stand tall by forcing him to bow and shrink in fear. Half my time is spent undoing the damage you have done to him."

I had never seen him so angry, but I suppose I should have known he would show it by lowering his voice. I doubt anyone but my grandfather and I could clearly hear what he said.

Otso-ka was nearly speechless. "You allow him to treat you so disrespectfully? This is not what an aloka should learn!"

"Would you strike me the way you struck him?"

My grandfather's eyes widened at the question. "Of course not."

"Why not?" My sponsor's voice remained low, but I hoped with all my heart that my grandfather recognized the dangerous light in his eyes.

Otso-ka chose the diplomatic answer. "Because I respect you." That, and the fact that it would be his last act.

"Elathlo has earned my respect. If he hasn't earned yours, that is your failure to recognize his worth, not his. You should be proud of him." My sponsor softened his voice slightly, though it was still stern. "You lead your people. How can you expect them to follow him if you don't show them how? If you respect him, they will too. It is in your hands whether he can lead."

They stared at each other in silence.

"Elathlo, please sit." The general indicated the seat next to him. He refilled my imea cup for me, a deliberate courtesy that Otso-ka watched, his expression unreadable.

"We were speaking of his progress in training. He is excelling. He works hard, and has good timing when we spar. He needs to work on his speed, but for a boy of his age, he is skilled. He is training for unarmed combat as well as with the scimitar and longsword. Next month we will begin training with the staff. He is also studying reading and writing in Common, history, arithmetic, military affairs, and diplomacy. He is a bright and studious pupil who has much potential as a leader. Before we departed Stonehaven, he participated in the reception of the Ophrani ambassador."

My eyes widened at his words, and I bowed my head to hide my surprise. Participated? I had eaten dinner at the same table without saying a word. Nevertheless, his praise so pleased my grandfather that he did not have to elaborate.

The tension in the air lessened a little, and my grandfather ignored me for much of the rest of the time, speaking as though I were invisible. This I did not mind, though I wished I had his approval.

He nodded toward me once. "It is good to hear you have not disappointed your sponsor."

I merely bowed. Any further acknowledgement would mean that I felt the general's praise was justified. A sponsor's praise is a rare and beautiful thing. To be allowed to live is approval, to be graced with the sponsor's time and effort in training is much to be coveted. The general had already so exceeded the responsibilities of a sponsor that this deliberate praise before my grandfather made my throat tighten with emotion.

As we walked out of the tent, my sponsor said, as if it was a thought that had only just occurred to him, "Did you notice that Elathlo did not spill the alamaa?"

Otso-ka grunted.

My sponsor turned to him and asked, "If Elathlo had a knife, do you think he might have been able to use it on you?"

Otso-ka snorted. "Alokas are not armed. Besides, the boy is hopeless with a blade."

My sponsor only smiled.

WHILE THE WOMEN prepared dinner, my sponsor took me some short distance away from the tents, onto a hillside. He stood for several long minutes and looked out at the tundra, the tufts of scrubby grass grazed short by our few sheep and horses. Swirls of snow formed faint eddies, though no more fell from the sky and nothing covered the ground. Then he turned to face the camp, his eyes ranging over the figures scurrying from tent to tent.

"After any skirmish, it is customary to have an after-action discussion, to learn from what happened. Tell me about what just happened in your grandfather's tent," he said finally.

"My grandfather was angry because I should not have spoken for you, sir. He was right in that. I'm sorry, sir." I bowed in the Erdemen style.

"You did nothing wrong!" It was the first time he spoke sharply to me in our months together. I should not have flinched. I knew by then that he wouldn't strike me, but it was reflex.

He spoke more gently then. "Here." He pulled his handkerchief from his pocket and poured water from his canteen over it. "Tell me first what you observed and what you thought. Then I will tell you what I thought."

I pressed the wet cloth to my split lip. The water soothed the pain and swelling, and I hoped it didn't look too bad. Blood streaked the cloth, but I didn't think my lip was bleeding anymore.

I tried to gather my thoughts into the calm logic that my sponsor always demonstrated. "Sir, the man across from me, Joreth, would not have obeyed an order to attack you. He put his hand on his sword hilt to intimidate you, but he does not like my grandfather and would not die for him. The other two whose faces I could see would have fought for him, or at least fought against you. They may not care for Otso-ka, but they wouldn't want to back down. I'm not sure about the one near me. I couldn't see his eyes."

The scene replayed itself in my mind, and I realized something else. "They were all of different tribes, and they wouldn't have known how to fight together. They were probably meant to report back to their chiefs about the meeting, not to guard Otso-ka."

I hesitated, and my sponsor waited, glancing from me to the tents and back again. His patience no longer surprised me, but knowing he waited for my words made me nervous. "I don't think any of them, except perhaps my grandfather and I, understood that you could probably kill them all, even if they attacked at once."

"Anything else?" He did not react at all to that statement, either to confirm or deny it. He had no need assert his skill, and that, more than anything else, told me I was right.

I hesitated, then shook my head. "No, sir."

Another thought occurred to me, although I didn't voice it. The guards and my grandfather had been armed with scimitars, meant for full-armed, slashing strokes from horseback. They were not suitable for stabbing or thrusting strikes, and thus were so impractical as to be nearly useless in such a small space. My sponsor had chosen his short sword for practicality, knowing that a confrontation in a confined space was possible. Perhaps he had even foreseen that it might occur while he was seated; his longsword would have been difficult to draw while seated and wouldn't have been easy to use in such a small space. My sponsor was as wise and canny as the wolf, though more merciful.

He studied my face a moment, then glanced back up toward the tents. "I agree about Joreth, the one who would not have fought. I think he agreed with me that your grandfather's harshness with you is counterproductive. He might even believe you would be a better leader than your grandfather."

I blinked.

My sponsor continued, "You did well not to react in anger or fear when your grandfather struck you. Many boys your age would have. It is better to wait and calm a disagreement than to engage, unless absolutely necessary." He looked down again and waited until I met his gaze. "But if you ever think of using your boot knife, don't glance at it first. Or at your target. If you have to fight, don't let your opponent know what you're going to do until it's too late for him to counter it."

I swallowed. "Yes, sir."

He took the cloth from my hand and raised my chin. "You'll be fine. Just a split lip and a bruise." He poured more water over the cloth and wrung it out, then sighed heavily. "I see better why you were so afraid of me when you first became my aloka. But you don't need to be.

Every man has flaws, Elathlo. I have many of my own. Your grandfather also has some. One of his is a failure to understand how to build up a man, to strengthen his strengths and shore up his weaknesses. You have a good heart and a quick mind. You work hard, and you're humble. Stay that way, and you'll be a better chief than he is."

I brushed at my eyes, feeling sudden, surprised tears of relief and pride well up. His voice changed, and I glanced up to see him smiling a little.

"When I agreed to take you as an aloka, I did it because I wanted the treaty. I did it for my king. Your grandfather risked much for that treaty, and I wanted to give him something in return that he would value, so that he would be bound by gratitude to Hakan. But I spoke the truth when I said it was an honor to teach you. You've earned my respect, regardless of what your grandfather thinks."

My emotion choked me, and my whisper was barely audible. "Thank you, sir."

He clapped a hand to my shoulder. "Come. I think they're ready."

He didn't speak again until we reached my grandfather's tent, where the food was steaming in the cool air. But my heart was full. The general was never a man of many words, and so many kind ones spoken directly to me, as if I were a man, was a gift I cannot describe.

DINNER, DESPITE THE HONOR they meant to accord him, seemed small and mean in comparison to the luxury I had almost become accustomed to. My sponsor showed only appreciation for the meal, without a hint of disdain. My grandfather and the men around him could not understand how generous that was.

My sponsor stayed the night in my grandfather's tent, which was another honor, but I imagine it was terribly awkward for both of them. If the king had known that his champion slept under the tent of a man who had wished him dead so many times, he probably wouldn't have been pleased.

After dinner and before it was time to sleep, I took him to my mother's tent. He looked like a giant under the low ceiling; he could not even stand at his full height. My mother sat him at the place of honor at the head of the low table and served us a second smaller meal of roasted lamb and beans, an extravagance that he probably couldn't appreciate. He requested that she sit with us, but she refused until nearly the end, both from tradition and from fear of him. She spoke very cautiously to me with anxious glances at him. I translated between them because my mother spoke no Common at all. He praised me to her and complimented the food she made for us.

She asked me about my bloodied lip; she thought he had done it. When I ducked my head and explained that it had been Otso-ka, she nodded in understanding. Her relationship with Otso-ka had been strained as long as I can remember. His discipline was not unusual. Every Tarvil boy goes through the same discipline and training, but all the same it is not easy for a mother to watch. I think Otso-ka was even more demanding of me, since he hoped I would lead after him.

My father was much the same; he'd learned from Otso-ka. She comforted me when Father and then Otso-ka disciplined me, and she encouraged me when I felt I could never earn their approval. Now that I was nearly grown she didn't embrace me so readily, but still I could feel her sympathy. I told her that my sponsor had defended me, though I didn't say how close we had come to bloodshed, and she was both astonished and grateful.

She bowed to him in the Tarvil way, and my sponsor looked at me for an explanation.

"Tell her that I did only what any man should do. Tell her also that it is an honor to teach you."

"Sir?" My eyes widened again. He might say it to me, and that was unusual enough. But an aloka never praises himself; even to relay the words would be unprecedented.

He smiled, a brilliant smile that lit the room. "Tell her. They are my words, not yours. You're not being arrogant."

I did translate, with an apologetic bow to my mother, and she stared at him in shock before putting her face on the ground before him. She bowed in respect, but she was also smiling, and for a minute I knew they didn't need me to translate any more. She loved him then for his generosity and his kindness to me. I think that memory gave her comfort when we left the next morning.

That night I slept in the familiar pile of sheepskins and fox furs, surrounded by the scents of leather, arsana wood, sheep, dog, dung, smoke, and the lingering scent of roasted lamb, beans, and flat cakes.

BEFORE WE DEPARTED, my sponsor suggested to Otso-ka that we demonstrate a little of what I'd learned in my months of training. Of course Otso-ka was delighted, and called all the men to watch. He was beaming, proud that my sponsor thought I already knew enough to offer a demonstration. He wanted everyone to see and appreciate the success of my aloka placement, and to use that to strengthen my claim to the blue sash of chief when the time came. The women gathered as well, with the children in a little cluster in front of them. I saw Tirta standing at the edge of the men; like me, he was not yet a man, but he was too old to be included among the women and children.

My belly fluttered with nerves, but my sponsor was so calm and confident that I felt myself relaxing a little. After his words of the night before, I knew he didn't mean to shame me in front of the men. If I was embarrassed, it would be my fault and mine alone.

"Let's do the *matosu* partner drill first," my sponsor murmured. "I'll attack."

We bowed to each other. I was acutely aware of everyone's eyes on us. My sponsor attacked, at a fast but not overwhelming speed. The moves were not yet wholly reflexive, but he'd chosen a sequence I knew well. It ended with me slipping close inside a kick at my head and sweeping his supporting foot from beneath him. He fell and slapped the ground with perfect form, then rose to bow to me again.

"The punching drill we worked on last week. Do you remember it?"

"Yes, sir." It was exhausting to do it dozens of times in succession, but one or two repetitions would not be difficult now. I tried not to think about everyone watching. My sponsor defended first, then attacked me with the same sequence.

He bowed to me again, and then seemed to think a moment. "What else? Oh, perhaps some knife work." His gaze held mine, then his eyes flicked toward my feet and back. "Elathlo, I'm going to punch you in the mouth."

He waited until comprehension dawned in my eyes, then punched at my face. Not at his full speed, but quickly enough to awe anyone watching. I sidestepped and deflected his punch even as I pulled the knife from my boot and pressed it to his side, just under the ribs.

He stood still for a moment, then stepped back and nodded. "Excellent."

We bowed to each other, and he smiled. I looked up to see that Otso-ka had paled, his gaze bouncing between my knife, my face, my sponsor's face, and back to the knife. One of the men who had been in the tent with us during the confrontation turned to stare at Otso-ka, then back at me.

My sponsor bowed again toward my grandfather. "I thank you for your hospitality. If you will excuse us, I must return to Stonehaven. Work awaits me."

Otso-ka bowed clumsily. My sponsor also gave him the Tarvil salute, and the men returned it.

Tirta spoke to me as we saddled our horses. "Did you always have the knife?"

"Yes. He gave it to me months ago." I grinned at his shocked look. "I told you. He is a wonderful sponsor, Tirta."

I wished I had time to tell him more, about the wedding, the market, the palace, and the king himself. About the soldiers and servants, the farmlands, the wildflowers. The music. Lani. There was no time, but I thought about everything as we left.

I waved to them as we trotted away, my mother and Tirta and my grandfather, the people who had known me as a child. The people who had once understood my life and no longer did.

We rode in silence until my gratitude could not be contained. "Thank you, sir. Thank you for everything."

He glanced at me and smiled. "You're welcome."

That was all. It was enough.

MY SPONSOR VOMITED twice during the relatively short ride back to Izotz. When I asked, he said it was the food, but he would be better soon enough. He was right; it was the alamaa that was the main problem for him, and he had taken none of it. I regretted my discourtesy, but I was pleased to know that I had managed to serve him in some useful way, flawed though my effort had been.

We stopped near a small stream shortly before we reached Izotz to let the horses drink. Ice crusted the edges, and my sponsor had his horse step into the water to break the ice before we dismounted to drink and refill our canteens. He gave me his handkerchief to press icy water against my lip again, then inspected my face with a faint frown. But he said nothing else about it, either then or later.

My heart and mind were full of everything that had happened. I wondered when Tirta would be placed as an aloka, and whom he would serve. Sympathy twisted inside me; no matter who he got, he would suffer.

While we were waiting for the horses to drink their fill, Tirta came galloping up on his father's horse. He gave the Tarvil salute to my sponsor.

"Will you ask if we can talk a moment?" he asked me.

I did, and my sponsor nodded. He walked a few steps away, giving us privacy for the conversation, although Tirta only spoke Tarvil and my sponsor didn't speak it at all. It was another courtesy I didn't know how to thank him for.

"I heard something after you left and thought you should know about it. You know the guards in the tent with you and Otso-ka yesterday? Two of them were talking, the ones from the Black and Red tribes. They don't know I heard them through the tent wall. One of them wondered whether you'd grown so much because of demon enchantment. Because the Erdemen are so big, and your sponsor is the largest of all." Tirta stopped and stared at me.

I shook my head. "I don't think so. He's human. I eat better. Maybe I'm just growing."

He gave me a skeptical look. "Well, the other one said he didn't care if it *was* demon enchantment. He likes you, and thinks you'd be the best high chief in generations. He said you could have been chief already several times. Your sponsor could have killed Otso-ka and no one could have prevented it, and no one could have argued if your sponsor had named you high chief." He stopped again, waiting for my reaction.

I nodded. "Yes, he could have. But he wasn't trying to provoke them. He was defending me." My throat tightened again with gratitude toward my sponsor.

Tirta gave a half shrug. "That's what they said. They also said you could have killed Otso-ka and claimed the crown yourself. It would have been legitimate. But you didn't."

I blinked. Although the demonstration that morning had shown everyone that I was armed, and that I knew how to use my knife, I still had not truly considered the possibility of killing my grandfather. If I'd thought of using my knife at all, it was only in the context of defending myself and my sponsor from the guards, not in order to claim power.

"I suppose I could have. But..." my voice trailed away.

Tirta smiled a little. "Anyway, the guard overheard what your sponsor said to Otso-ka about what makes a good king and what he's teaching you. They like your sponsor now, and they like that you held your temper. Otso-ka isn't so bad; he negotiated a good peace with Erdem, and he's kept us alive through some harsh winters. But they agreed that they like you more, and they'll support you when you make your move."

My mouth felt suddenly dry. "Does anyone know you told me this?"

"No. I told my father I wanted to congratulate you on your progress. I need to go back in a moment." He glanced at my sponsor, who was standing with his hands clasped behind his back some distance away, studying the far-off mountains. "He's a good sponsor, isn't he?"

In that one question, and in the sudden desperation in his eyes, I read Tirta's fear and envy, his happiness for me and his despair, knowing his own sponsor wouldn't be half as generous.

"Yes." My voice cracked, and I put one hand on his shoulder in sympathy.

He took a shaky breath, then nodded curtly. "Tell him I thank him for letting you speak with me. I'm glad for you, Elathlo." He forced a smile, then jumped back on his horse. He saluted my sponsor again and then galloped away.

We stayed the night at Izotz, where my sponsor reported that our meeting had gone well. So far as I knew, he didn't tell anyone what had happened, either the threat to his life or his own generosity. Perhaps he put it from his mind entirely, or perhaps he merely didn't think to tell of it, because he wasn't one to boast. His reserve no longer surprised me.

I understood, even then, that what he'd done would benefit his country and his king. Buying my loyalty by defending me would have been a shrewd political move. Ensuring that the next Tarvil high chief owed some allegiance to Erdem, or at least the Erdemen military commander, was intelligent, perhaps even cunning.

But when I replayed the day's events in my mind, I could not forget the kindness in his eyes. When I'd first gone south, I'd been unable to read his face, seeing only the harshness I'd been told to expect. Now, after months

192

with him, I could see the small kindnesses that had always been there. I remembered how he'd given me his pallet that first night, when I'd been terrified and he'd been ill from the alamaa Otso-ka had pressed him to drink. That was not some canny plot; it was compassion.

When I drew my knife and pressed the flat of the blade to his side, he didn't flinch. His eyes were proud.

The events of the day may not have been entirely unexpected, but they were not some devious scheme either. He might have served his country, but when he gave me his handkerchief, when he praised me to my mother, even when he drew his sword on my grandfather and when he demonstrated with me in front of the men, he did it out of kindness.

THE NEXT MORNING we woke early, ate the first flat cakes and bacon that the cook prepared, and began our journey south. The school that would train Erdemen and Tarvil boys together was not at Fort Kuzeyler, but at Ironcrest, a military installation I had not yet visited. We stopped there on our way back to Stonehaven for my sponsor to inspect the buildings. They were almost complete, and my sponsor was pleased by the progress. He spoke to the man in charge of the construction, and then sent word back to Izotz that Otso-ka and the men should select the Tarvil boys for the first class, which would begin in two or three months.

I hoped Tirta would be selected. He had a good chance; there weren't so many boys in our tribes of the right age that many would be left out.

We returned to Stonehaven in the first real snowfall of the year, dry and powdery, layering everything in white flakes two hands deep. We hunted deer and fat hares near the pool beneath the Silverfall for a few hours before moving on. My sponsor tried to make the journey pleasant for me, and I was grateful to him for it, but I could see he was eager to return home.

An hour outside of Stonehaven, as the sun was beginning to lower behind the tallest of the trees, he said, "Elathlo, do you want to do something to earn your training?" He made it sound like a question rather than a command.

"Yes, sir!"

He glanced at me and the dappled light caught his smile. "I'd like you to tell me about your grandfather and your people. Write about them. I think our people need to understand each other better."

I blinked. "Yes, sir." I couldn't help my next words. "It doesn't seem like enough." I hoped he could hear my gratitude in my voice.

"It will help the king. And me. It's important work." He smiled at me again, and I felt myself flushing with pride. "And when you're high chief, we'll keep the peace."

TWENTY

KEMEN

We rode into the palace courtyard in a flurry of snow and shouted greetings. I told Hakan all was well, bid Elathlo goodnight and sent him off for dinner, and headed to the estate to greet Ria. My heart had been full thinking of her.

I jogged up the steps and Glaw opened it just as I reached for the handle. "Good day, sir. How was your trip?"

"It went well, thank you. Where is Riona?"

"Lady Sendoa is in the south study taking a late tea with Lady Citulali Creston." He bowed slightly.

I almost asked him whether I should bathe before intruding on them; he undoubtedly had more knowledge of noble etiquette than I did, and I didn't want to embarrass Ria before a potential new friend. But Ria was my wife, and I had longed for a kiss for weeks, and I knew she would forgive me, even if I stank.

"Thank you," I said.

I strode through the hallways, still feeling out of place in my own home. Yvet, one of the new maids, curtseyed and I stopped to bow to her, reminding myself that I shouldn't be rude to the staff simply because I was impatient to see Ria.

I opened the door to see Ria and Citulali sipping tea across from each other at a small table by a window, with a platter of delicate pastries between them. The sunset reflected off the snow behind them to light the room with orange and gold.

"Lady Sendoa, Lady Creston." I greeted them with a bow, then stepped into the room.

"Kemen!" Ria's delighted smile made my attempt at respectful courtesy crumble. I pressed a kiss to her fingers, then her lips, not caring that Citulali was staring at us, looking a little shocked.

"I'm sorry, I should have cleaned up, but I wanted to see you." Her eyes were so blue I could barely marshal my thoughts into coherence. "Forgive me for intruding."

"I missed you." Her smile was warm and she kept her hand in mine as she turned to her guest. "You've met Lady Citulali Creston?"

"Yes, though it's been many months." I bowed to her and she gave me a sweet, shy smile.

"I didn't know if you'd remember me, Lord General Sendoa. But it's good to see you again."

I blinked at the title. Was I a lord now? "Of course. I never forget a kind face."

Lady Creston blushed and looked down.

I turned to kiss Ria again, full on the lips, though it was probably scandalous. "Ria, I'll see you for dinner."

Our eyes met for a long moment, and she smiled again, her cheeks turning a lovely shade of pink.

My hot bath was a relaxing reminder of the luxuries that now surrounded me, and I mentally thanked Hakan again for his generosity. Months before, Glaw had attempted to attend me during my bath, as it was apparently customary for noblemen to request wine, cheeses, and assistance with soaping and bathing themselves. I'd given him an astonished look and said that such assistance was unnecessary; I'd managed to bathe myself without assistance for thirty-four years of my life and hadn't forgotten how. In fact, the short time alone in the bath was a welcome bit of solitude in my otherwise busy days.

Refreshed, my hair still damp and buttoning my shirt, I walked out of the bathing room and made my way to our private sitting room connected to our bedroom. Glaw was refreshing the water in a glass of cut blooms on the table, and he bowed as I entered.

"What time would you like dinner, sir?"

"Whenever Ria will be hungry."

He bowed again. "In an hour, then. Lady Sendoa should be here shortly, sir. She chose to walk Lady Creston to the door." I could hear a hesitation in his voice, and I wondered what he thought of us. "Sir, if I may say…" he hesitated, and I nodded for him to continue. He swallowed and glanced away from me, then fixed his eyes on the center of my chest, as if he were embarrassed and didn't want to look at me directly. "It is a pleasure to serve you and your lady, sir. You are both very kind."

"Thank you, Glaw." I bowed to him, and his eyes widened, as if the bow surprised him again. "I hope you're happy here."

"Yes, sir." He bowed deeply, and I smiled at the top of his head.

A few moments later, Ria stepped into the room, her steps more like those of a servant than those of the lady of the house. Glaw slipped out with the subtlety of the well-trained servant. I wrapped my arms around Ria and we simply stood for a moment, her head resting against my chest and my face in her hair.

"I missed you, Ria."

She tightened her arms around my waist. "I missed you too."

Glaw brought our food soon after. As we ate, she told me about her attempts to make friends among the young noblewomen. She asked about our travel, and I told her how Otso-ka treated Elathlo.

"That's horrible!" she murmured, her eyes wide with sympathy.

"Yes. And I'm not..." I hesitated. "I'm not always good at being as warm as a child needs. But he's young, and he needs someone to be kind to him. I'd like to have him with us for dinner sometimes, if you don't mind."

"Of course I don't mind." She reached out to slip her hand into mine, white skin against olive.

I stared at the contrast for a moment, the slim pale smoothness of her fingers against my rougher skin, faint scars across my knuckles, the back of my hand tanned darker than the palm. Her hands were fine-boned but smooth, the callouses of her work beginning to fade already. Mine showed the lines of veins and tendons as they worked beneath my skin, efficient perhaps, but not beautiful as hers were.

"What are you looking at?" she asked.

"You're so beautiful." My voice felt rough with emotion I could not express. Gratitude, perhaps, for her patience with me, for her love, for her warmth, for her existence. Love that woke me each morning and soothed me to sleep each night, that kept my heart beating when I should have died.

She laughed, a soft, light sound that made my heart beat faster, and raised my hand to her cheek. "You have no idea, do you, Kemen?" Her skin felt like silk as it moved against the back of my fingers.

"About what?"

"How much I love you." Her smile lit the room, and she got up to stand beside me. She wrapped her arms around my shoulders and I leaned in to her, eyes closed. I inhaled the clean scent of her, the paints she'd used that afternoon, the faint warmth and sweetness of our pastries, soap, and the starch in her dress.

"I believe you," I murmured, my eyes closed. "It just surprises me. I don't understand."

"Because you're not an arrogant cretin like most noblemen. Come, Kemen. You're tired, and it's time for bed."

I thought of protesting, because I had much work waiting for me. Then I saw the gleam in her eye, and as much as I loved Hakan, and loved my work for him, Ria was my wife. For reasons I couldn't fathom, she not only loved me, but desired me, and no work should come between a man and his wife, especially after an absence.

We did not entirely make up for my weeks away, but we made a good start.

IT WAS ONLY from force of long habit that I woke so early the next morning. Ria's arm was draped over my chest, her face resting against my shoulder. Ria had adjusted to sleeping together more easily than I had. Years of reflexes kept me half-alert even in sleep, and every slight movement she made jerked me up toward wakefulness before I remembered that it was my wife (*my wife!*) who breathed beside me. After that first week, she had slept deeply, secure in my arms, while I took longer. Only now, after months of marriage, and nearly six weeks apart, had I finally slept soundly in our marriage bed. Soundly, but only for a few hours. Ria could sleep until long after the sun rose, if she chose, but I had work.

"Sweet Ria, I must go."

"Mm," she murmured. I pressed a kiss to her forehead and extricated myself as gently as possible, pulling the cover up over her shoulder as she liked. She frowned and turned her face into the pillow like a sleepy child.

At the palace, I exercised for an hour before going inside to wake Elathlo. He would be tired too, though he would likely not have stayed up as late as I had. Certainly not for the same reason. We trained for an hour, then ran, and I sent him inside. I worked on the balance moves and strength a while longer before returning to the manor for a bath. Walking through the garden between the palace and the manor, I stopped and looked around. For a moment, I had the uncomfortable feeling of being watched, but I saw no one. No movement stirred the bare branches of the bushes and trees around me. I pushed the feeling to the back of my mind, though I remained alert.

Once I was clean, I escorted Ria to the palace for a late breakfast, where we had a quiet, casual meal with Hakan and Kveta. Elathlo ate with the servants in the kitchen. I felt a little guilty for excluding him, but we would invite him for dinner. Besides, I hadn't seen Hakan and Kveta for weeks.

Though I listened as they chatted, my attention was focused mostly on little Kem, the tiny prince of Erdem. His pale hair was soft as duck down, and his wide blue eyes fixed themselves on me. He gave me a toothless grin and waved his arms. I took him from Kveta and let him rest against my chest. He snuggled into my shirt for a moment before deciding that he was more interested in looking around.

Kveta said with a smile, "Kemen, you should give him back."

"Why? I was thinking of keeping him." I rested my cheek against the feathery fuzz atop his head.

Ria smiled affectionately, and the warmth in her gaze made me smile too.

"Because we're all finished eating and you haven't started yet." Kveta grinned. "He's beautiful, isn't he?"

I let her take Kem from me. "Yes, he is."

Kveta and Ria went away to play with Kem and put him to bed for a nap. I told Hakan about the school and we made plans to begin interviewing instructors and selecting students soon. The first class of boys would be selected from the sons of merchants of Stonehaven. Later there would be an application process and boys from around the nation might be selected for this or the other schools to be opened to commoners. We agreed that the boys selected for this class would be selected more for personality than academic aptitude. Perhaps later it would be possible to select based on academic potential, but for now it was more important to ensure that the boys were as agreeable and friendly as possible. Having the class end in bloodshed would negate any benefit of this experiment.

Noriso suggested the initial list of boys; he was far more than a servant, but a source of much knowledge about the palace as well as Stonehaven and its occupants. I knew few of the names, so I wasn't much help while he and Hakan refined the list. Then Noriso prepared a pile of invitations, which Hakan signed before Noriso took them to be delivered.

I asked him if there had been any other worrying incidents, and he said he hadn't noticed anything. But I could see the strain in his eyes. He hid it well, but I knew him better and he could not hide it from me.

Sirkhar had found nothing useful. I wondered how hard he'd looked.

By then it was nearly time for dinner, and before we ate, I took Ria on a leisurely walk through the garden. We didn't speak much, but even the silence between us felt warm and comforting. She leaned close to me in the cold, and I wrapped my cloak around her. Ria said that she and Kveta had been painting together, which she enjoyed despite her embarrassment at her inexperience. Kveta, of course, was a well-educated princess, and much practiced at many artistic endeavors. Ria said she was kind, though, and offered advice only when it was requested, and encouragement much more frequently.

After dinner we would share our pictures with each other. I cautioned her that I was no brilliant artist either, and she laughed and said I was more talented than I knew. Like everything else she said, her words were kind, but I knew the truth. I could see the awkward angles in the rose petals I drew and the too-small eye of my horse Kanti when I sketched her. Perhaps, though, she didn't mind those imperfections, as she chose not to mind my other faults.

Twenty-One

Elathlo

My lesson with Colonel Bekendi was short that first day back in Stonehaven. He said he could see I was tired. I was instructed to take a nap in the middle of the day, which I did, feeling guiltily grateful for the indulgence. I slept without dreams and woke to a knock at my door. Sinta said dinner would be ready soon and I was invited to eat with my sponsor, Lady Riona, and the king and queen in one of the small dining rooms.

As always, the food was delicious and plentiful, arranged artistically on the porcelain plates. After our visit north, I appreciated the luxury even more. I'd never grown entirely accustomed to it, but I'd forgotten how grateful I should be. I remembered how my sponsor had praised my mother's roasted lamb and thin bean slurry with unfeigned gratitude.

After dinner my sponsor accompanied me to my room to help me begin the task he had given me.

I sat at a table with a stack of blank paper in front of me. "I don't know what to write about." I bit my lip and looked up at my sponsor.

"Everything. Your customs. An aloka's training. How your father would have become high chief. How your grandfather commands the tribal chiefs. How men and women are married. Everything." My sponsor smiled. "I don't expect you to finish tonight. Be thorough. Take as long as you need."

I stared at the parchment and thought. Finally I began, tentative, practicing my still-sloppy Erdemen characters. Otso-ka became high chief when he defeated El-mal-ka. Elmal-ka's status had been questioned in a council of the tribal chiefs after his defeat by Rikutan soldiers in the year... I had to stop and think, because years were counted differently in Erdem. ...301, which my people called 947. Now it is also called the Year of Winter Silence, a joke, because there was no conflict between the Red Tarvil and the Black Tarvil. There was no conflict because Otso-ka's victory over Elmal-ka was so swift and so merciless that the Black Tarvil took themselves to the high hunting grounds to consider their next move, afraid Otso-ka would want more blood.

My sponsor left some minutes later, but I continued writing. The glow of sunset through the window faded and I lit the lantern on the table and stretched my shoulders before focusing again on my work. The window across the room was open just a crack, and the room grew chilly. I ignored it, focused on finishing the story of Otso-ka's first year of rule. I knew it well, because I'd heard it many times, a cautionary tale about Elmal-ka's errors in both war and in his dealings with the outlying tribal chiefs.

I shivered in the chill, glanced up, and gasped. A man stood next to the window, his cloak edged by the faint lamplight.

"I would not run if I were you."

I swallowed. His voice was low, with a cruel edge to it that made my heart pound. I couldn't see his features in the deep shadow of his hood.

"I came to give you this message. What was done to you in the market can be done again. I want a little information."

I swallowed, not sure what to say.

"I want to know when and where the king next plans to leave the palace."

My mouth felt dry. "The king has been nothing but generous and kind to me. I won't do anything to put him in danger."

"I said nothing about danger except yours. But it would be easy enough to punish your little friend Nalani if you have any thoughts of deceiving me. Would you like to see what we could do to her?"

I gasped.

"Not so brave now, are you? She's pretty, isn't she? She wouldn't be after we finished. Would you risk that for a little information?"

I felt sick at the thought.

"I want an answer tomorrow, boy. Don't tell anyone."

I nodded.

He climbed out the window again, a dark shape that disappeared into the shadows. I closed and locked the window immediately, then pulled the curtains, feeling exposed with the light on my face and everything before me black and indistinct.

I left the light on for hours, though I could no longer focus on my writing. Even when I finally blew out the lamp, I was unable to sleep, turning the threat over and over in my mind.

I assumed the threat was against the king's life, although I couldn't be sure. Perhaps the intruder wanted to know for some other reason, but assassination was most likely. It might have been some kind of test, to determine how easy I was to manipulate or how trustworthy I was or something else I could not guess. If so, I couldn't imagine my sponsor devising such a test. He was cunning but not devious.

Assassination is not uncommon among men who want power. My own father had killed without warning before, as had Otso-ka and many others. I didn't like the idea, but my dislike was more a sense of squeamishness than a moral objection.

I owed no particular allegiance to the Erdemen king Hakan Ithel. I didn't hate him, but I didn't love him either. He was, to my knowledge, a good king for the Erdemen people, but they were not *my* people. He'd been generous to my people in the peace treaty, but that was as much my sponsor's doing as the king's. I stayed in his palace, under his roof, but the generosity with which I was fed, clothed, and trained was that of my sponsor.

Lani was my friend. I owed her nothing, but I liked her. She was kind to me, even though she didn't have to be. If I had to choose one of them to die, I would let the king die to save Lani. The choice was simple.

If Hakan Ithel died, who might replace him? I tried to think. The Erdemen crown passed to the eldest male heir upon the king's death. The king already had a son, but the boy was an infant, so a regent would be necessary. My sponsor would be the most likely candidate to serve as regent while the son grew.

Logically, my sponsor was the most likely person to threaten the king's life, but I knew that was impossible. If it was someone else, they would not likely be pleased with the idea of my sponsor serving as regent. They might threaten his life as well.

Although I felt no real loyalty to the king, I would have died for my sponsor. I owed him everything. But I didn't truly fear for his life.

Instead, I knew, with sickening clarity, that if I did not tell my sponsor, if I did not attempt to save the king's life, my sponsor would be disappointed in me. I would have betrayed not only the king, but my sponsor.

He'd trusted me to defend myself against his attack with a sharpened knife, allowed me to press the keen edge against his side. We'd never practiced with sharp knives, only dull practice knives. One thought of retribution, or one simple mistake or ill judgment, would have been enough for me to slip the knife beneath his ribs. But he trusted me. He trusted me enough to do it in front of my people, to demonstrate my skill to them. To earn their respect for me.

How could I betray him?

My sponsor would have died for his king, almost had several times.

I had to tell him.

If I was going to tell my sponsor, I would have to be discreet. Someone knew to threaten me, perhaps thinking that I was the most likely person to betray the king. Perhaps he was right. I *was* the most likely, but not likely enough. Not anymore.

He also knew how to threaten me. Lani's safety was a more effective threat than my own life. I would not call myself brave, but there are some things worth dying for. Even if I was terrified, I would die for Lani, for my sponsor, for my mother, perhaps Tirta.

Both those facts meant that the person who threatened me, or at least the person who informed him, was in the palace. I'd barely been outside the palace in all my months in Stonehaven, and no one outside the palace could possibly know how much I liked Lani. Even Lani didn't know.

I would have to be careful.

I DRESSED and waited for my sponsor to knock on my door as he always did. I knew he trained for at least an hour before he woke me, and I could have gone to meet him earlier. I was awake, not having slept all night. But if I meant to be discreet, I must act as normal as possible. So I waited, jittery and tired, for my sponsor's knock.

He was already sweating, and the damp skin of his arms pricked with chill when we went outside. We did the strengthening exercises first, and I had no breath to spare to mention anything to him. He held my feet while I tried unsuccessfully to do the handstand pushups.

When we finished, we did technique drills for a while, practicing kicks, sweeps, punches, and grappling moves in slow motion. The warriors of my tribe never practiced their fighting slowly, and it had taken me months to understand why my sponsor did so. He said that clean technique was faster and more efficient than sloppy technique, and practicing slowly allowed us to make sure our technique was as close to perfect as possible. At first I had been skeptical, but I saw that what he said worked.

Then he showed me a new grappling move, and we went over it several times. It was my chance. We were close together, with no one nearby to hear us and every reason to be speaking to each other. Just as we did every day.

"Sir, I need to speak with you without anyone knowing," I said. "Anyone at all."

"I'm listening." His expression did not change, and he demonstrated the move again.

I'd told myself I was brave and remained calm so far. But my thudding heart reminded me that I was actually terrified, no matter how well I hid it. "Someone came into my room last night and threatened me. They want information about the king. I think someone wants to kill him."

He didn't say anything for one moment, only adjusting my grip on his wrist for a moment. "Try it again. A little faster this time."

At first I thought he hadn't heard me, but then I realized he was being discreet, just as I'd hoped. If someone was watching, even our actions must not betray us. So I did it, moving through the sequence again a little more quickly. The move placed pressure on his wrist and forced him to one knee. My sponsor said he'd used it once in a wrestling match. The thought of my sponsor using it on me at full speed made me cringe in sympathy with the unknown opponent.

He rose and brushed off his knee, then pulled his boot knife and knelt again. He drew a rough map of Erdem and the surrounding areas in the packed earth of the courtyard. The edges of his lines were sharp, glittering with frost. "This should give us reason to stand and talk," he murmured. "What happened?"

I leaned over and pretended to look at the map. "A man came into my room last night and wanted to know when the king would next leave the palace. He said he would come back tonight for the answer."

"Could you recognize him?" He pointed at different points on the map, as if in relation to what he was saying.

"I don't think so, sir. He kept his face covered by his hood and I think he tried to disguise his voice."

My sponsor used the point of his knife to add the lines of rivers to the map. "Thank you for telling me. I will speak with Hakan and we will decide what to do."

"He said not to tell anyone."

He sat back and stared at the map, then leaned forward to draw several passes across the mountains into Rikuto. "Hakan has a right to know."

I swallowed, my mouth dry, then knelt to point at the ground. "He threatened Lani. He said that what was done to me in the market could be done to her. And worse."

Only because I was so close to him, and so alert to every little motion, did I notice how his lips tightened and the lines of his face became a little harder. His voice did not change when he repeated, "Hakan has a right to know. Lani will be safe."

"Yes, sir." With those two words, I told him, and myself, that I trusted him.

He waited a moment longer, perhaps to see if I had anything else to say, then rose. He stretched his shoulders and said, "Let's do the sequences in order before we run. How many do you know?"

"Nine, sir."

He nodded for me to begin. First I did each one slowly while he corrected my form and technique. Then I did it at speed, and he commented on each one. Then we did it together, so that I could copy his rhythm. Then he did it alone, so that I could watch and see how it was meant to look. By the end of the sixth, I was breathless, barely able to catch my breath while I watched him. We drew some water and drank before we ran. He said nothing else about it, and indeed if I did not remember the conversation, I would never have known it happened.

We ran sprints that day, which did not take as long as the distance runs we had begun, but left me every bit as exhausted. We jogged to the hill behind the palace, then sprinted up it eight times, until I felt my heartbeat pounding in my ears and my stomach threatening to vomit up the emptiness inside me.

My sponsor let me set the pace on the way back, which meant he accompanied me as I staggered down the hill, barely able to keep upright until I had caught my breath.

"Go get a bath and breakfast. I'll see you at lunch."

"Yes, sir."

Twenty-Two

I f someone was watching, I should not deviate from our routine. So I went back to our estate and bathed. I dressed and ate a quick breakfast with Ria, then bid her farewell for the day and returned to the palace. Hakan and I had a meeting scheduled to interview some teachers, so it would not surprise anyone if I spoke to him before it.

I may have been excessively cautious, but I requested that Hakan join me in a short walk outside. I didn't want to risk anyone hearing through a door, and in the open air I knew no one could lurk unseen. Hakan agreed and followed me out toward the stable. Even there, I didn't speak freely, but only talked of the horses until we moved out to the fence surrounding the smaller paddock. He leaned his elbows against the fence and watched the horses nibble at the frost-covered grass. I watched for a moment too, then turned to lean my back against the fence rail, stretching my arms as if I were utterly relaxed.

"Someone threatened Elathlo last night, wanting to know when you'd next leave the palace. I assume to make an attempt on your life."

"He told you?" Hakan maintained his calm admirably, though I saw his shoulders tense.

"Yes." I told Hakan everything Elathlo had said, including the threat against Lani. "I intend to wait in his room tonight to catch the intruder."

"Use him as bait."

"Yes."

Hakan's eyes flicked around, and I knew he was nervous. He did well hiding it though; if I had not known him so well, I would not have been able to see the tension in his jaw or the way his nostrils flared as he thought.

"Someone in the palace is involved, then. If they threatened him through her."

"Yes," I said. "That's why we're speaking out here."

His eyes returned to the trees some distance away, and I imagined he was wondering if anyone could shoot him with an arrow from there.

I answered his unspoken question. "I doubt it. Perhaps a trained archer, but they asked when you would leave the palace. I assume that means the palace grounds; if the traitor inside could strike at you directly, he probably already would have."

His lips twitched. "Not necessarily. It depends on what they want." He sighed and turned to look back at the palace. I turned as well, alert for any movement in the trees that might not be caused by the wind.

"I'll tell Sirkhar, and he can look into the matter."

"Don't. What if he's involved?" I asked.

He glanced at me. "I doubt it. He served my father for years. He's had a thousand opportunities to kill me."

"I don't trust him." I tried to keep the hardness from my voice, but I'm sure he heard it.

He frowned but nodded. "I don't either. I just doubt he'd want to kill me. We'll wait though. Try to catch the man tonight. What do you need from me?"

"Be careful. Be ready tonight." I forced a smile and we meandered back in. I asked him a few questions to help form my plan, which he answered as we walked. Hakan gestured toward the field, as if that was what we had been discussing the whole time.

We ate lunch with Riona and Kveta after the meeting, then worked for most of the afternoon. Hakan had already grown more adept at hiding his nerves. He was no longer the boy I had found in the snow.

Perhaps Kveta saw his tension, but she said nothing. She had lived all her life among nobles, and I imagined she knew that even a palace is not always a safe place to speak freely. Despite her years in the palace, Ria didn't know Hakan well enough to see that he was any different than he usually was.

The evening sparring session gave me a perfect reason to stand around afterwards chatting with Kudret, Eneko, and Shui. I explained that there was some possibility of trouble that evening. I would be occupied until late, and I would appreciate it if they would guard Ria while I was unable to. Of course they agreed.

Twenty-Three

My sponsor invited me to eat dinner with him and Lady Riona that night. Several of my sponsor's friends from among the army officers were also guests for dinner.

Lady Riona asked me about our trip north, about hunting, about my friends and my mother. Answering her questions distracted me from my nerves, and I found myself smiling as I told her my mother was grateful for my sponsor's generosity and kindness to me. I didn't tell her everything that had happened between my grandfather and my sponsor, but I did tell her how he'd demonstrated with me in front of the tribe. My throat tightened at the memory, at everyone's astonishment that I was armed, and at the skills my sponsor had already taught me. She reached out to touch his hand, and he smiled at her, entwined his fingers with hers. I felt privileged to see their affection. I knew he loved her, but it was a gift to be allowed to see him show it.

As my sponsor walked with me back to the palace, I was glad I'd told him about the threat. Terrified as I was, I could not imagine the guilt that would twist within me if I had not told him.

I readied myself for bed with the curtains drawn and the window locked. My sponsor stepped into a corner from which he could easily see the windows, and nodded to me. I blew out the lamp and waited a moment for my eyes to adjust to the darkness, then unlocked the window. It was cold outside, and I didn't want to open the window completely, so I pushed it open just a crack, so that it would be easy for the intruder to enter. Then I settled into bed.

I lay with my face toward the window, feeling the slightest breath of cold air from the window brushing my cheek. Faint silver light touched the windowsill from the slim crescent moon. In the silence of my room, I heard every distant sound of the palace, occasional muffled voices from another hallway and the soft footfalls of servants passing by. It would have been easy to forget my sponsor was there; he made no sound, and in the shadow of the wardrobe, even his tall form was only another dark shadow.

Sleep did not come, but despite my best efforts, I found myself less than fully alert when the intruder finally entered. It must have been near midnight, the light no longer slanting in the window.

The window creaked softly as he pulled it open, and I waited, my heart thudding, as he clambered in. He wasn't graceful, but he kept the hood fully over his face and he was quiet. He stood for a moment with his back to the light, and I imagined he was letting his eyes adjust to the darkness before approaching me.

I sat up, not wanting him to wake me with a knife to my throat.

He stepped closer to the bed. "What is your answer?"

I never saw my sponsor move, but the man bit back a cry of surprise and pain.

My sponsor said, "Close the window and the curtains, Elathlo. Don't light the lamp."

I did as he said.

"Now look out in the hallway. If anyone is there, close the door again."

I looked. "No one, sir."

"Then come."

He maneuvered the man out into the hallway, down the length, and down a stairwell into a basement area which I had never entered. We went down another flight of steps into a dark stone hallway and into the first door. The room was a cool, dry stone cell, with a heavy wooden door and a lamp sitting on the floor shedding flickering light. My sponsor spun the man around, pinned him against the wall, and pulled back his hood. He examined the man's face for a moment, then clanked manacles around his wrists. The man barely resisted, though he spit a curse as my sponsor turned toward me. He ushered me out and closed the door behind us, leaving the lamp on the floor just out of the man's reach.

A moment later, the king arrived, carrying his own lantern. "You caught him?"

"Yes." My sponsor held the man's knife out for the king to see, then slipped it into his belt. I'd assumed the man was armed, but I hadn't actually seen the knife. My sponsor had disarmed him so smoothly I hadn't even realized when he did it.

"Do you know him?"

My sponsor shook his head. "I've never seen him before."

The king peered cautiously through the little peep hole in the door for several long moments, then stepped back and slid the cover back over the hole. "I don't recognize him," he said in a low voice. "We need to question him. What does he want? Who is behind it? How many people are involved?"

My sponsor's frown deepened. "I can ask him, but it's not really my area of expertise." He bent to look through the hole himself. "He doesn't strike me as the mind behind the threat. He may have information, but..." he hesitated again. "Hakan, I'm a soldier, not an interrogator. Beyond the basics, I wouldn't know how to get information out of him."

I finally spoke up, feeling myself useful for once. "Getting information out of a man is easy. I can do it."

The king snorted, trying unsuccessfully to hide a smile. "What do you know of interrogation?"

"I haven't done it myself, but I've watched questionings many times. If he's not used to it, he'll give you whatever answer you want without any trouble. Hot coals on the bottoms of his feet would be quick. Pinches of skin torn out. Eyes are very sensitive, as are fingernails. It's not difficult."

They stared at me a moment, then looked at each other. "No." They spoke together, quiet and firm.

I blinked. "Why not? Wouldn't it help get the information you need?"

My sponsor spoke first. "You did not come to Stonehaven to practice torture. If you already know how, I can't make you unlearn it, but I'll not have you increase your knowledge here. Especially not on an Erdemen citizen."

"Yes, sir." I felt my shoulders slump in the face of his anger. His voice was controlled, of course; he never raised it and he did not then either. But the fury in his tone could not be mistaken. "I'm sorry. I only meant to help." My apology was nearly a whisper.

The king's voice broke into the silence. "I'll ask Sirkhar to question him. That was one of his duties for my father. Supposedly he was quite good at it." He didn't sound pleased with the idea.

"And if he's involved?" my sponsor asked.

The king glanced down the hallway. "The next room is an observation room. My father had it made with mirrors through a little tunnel in the wall; you can see most of the room and hear everything. Sirkhar must know it, but I doubt the prisoner does. He may betray Sirkhar when he enters, if he's involved."

My sponsor nodded and pushed open the door to the observation room. It looked much the same, as the holding cell next door.

"As you say. Elathlo should stay out of sight. Assuming more men are involved, someone may have noticed that our prisoner didn't return from threatening Elathlo and may wish to silence him. Lani as well. And you, of course. Stay here and wait. I'll bring Lani and Sirkhar." He waited for the king's nod.

Only later did it strike me how much the king relied upon my sponsor. In this, when the king's life was at stake and even his most trusted servants and staff were under suspicion, my sponsor's honor was beyond doubt.

My sponsor unbuckled his sword belt and handed it to the king, along with the intruder's knife.

"Sirkhar is probably asleep. His quarters are below mine and one hallway to the east."

My sponsor nodded. "Be cautious." He held the king's gaze until the king nodded. I wondered if he was really a little pale, or if it was just my imagination.

My sponsor stepped out into the hallway, leaving us the lamp. The king buckled the sword belt around his hips and waited, leaning against one wall with his arms folded. The relaxed posture did not entirely conceal his tension, but he glanced at me with a wry smile, as if to say that he knew I was nervous too.

I was glad I'd told my sponsor. I did not want the king to die.

TWENTY-ONE

KEMEN

I went to Lani and Ena's apartment first, because I wanted to assure myself Lani was safe. Ena opened the door after my second knock, her hair tousled and eyes bleary.

"Sir?" She blinked up at me, looking sleepy and confused.

I slipped inside the door without being invited and closed it behind myself. Her eyes widened and she stepped backward, almost stumbling.

"Can I help you, sir?"

"Is Lani here? Safe?"

"Yes, sir. She's asleep."

"Good. Wake her. She's in danger and needs to come with me."

She stared at me. "What are you talking about?"

I tried to keep my voice quiet, but time weighed on me. "She's been threatened as part of a plot against the king. I will protect her, but I need her with me."

"We should stay together."

"If you wish. Hurry."

I waited impatiently, trying not to tap my foot, as she woke Lani and they dressed. Finally they reappeared in the tiny sitting room.

"Come quietly." I turned, and they followed me out, asking no more questions.

I led them to Sirkhar's apartment, a door with no sign or indication of who lived there. Somehow I knew it was his, though; a door beside one of the king's studies and on the hall Hakan had said.

I knocked.

Sirkhar opened it only a moment later, clothes rumpled but eyes alert. Perhaps he was more like a soldier than I had thought at first, able to go from deep sleep to fully awake in seconds.

"What is it?" His voice was raspy with sleep, and he didn't bother to hide his dislike of me.

"The king has need of your skill at interrogation. Come."

He nodded, then glanced behind me at Ena and Lani. His eyes narrowed, but he said nothing else as he stepped into the hallway.

We hurried back down to the prison where Hakan and Elathlo waited for us. Hakan nodded for me to explain what had happened. I did so, careful to keep my voice low in case the prisoner could hear us as easily as we might hear him. I gave only as much detail as necessary; if Sirkhar was involved, I did not want to let him know how much we knew. Which wasn't much, to be honest, but I did my best. If he knew anything else, perhaps he would betray himself somehow.

Ena and Lani sat on the floor, their heads leaned against each other.

Before Sirkhar left our observation room and went next door, I stepped away from him and Hakan and went to Lani. She was trembling a little, though I wasn't sure whether it was fear or cold that made her shiver. I murmured to them that they would come to stay with Ria and me at our estate. They would be safe.

Sirkhar gave Elathlo a sharp look before he left, but he didn't say anything. I'm not sure whether he suspected the boy, or simply disliked him, but it didn't really matter.

Hakan and I stood at the viewing station, two holes near the door through which we could peer at mirrors that reflected the image of the room. The mirrors were far from perfect, and the expression on the man's face was a little distorted, but we could see him well enough, given the limited light of one lamp. The chains prevented him from leaving our sight, though they gave his arms some movement. We couldn't see Sirkhar immediately, but we could hear his steps.

If the man begged Sirkhar to help him escape, or looked relieved at his entrance, Sirkhar was probably involved. At least Sirkhar could not be trusted. If the man looked frightened, did that tell us anything? If more than one group was involved, it might not tell us definitively that Sirkhar was innocent, but it might indicate that Sirkhar wasn't part of this particular plot. The previous attempts on Hakan's life might have been by another traitor or another group.

Sirkhar waited several moments before we heard the door creak open. I hoped he was waiting for us to get into position, and hoped that was a good sign, rather than composing his method to deceive us most effectively.

ELATHLO PROBABLY THOUGHT I was angry at him after he suggested we torture the prisoner. But my fury was more at Otso and the Tarvil people, who subjected children to such brutal sights. Even I, who had been in battle more times than I could count, felt sick at the thought of slow, deliberate cruelty.

What must seeing such things do to a child? No wonder he'd been terrified of being at my mercy for an entire year. Terrified at the idea of being sent back home. He'd spoken of beheading as a quick and easy death, but I had not truly imagined the horrors he envisioned.

I wondered what Sirkhar would do to the intruder. I didn't want to watch torture. I didn't want Hakan to watch it. I certainly did not want Lani and her mother to hear the man's screams. If it became too brutal, I would escort them away.

The door squeaked as Sirkhar pushed it open and stepped inside, then closed the door again. He stood without speaking for a minute. The man stared at him. No obvious sign of recognition crossed his face.

After a moment, Sirkhar said, "We can talk quietly for a time. Do not raise your voice or you may alert the guards. I have questions for you."

"I have nothing to say." He set his jaw, as if he meant to look stoic.

"Do you know who I am? My name is Baretz Sirkhar. I worked for the old king, Hakan Emyr."

At that, the man's eyes widened, and fear flashed over his face. "I know *of* you. You of all people know I'm bound by the codes to keep silent."

Despite the brave words, he pressed his shoulders back against the wall, as if he wished to burrow into it.

I glanced at Hakan, whose lips had thinned in a faint expression of distaste. No doubt he guessed, as I did, that Sirkhar was well-versed in torture.

Sirkhar snorted and stepped forward, giving us a view of the back of his left shoulder. "I know of your code, and we both know I could make you talk. I'm not here for that sort of information. I told you, I worked for the old king. I did not say I worked for this one. I ask my questions as one professional to another, for my own insight and purposes."

He paused, giving us ample time to see the man's fear turn to wary confusion.

"What you attempted had no chance of success. The palace was warned in advance by a certain nobleman that an attack would be coming from the Guilds. If a noble has the information, it's not very secret that the Guilds are attempting a coup. I've heard such rumors on the street from a dozen sources. The nobles and the king will use this to rally the citizens to bring all of you to light and eradicate the Guilds from Erdem. Even those who are normally happy to deal with the Guilds wouldn't condone this." He paused, then added, "This does not benefit me or my plans for the future. At all."

Hakan's face was set in a hard, unhappy expression. I tried to parse through what Sirkhar was saying. He knew we were watching, or should have known. Therefore he was lying. Wasn't he?

Sirkhar continued, sounding confused and irritated. "But I don't understand. This move on the part of the Guilds was beyond stupid. It was pure insanity! Even if it succeeded, I can't see how it wouldn't destroy the Guilds. Certainly the king will make things harder for us, who work outside normal expectations. But what did *you* expect to result from this? After assassinating the king, every hand would be against you, every eye looking for you."

Sirkhar stepped forward, his posture intimate rather than threatening. "What the keffing dung heaps were the chiefs thinking? And you... how could you expect to survive this? Even if the plan to kill the king was successful, you would have been killed immediately to keep you quiet."

The man sagged against the chains, his expression shifting from shock, to horror, to defeat. "But I... we..."

"Fine. So the Guilds have spoiled my plan and effectively committed suicide in an astonishing display of ineptitude. How did you think this might possibly work out, if all went as you intended? Or did thinking enter into the process at any point?"

The man frowned, looking away from Sirkhar and staring at his own boots. His head jerked up, his eyes suddenly angry. "Tell me, was it Lord Daiko who tipped you off?"

"... I ... can't tell you that. But what if it was? How ... What difference does it make?"

"We were betrayed! The guilds didn't come up with the plan. Lord Daiko hired us! Obviously so he could turn around and warn you about it!"

Sirkhar shifted and scratched the back of his neck thoughtfully. "That would gain him favor, especially since he hasn't previously shown himself to be a strong supporter of the new king..." his voice trailed away. He tilted his head. "No, that does not ring true. How would such a noble contact you? Do you claim long history of dealing with him? Even if the new king didn't, I think I would have suspected if that were true."

The man leaned forward. "No, Lord Daiko had Gershon Murtars brought to his estate. Murtars deals with the Black Rats all the time, and sometimes with the

Snakes. He's hired us, the Blades, twice. Once to persuade other merchants to leave a particular bit of business to him, and once to keep someone from spreading a piece of particularly interesting information about him. Lord Daiko asked Murtars how to contact us."

"And that was it? Murtars knew who was in charge, and it was as simple as that? Is there no concept of security in your operations?" Sirkhar's interested pose vanished, and he threw up a hand in disgust.

The man scowled at him. "No. He told his Black Rat contact, who relayed it to his chief. His chief sent a courier with a letter to Daiko, asking him to meet in a deserted barn, just the noble with only two retainers. The barn and the approaches were watched. Only when Daiko arrived alone did the chief leave. I heard he enjoyed making the nobleman wait for him, too; he took his time." He smiled a little. "The deal was outlined. Tarinko didn't agree at once, he saw the risks, but he also saw the possible rewards."

Sirkhar nodded. "I begin to see how this did not look as insane as at the beginning." His voice was more respectful now, as if he and the intruder were equals rather than an interrogator and a prisoner. "But did everyone just comply with what he said? Do they dominate you others so much? It wasn't like that before."

"No, he spoke with the other Guild Chiefs. They agreed we would—actually had to—help. I was chosen to gather the information for the assassination. It would have been from a distance, using archers. And Pirts wouldn't have had me killed. I don't believe it. We've known each other since we were boys together, and I've known enough to hang him for years. More can't hurt; you can only hang once. And he'd need people he could trust more than ever. He shared all this information with me because I needed to know how to plan, and he needed my commitment. What was my alternative, once I'd been told the job was mine? I couldn't say no! Then I *would* be killed, because they couldn't trust me anymore."

Sirkhar nodded. "Yes, I see." He rubbed his jaw thoughtfully. "I doubt it was difficult for a man of your skill to enter the palace. But how did you get such good information on the Tarvil brat? He could have been in any room in the palace."

The man smiled a little at the compliment. "No, it wasn't hard. You know about the informants in the houses?" Sirkhar nodded, and he continued. "In the palace, you can't push them too far. They think they're only supplying gossip. Asking for sensitive information would make them suspicious, and they'd either report us, or just go silent. I needed more leverage and less loyalty. The Tarvil brat is perfect for both. I asked for information about his friends, maybe a little lover, and then about the relative locations of their rooms. He thought I suspected illicit nighttime visits, of course, and told me that was unlikely. But I got what I wanted."

Sirkhar nodded again and took a few steps across the cell, then back, careful not to block our view of the prisoner's face. He ran a hand through his disheveled hair. "I can't think of who could possibly know enough about the boy to be useful, and would go out of the palace enough to speak with you without arousing suspicion. Most of the servants are fairly bright, and they're all loyal. And most don't have much opportunity to watch the Tarvil enough to detect his affections... they're not obvious. Unless... Ah! It's someone in the stables. They've had some new boys lately, and fewer warnings given to them by Noriso about keeping their tongues quiet while they're out. A subtle weakness. You were wise to exploit it."

The man nodded. "Yes, one of the stable boys. He's just done cleaning the stable when Sendoa and the Tarvil begin exercising in the courtyard and he watches them. He was only too glad to talk scandals about the girl joining them."

Sirkhar rubbed his hand over his jaw again, then nodded. "Thank you." He stepped out of view, and a moment later we heard the door close and the lock clank.

Hakan stepped back to wait Sirkhar's entrance, but I kept watching through the hole a moment. The prisoner had a self-satisfied look for a moment that slowly faded into puzzlement as he stared at the closed door.

Sirkhar stepped into the cell we occupied and murmured, "It would be better to discuss my findings a little farther down the hall, where he cannot hear so easily."

Hakan nodded. We followed him out and down the hall to the guard station at the end. There were two tables with rough wooden chairs. Ena, Lani, and Elathlo sat at one table, and Hakan, Sirkhar, and I sat at the other.

Sirkhar leaned forward with his elbows on the table. "Your Royal Highness, you know of the criminal groups in the city?"

Hakan nodded, then glanced at me. "Well, not much. I know they exist."

"They call themselves the Guilds. There are four main ones: the Black Rats, who deal in smuggling; the Snakes, who deal with petty theft; the Clerks, who deal with embezzlement; and the Blades, the assassins and enforcers. The first three have agreed not to form their own enforcer teams to prevent inter-guild wars. The Blades have agreed not to take on contracts except with the agreement of each of the other three guilds. This ensures that each guild remains at peace with each other.

229

More or less. There are always little disputes, but the Blades like the arrangement and so it works."

Hakan frowned. "So all four guilds agreed with the assassination attempt?"

Sirkhar gave a faint nod. "Yes." He paused a moment, then continued, "The guilds are not large, and the Blades are not especially skilled or intelligent. Assassination is something they probably would not have attempted on their own, even if they'd thought of it. Their usual business is intimidating one merchant on behalf of another, generally at his home or his shop. Threats or violence against nobility are unusual, much less against royalty. They tend to use methods that have been successful in the past; they're not especially innovative or ambitious. They've never really gone up against anyone who would oppose them."

"What about my father?" Hakan asked in a low voice. He kept his eyes on the table.

Sirkhar hesitated. "He found it not worth the effort to oppose them."

"And you?" Hakan looked up, clear blue eyes holding Sirkhar's gaze.

"I have little use for men who serve only themselves." Sirkhar gave a tight smile. "My allegiance is to this country, not every individual within it."

Hakan's eyes narrowed a little, as if he were trying to decide if that was a promise of support or a threat. Then he returned the smile and nodded. "Go on."

Sirkhar continued, "Aside from Taisto's coup, there has been no real rebellion against the crown for over five hundred years. The nobles jostle for position close to the crown, they attempt to influence the crown, but they do not normally seek to replace the crown. Most of the nobility support you, or at least would not support insurrection or a coup. So those who oppose you must try something more subtle.

"My guess is this: Lord Daiko is either the mind behind the attempt on your life, or the one chosen to speak for him. I'd guess he's in charge, though; no underling would be trusted with that initial contact. He is also powerful, and unlikely to accept a subordinate position, even if it was not his idea originally. There is a small group of nobles that supports it, probably close friends of Lord Daiko. Once the instigator came up with his plan, he told this small group, and once they have been told, they are bound to help or to report him. Since they did not report him, we can assume they support the plan. He's a man of standing, so between him and his friends, they have money and some small measure of force. However, they don't have the force necessary to directly oppose you.

"To my knowledge, Lord Daiko has no real connection to Taisto, and was uninvolved in any plots before now. I assume that means he and the others with him dislike you because of your policies, not because you are your father's son."

Hakan nodded. "I agree."

I glanced at Hakan. "What policies have you implemented that would provoke such a response?"

He frowned. "I'm not sure about Lord Daiko in particular, but the taxation changes late last year were very unpopular with the nobles holding hereditary lands. Most of them contribute nothing to the treasury and just sit on their lands, getting richer off their tenants. I didn't think the changes were especially harsh, but since they haven't paid anything in generations..." he let his voice trail away and steepled his fingers in front of him. "Anyway, what else did you find out?"

"Any coup or assassination attempt must be considered in light of a possible replacement. Your son the prince is an infant; if you died, a regent would rule for years. They would suspect you would have already designated General Sendoa," he glanced at me with an unreadable expression, "but since he has reportedly rejected power before, there is a good chance he would have done so again. If he wanted political power, he would have requested it and you would have granted it before now. Perhaps also, they imagined that if he did accept the title of regent, he would be easy to manipulate. He is not viewed as politically savvy."

Sirkhar glanced at me again, as if he thought I would be angry at that. I remained silent; nothing I could say would contribute anything useful to Hakan's knowledge.

Hakan spoke then, with a faint, wry smile. "Yes, if he wanted power he would have it. But they underestimate him if they think he's naive."

Sirkhar nodded, giving me another unreadable glance. "I'd guess they judge it more likely that you would have appointed one of the most powerful nobles as regent to rule in your stead, unbeknownst to them. One whom you presume completely loyal. Even someone not in their group would likely be sympathetic to their ideas of good policy. If you have not yet designated a regent, Her Royal Highness would reign, but she would have little real power. They would form a council to select their own regent, with the goal of selecting one of their own, or at least someone they could tolerate. By law, the queen has the power to veto their choice, but I could imagine she might be pressured or deceived into accepting their decision.

"If the regent is acceptable to them, they would hope to make him king when your son suffers an untimely death in a few years. Or perhaps they would hope to mold your son into their views and assist him in taking power early, when he is easiest to manipulate. In either case, both your son and the queen are at risk."

"So what do we do?" Hakan asked. "The stableboy has to go, of course."

"Yes. I doubt he knew what he was doing, though. It's not hard to recruit informants like him. You ask for a piece of trivial information, such as what color robe the master wore that morning or what type of cake the mistress prefers. Pay the informant. Ask for more information, similarly harmless. Pay increasing amounts. By the time you ask for tidbits of information that add up to anything useful, the informant relies on the money you provide. He's afraid of being let go, and so he'll keep quiet, even if he's uncomfortable with the questions you're asking. At most, he'll clam up and avoid you.

"If you need the information, you can threaten him, but usually it's easier to cultivate another informant. None of them know every piece of information you're getting; each bit is worthless on its own, but together they form a picture you can use. The stableboy knew it was wrong to accept money for information, but he probably had no idea the Tarvil boy would be threatened, much less you, Your Royal Highness." Sirkhar shrugged slightly. "Though I'd still let him go. Even harmless gossip is betraying the trust of the master of the house. Even more so when the house is the palace."

Hakan nodded, frowning.

I glanced over at Elathlo, Lani, and Ena. They all looked sleepy, slumped over the table, though Elathlo watched us with wary eyes. I thought also of Ria, and hoped she was not too worried yet.

Sirkhar tapped his fingers on the table thoughtfully. "I recommend you do nothing yet. I will investigate. Un-

233

til now, I haven't had enough information to pursue the guilds, nor was doing so on your father's list of priorities. This changes things. I will identify the guild leaders and as many of their deputies as possible. Then you can make your move against them."

Hakan sighed and leaned back in his chair. "How long will it take?"

Sirkhar thought for long minutes. "Probably a matter of two or three days to identify the guild leaders, their deputies, and the nobles involved. If it takes longer, they will either flee or attempt to attack by force. It wouldn't work, but it would be messy. I must move quickly, before they realize how much has been exposed. I recommend letting no one in or out of the palace unless absolutely necessary, but don't make it obvious that the palace is closed. I'll handle the stableboy."

"Who is it?" I asked.

He glanced at me. "Gareth."

I nodded. I knew the boy by sight, though not much more than that. He'd brushed down Kanti a few times when I'd returned from riding.

Sirkhar said, "There is also the matter of the spies in the households. The Blades, the Snakes, and the Black Rats identify their members with tattoos. The Clerks like to remain less visible. Most of the spies are probably either Snakes or Clerks. We can identify Snakes in the households by looking for snake tattoos on the inside of the left ankle. Blades will have a linear tattoo on the inside of the right arm, and Black Rats will have a round or oval shape just behind the right ear."

Sirkhar continued, "Clerks will be a little more difficult, but I have a few contacts I can pressure. Once I have a few names, I will make faster progress."

Hakan nodded. "What do you need?"

Sirkhar glanced at me. "Nothing yet. Don't kill the prisoner. I may need to question him again."

"I wasn't planning on it." Hakan blinked.

Sirkhar appeared almost ready to stand, then paused. "I doubt Lord Daiko is aware of the infiltration tonight. The guilds know a little about how to keep secrets. So even though the guilds will know that something went wrong tonight, Lord Daiko may not find out immediately."

He glanced at me again. "The boy should disappear. Let a rumor get out that he killed an intruder in his room tonight, but died in the fight. General Sendoa found them both dead in the morning when he arrived to wake the boy for his morning exercises. Don't deliberately make it public; let the rumor get out secretly, as if it is not meant to be known. I will make sure the stables hear of it. The guilds will think that this mission to gather information failed, but in a way that did not damage the overall plan. They may or may not inform Lord Daiko, but if so, it will only be to let him know that they will proceed more slowly. It will buy a little time without alerting them."

Hakan nodded. "If Elathlo is said to be dead, it's safe for Lani and her mother to return to normal duties, isn't it? There's no reason to threaten her."

"Yes."

I frowned. "Perhaps. But they are not accustomed to keeping secrets, and if Elathlo is supposed to be dead, she would be grieving. Excuse Lani from her duties to mourn him, and her mother in order to comfort her. They can stay with Ria and me so they aren't questioned."

Sirkhar gave me a long, thoughtful look. "Yes, that is wise."

Hakan licked his lips. "Is the queen in any danger?"

Sirkhar shook his head. "I doubt it. They couldn't even strike directly at you, and they have no reason to target her. But a guard would not be amiss."

Hakan looked at me. "Choose someone you trust."

I nodded, then thought a moment. "If we know Lord Daiko is in charge of the coup attempt, is there a reason not to arrest him now? Then arrest the other conspirators after questioning him?"

Sirkhar shook his head. "If he is attacked, he has nothing to lose by fighting, hoping others will join him. I doubt anyone would, with the possible exception of his co-conspirators if it looks like the fight is going his way, or if they think they are already known to be on his side. But since we don't know who they are yet, they could cause more damage than their numbers would justify."

"Agreed." I nodded, and Sirkhar gave me another odd look.

Hakan frowned but nodded. "I agree as well.

I said, "If I understand correctly, many of Lord Daiko's men would probably fight for him only if they did not know what he was plotting. They're not lords and they probably stand to gain by the tax changes. They have no reason to oppose the king, other than loyalty to Daiko. Even if only half of them left Lord Daiko, that would reduce his forces such that a fight would be hopeless. The ones most likely to switch would be the veterans, especially retired officers. They would also be the best he has, and probably the leaders. Many of the others would obey them." I caught Hakan's eye and said, "Perhaps I can coopt Lord Daiko's men before he realizes it."

Sirkhar studied me, pale blue eyes on mine. Finally he gave a cool smile. "That might work. How would you do it?"

Hakan also turned to me, and I pondered a moment. Indeed, how would I do such a thing? "Hakan would send a royal messenger to Lord Daiko, urgently request-ing permission for me to consult with some of his officers about the school in Ironcrest. Flatter him. He has money, so he'll have some of the best retired officers on his staff. We'll include a list of the officers I wish to consult. The letter will confidentially inform Lord Daiko that Elathlo was killed, and this has upset me personally. It will also complicate relations with the Tarvil, once word reaches them. For both reasons, work on the school has been ac-celerated. Hakan wants to keep me busy and mend rela-tions with the Tarvil. Lord Daiko should not discuss Elathlo's death with anyone until there is an official statement from the crown. I'll follow the message by a few hours, trusting in Lord Daiko's understanding and cooperation. Because of the short notice, it is understood that not all of the requested officers may be available, but I am to begin working immediately. With all appropriate thanks, of course.

"I'll visit Lord Daiko with a small group of men, drawn from Hakan's guard and the officers visiting for their advanced training. I'll meet with Lord Daiko's offi-cers and move outside to show them some training exer-cises we've been working on. Out of earshot, I can speak to them about Lord Daiko's plan and gauge their support of it, then either secure their promise of assistance or re-move them from the conflict as appropriate. Then we'll see what happens."

Sirkhar stared at me with narrowed eyes. "Yes," he said slowly. "Yes. It is a good plan. While you are visit-ing Lord Daiko, I will identify and secure the guild chiefs."

Hakan nodded. "I'll write the letter to Lord Daiko. We'll send it in two days, in the morning, with your meeting around noon. Is that enough time?"

Sirkhar nodded.

Hakan took a deep breath, glanced at the other table, and lowered his voice even more. "Sirkhar, we need to understand each other. You said you served the old king, but not this one. I know you lied to him, and I understand why. But you've never actually *said* you're loyal to me. Where do you stand?"

Does he mean to have this conversation in front of me? Will Sirkhar be honest, knowing that I hear his every word? Yes, Hakan does not want to be alone with him until he has a better idea of Sirkhar's loyalty.

Sirkhar blinked slowly, as if formulating his response, then said, "Yes, I lied to him. But not much; mostly I let him infer the wrong thing. I let him think I was on his side. It's better to avoid blatant lies when possible, since you have to keep them straight. That's one way I gain information. Ask about details, preferably out of order. Do it over days, taking time to review the answers elsewhere and going back for clarification on what seems contradictory or confused. Eventually a liar's story will break down, either through internal contradictions or through contradictions with known facts. It's much harder to break down a world created by implications and inference. He fills in what he expects, and he'll never know I lied to him."

He spread his hands on the table and looked at them for a moment, then looked up. "But your main question is whether I serve you. Not exactly. I serve Erdem. I served your father the old king because he was a tolerable king. He was not my favorite man, but he was the leader of my country. Serving even a mediocre king is better than starting a cycle of coup followed by coup followed by civil war."

Hakan asked, "But what about when Vidar, or Taisto I suppose, usurped me? Where were you? He

238

killed my father, and he tried to kill me. I didn't see that you did anything. Am I wrong?"

"I had done no work for your father for some time. I did not know there was a plot against him. After his death, I suspected he may have been murdered. I looked for proof, but I found nothing besides circumstantial evidence. Vidar, and then Taisto, served as de facto king in your absence.

"I would have judged Taisto a mediocre king, perhaps a little better than your father, aside from his questionable claim to power. You were probably dead. Even if you were alive, I had no reason to believe you would be a better king than Taisto would be. Probably worse. If you were alive, it would take a civil war for you to regain the throne. You might die in the war, or the war would fail. In either case, the conflict and destruction that followed the civil war could last for decades.

"Perhaps I could assassinate Taisto. That might be justice, but it might not. It wouldn't make you king. One of the other nobles would seize power long before you could make your move with any force. It was better for Erdem to let things be. Most people would be better off.

"Now... you're king. Legitimate, and wiser than I'd expected. Better than Taisto, and better than your father. I'm not sure I think everything you're doing will work, and I doubt this is the first time you'll face resistance. But that's international politics and economic policy. I'm not an expert in those.

"I don't know yet that I like you personally, and I definitely don't like General Sendoa."

He glanced at me then and paused, his eyes narrowed as if he was reconsidering those words. I tried to remain impassive; it was not as if his dislike was a complete surprise to me, although I was surprised that he would state it so openly.

"But my personal likes and dislikes are irrelevant. I will serve you as king because it serves Erdem." He held Hakan's gaze.

Hakan licked his lips. "I thank you for honest answers. Most men would have said what they thought I wanted to hear. My father paid you, but there is no mention in the records of your pay other than a monthly salary. I assume that was only part of your pay, and that you were also paid for individual... assignments. What was the arrangement? How should you be paid?"

Sirkhar gave a slight nod. "The records are correct. I am paid only by salary. It is the standard pay for a general administrator of the twelfth rank, and my pay changes only when that standard changes. I expressly refuse to be paid for individual jobs, or for specific information, or to be eligible to receive a raise for service that pleases the crown. My pay is fixed. It may not be high, but it is comfortable."

"It can be adjusted," Hakan offered.

"To accept reward for providing damaging information on others or for performing even more unpleasant activities gives me an incentive to do so. I like to think I would ignore such incentives, but it is best for everyone if my judgment is not tempted. It also makes my testimony against or for any individual more trustworthy. I do not wish to be bought, by the crown or by anyone else." Sirkhar's eyes flashed with the first hint of emotion I'd seen from him all night.

Hakan said, "That's admirable. But if you're paid the same whether you do something or do nothing at all, your motivation might be to do nothing unless absolutely required."

Sirkhar looked at Hakan impassively, the silence stretching out between them.

At long last, Hakan gave a faint smile. "I see. I'm impressed. Your pay will remain as you have said. I hope you come to like me. I think the kingdom we both serve is lucky to have your loyalty."

Twenty-Five

N o screams of pain or sounds of begging made their way through the holes through which my sponsor and the king watched Sirkhar and the prisoner talk. From where I stood, the conversation was muffled, and I heard little of the words, only enough to know that Sirkhar didn't torture the prisoner. This confused me, as did Sirkhar's apparent satisfaction with the results of the interrogation. The conversation that followed confused me just as much.

The king listened to Sirkhar and asked questions sometimes. Sirkhar's dislike of my sponsor was palpable, though my sponsor didn't acknowledge it. I wished Sirkhar wasn't necessary. I didn't hear all of it, since I was seated at the other table, but I heard the coolness in his voice when he spoke to my sponsor.

When they finally finished, my sponsor escorted Lani, her mother, and me to his estate. He said we would stay there until the threat had been addressed. Lani had fallen asleep on the table, and the fabric of her sleeve had pressed lines into her cheek. My sponsor was the only one among us who didn't look tired, alert to every sound in the garden as we slipped through the darkness.

His estate was smaller than the palace, but almost as luxurious as the living areas of the king's residence. His head servant met us at the door and let us in; I suppose my sponsor had already told him we would be up very late. He took us to quarters prepared for us.

My sponsor had thought of many things that I had not. The soldiers who had eaten with us, including Captain Askano, who had once threatened to cut off my hand, were there waiting for us. I assumed he'd asked them to protect Lady Sendoa, in case anything went badly that night.

The room I was given was on the second floor, with no easy way to climb to the window, which was locked from the inside. Lani and her mother were next door, in a similarly prepared room. One of the soldiers sat in a comfortable chair in the hallway just outside our doors with a lamp and a book. The other two were downstairs, keeping Lady Sendoa company while she waited up for my sponsor.

We were ushered upstairs immediately so I saw little of their meeting, but even I could not miss the relief that flashed across her face when she saw him. A few minutes later I was undressed and in bed.

I couldn't sleep for some time, despite my exhaustion. I wondered whether my sponsor would wake me in the morning for practice, then decided it was unlikely, since I was meant to be hidden. My thoughts bounced uneasily between the intrigue threatening the king and my concern for Tirta. He was my friend, but that was no guarantee he'd be chosen for the school in Ironcrest.

I considered what warriors might take Tirta if he were not chosen, and the results of my mental list were far from encouraging. Then I considered asking my sponsor if he would be willing to take another aloka, but discarded the idea as too bold. I already owed my sponsor so much; I did not have the right to ask him to take on another aloka.

Then, I had my great idea. Perhaps the school could replace service as an aloka entirely. After my demonstration, word of the superior Erdemen training would make its way through the tribes. Alokas served warriors, but perhaps the warriors could be persuaded to give up our labor in return for not having to train and feed us. I'd always suspected that the extra mouth to feed was part of why warriors disliked alokas so much.

Postponing service as an aloka until after schooling would be dangerous. Warriors would not want to accept older, more confident alokas, particularly if they were trained to use weapons already. But serving as an aloka before schooling would mean that boys would serve younger than before, perhaps younger than the warriors would wish to accept. Not too young to work hard, of course, but too young for it to be worth the warriors' time. Abusing, even killing, his aloka was a warrior's right, but killings were rare; the family might hold a grudge.

I would suggest it to my sponsor and see what he thought. Perhaps he would see it as beneficial too. He had decided to take me, without expecting me to earn my keep as a Tarvil warrior would have. He did not even take the price of my training from Otso-ka. He had done it for his own reasons; kindness was one reason, but not the only one. Perhaps those reasons would hold for others as well.

At last, as the faint light of dawn began to peek through the window, I fell into an uneasy doze. I woke not much later to the sound of a knock on my door.

A servant had brought me breakfast. I thanked him, and he gave me a faint, amused smile. "I've been instructed that you are free to visit with Ena and Lani when they awake, but they are still asleep. Until then, Lord General Sendoa says that you may read anything in the library, and he expects you to make a little progress on your cultural writing assignment today. Colonel Bekendi will not be visiting until Lord General Sendoa's current assignment is complete. You may also sleep more if you wish; I understand you were up late last night."

"Thank you."

I ate and slept a little more, then worked on my writing assignment until lunch.

TWENTY-SIX

KEMEN

I could not tell Ria everything; there was too much to say and do, and little time. For a few brief hours we lay in bed, the covers pulled up against the midnight chill. She slept immediately, her breath puffing softly into my shoulder as she nestled beside me. I did not, though I floated into the haze of drowsiness for a short while.

I kissed Ria and held her again before returning to the palace for an early breakfast meeting with Hakan. He'd already compiled a list of Lord Daiko's men and identified the veterans among them. I didn't personally know any of them, although I recognized a few names. The list was not long, eleven veterans out of thirty armed men who worked for Lord Daiko.

Sirkhar had been gone for hours. I wondered if he needed help.

Or perhaps he was planning something of his own. I tried to dismiss the thought, but it would not leave the back of my mind. Something was wrong with Sirkhar, something deep inside. Something about him made me think of a viper, expressionless and unthreatening until it suited him, then striking without warning. How much could we trust him?

Not long after I wondered, he stepped into the room with a quick bow. "Your Royal Highness, I have news."

"Come. Sit." Hakan gestured toward a chair. "Have you eaten?"

"No." His eyes were red-rimmed, and I thought he looked not only as if he'd been up all night, but as if he'd had a busy night of it too. Dirt was ground into the fabric of his jacket on one shoulder, and a shallow cut crusted with blood crossed his left cheek and the top of his ear.

I rose and stepped into the hallway, where I requested that Sinta bring us another plate and another pot of tea. Sirkhar was already talking when I slid back into my seat.

"...explain what I have done, because I will need more men for the second piece of our plan. I told you the guilds are not large, and most of the men in them live double lives. They have a normal job, or at least the appearance of one, or they pretend to have income from property. Many of them have families; crime is something they do behind the scenes. It enables them to live their lives as they wish, but it isn't necessarily something they are proud of.

"So, if you can identify a guild member, it is relatively easy to catch him. Most of them will probably talk to reduce their sentences or gain some consideration for their families. Perhaps even to explain how they were forced into crime so their families will think better of them.

"However, if you arrest all the criminals you know of in sequence, after the first two or three disappeared, the others would flee. Word would spread. If you arrest the flunkeys first, the leadership would disappear. As a group, it would be destroyed, because they wouldn't want to reappear again. They'd have to move away, and may not have planned to flee at all. They'd have few resources. The highest leadership may have a contingency plan with money hidden away, perhaps even a second house or identity. But that requires planning and money; they may not have bothered.

"The mid ranks are least likely to flee; they have a few resources but much to lose. They would probably think the arrests are aimed only at the leadership, and will hope they have escaped notice. The lower levels are too stupid, too poor, or too uninformed to do much of anything. Also they pose little threat.

"I have identified three of the four guild chiefs, as well as five of their deputies in total. I…" he stopped at a knock on the door.

I rose and took the teapot and platter from Sinta. Sirkhar glanced at the door to be sure it was closed before he resumed speaking.

"Thank you, General." He gave me a cool, thoughtful glance as he picked up a piece of bread. "I should have the name of the fourth by this afternoon, as well as another few of the deputies if things go well." He pulled a crumpled piece of paper from his pocket and slid it across the table toward Hakan. "These are the names and their addresses. I recommend that we move swiftly when we move, with a plan unique to each target. I can't supervise each operation, of course, since they should be simultaneous, or as close to it as possible. I have a few men I can use, but most often I work alone. Perhaps you could lend me some thirty soldiers."

Hakan looked at me, and I nodded. Sirkhar's eyes tightened a little at that; perhaps he thought Hakan asked for my permission. I took it as Hakan asking whether it was wise, and my confirmation that I saw no risk in it.

"The goal is to capture each target individually without alerting anyone who might be watching them. They can be arrested later. For now, the objective is to remove them from action as quickly and quietly as possible, so no one guesses they've been arrested, much less for treason."

Hakan and I nodded.

"Kemen, can you designate which men should go with you to Lord Daiko's estate and which should assist Sirkhar?"

"Aye." I thought a moment, then named the men I thought would best be able to fulfill Sirkhar's requirements.

Hakan's next question surprised both Sirkhar and me. "Last night you said you did not like my father. Would you have tolerated his assassination if you'd known of it ahead of time?"

"No. Politics are not my area of expertise. I had suspicions but no proof that your father died of unnatural causes. Taisto said publicly that he served only as regent until you were found. I do not have the right to interfere in even a messy transfer of political power. I am not a kingmaker." His gaze flashed toward me, and I finally understood why he disliked me so much.

"I respect that." My words surprised both of them. "It is admirable for someone in your position and with your responsibilities to remove himself from questions of succession. It would be too tempting to interfere for your own purposes."

Sirkhar studied me. "Your loyalty is to the king. You think like a soldier, not considering what is best for the nation."

I raised my eyebrows. "I *am* a soldier. I consider the chain of command. When I ask men to die for our country, my conscience needs to know that the man who commands us to risk our lives understands and respects our sacrifice. I can't command men to die on the orders of a man who rules by deception for his own personal gain. Hakan was naive, but he was a boy of honor who grew into a man of honor. The sort of man who is smart enough to take good advice where his own wisdom is insufficient. He wanted what was best for his country, even if it meant giving up power himself. I can serve a man like that."

Sirkhar stared hard at my face, then gave a faint, cool smile. "Perhaps I misjudged you, General Sendoa. I thought you were a simple man. We may not agree, but I understand you a little better than I did."

I smiled back with more warmth. "I am a simple man."

I think I understood him better than he understood me. He kept himself deliberately aloof from political decisions. Perhaps he feared the power he could wield, or perhaps he feared the consequences of choosing badly. Perhaps it was only his moral code that kept him from interfering. A man with his job had to draw a line between what he was willing to do and what he was not; otherwise he was only a hired enforcer or assassin. Political neutrality and patriotism were the line he drew. I may not have liked his work, but with such strong beliefs, I could trust that he served well.

He also probably believed I'd been precipitous in choosing to help Hakan reclaim the throne. Perhaps I had. We'd all been fortunate Hakan had grown into a man of character, stronger than he'd been at first. I might flatter myself that I'd helped him mature. But he could have made different choices. Things could indeed have turned out badly.

Perhaps, from Sirkhar's point of view, I had made essentially political choices without considering all the repercussions. I'd made choices I had no right to make.

From my position, I'd made the only choice possible.

Not much later, Sirkhar and I gathered the men I had chosen for the various duties. I asked Eneko to remain guarding Ria. I didn't expect her to be in any danger, but it made me feel safer to have someone I trusted with her. Kudret and several men from the palace guard would accompany me to Lord Daiko's estate, while Iretzi and the other seven men in Stonehaven for the advanced training seminars, as well as some others, were to assist Sirkhar in capturing the guild leadership. Siri Andar, one of the senior men of the royal guard whom I had met when Hakan first regained the throne, as well as some others he selected, were to remain with Kveta and Hakan.

I listened while Sirkhar explained to the soldiers what they were to do. He would return later with more details after questioning one more man in hopes of identifying the leader of the Clerks and his deputies.

"We'll strike tomorrow at noon. Bade Grammen is the leader of the Snakes. He owns a tavern, and at noon tomorrow he should be preparing for the evening meal. Four men will apprehend him, but only one will speak with him. Say that Flikurino has been taken ill, and there is a meeting of the chiefs to determine the way forward while he is unavailable. He may be confused, and deny any knowledge of what you speak. Tell him that you've been authorized to give him proof in the form of a token payment from the Black Rats. Give him the gold, and make sure he sees this."

He opened a small bag and pulled out three gold coins, as well as a length of thin, braided black leather knotted into a double loop. "It's not a definitive identification, of course; that would be too simple. But it is an indication that is sometimes used from the Black Rats to indicate that a message is genuine. He should go with you without any trouble. Bring him to this address." He handed over a piece of paper. "We will arrest him there, behind closed doors, and then bring him to the palace prison to be questioned later."

The other plans were much the same. I gained new respect for Sirkhar as he spoke. Every detail was planned, every capture unique. We spoke again after the men had received their instructions. In the courtyard, they practiced their conversations, and within each delegation selected the man who was most convincing.

Sirkhar turned to me. "You plan to leave this afternoon?"

"Yes. I could make it late tonight if I started now, but we'll take two days. It will be leisurely, with an unnecessarily luxurious camp tonight. The point being to distract me from my grief. If Lord Daiko sends someone to meet us, as is likely, he will suspect nothing."

Sirkhar nodded. "That is wise." He gave me a sidelong look. "You didn't strike me as a particularly devious man, General Sendoa."

"I'm not. I like to avoid fights when possible. But when that's not possible, I like to win. Giving an opponent warning makes that more challenging." I realized belatedly that perhaps my words sounded like a threat. So I smiled. "Captain Sirkhar, I realize you don't like me. I think I understand why. I don't even mind. I'm a patriot, and I think you are too. If you serve Erdem, and you don't threaten Hakan, you'll find we're on the same side, even if we have different tactics."

He gave a faint nod. "Perhaps."

I don't know if it helped. The words surprised me, as they probably surprised him. But he'd been open about his beliefs with Hakan, and I felt that perhaps a similar openness might help him trust me.

Twenty-Seven

Elathlo

My sponsor spoke with me briefly at lunch. He thanked me for telling him about the intruder. It seemed many things had been decided while he was gone, and he was departing that afternoon on the king's business. Knowing how busy he was, I should probably not have been so bold, but Tirta's future had weighed on me all morning. My idea had grown and shifted as I thought about my visit north and the things I had seen.

"Sir? I have a request."

He looked at me, waiting.

I stumbled over the words a little, though I'd rehearsed them in my head already. "My friend Tirta will be assigned to a warrior soon as an aloka. I'm afraid for him." The word afraid did not begin to cover the sympathy that nearly choked me. "I was wondering if perhaps the school might be opened to more Tarvil students. Erdemen training is so much better than what our warriors can offer. I thought also that perhaps Otso-ka might be able to offer more goods in trade than you and the king might be aware of. We have not considered certain things valuable, because they are not difficult for us to obtain, or they serve no purpose for us. But perhaps you might like them, and maybe they could pay the cost of the additional students."

I felt my enthusiasm faltering in the intensity of his gaze.

"Goods such as..." he prompted.

"Fox furs. Sometimes we catch white foxes. We use the fur to line winter tunics and shirts, because it's thick and soft. Once my father and some other warriors killed a white bear. They used the skin for many warm parkas and other things. Sometimes also they kill marseni. They're like your weasels, only larger; in the winter they have white fur, but during the summer it's brown."

I paused, and he nodded that I should continue.

"Mostly my people select furs based on what is easiest and safest to get. Sheep's wool is warm, and we have enough of it, so we seldom hunt other animals. We hunt for meat, not fur. But furs are more valuable here. I saw in the the market that a red fox fur was four golden eagles, and the white fur is much thicker and more beautiful. If my people knew they could trade such things to Erdem, perhaps they wouldn't be so desperate. We wouldn't be rich like Erdem, but life would be better."

He nodded. "I can't make any promises. But I'll speak to the king about it." He gave me a quick smile. "I'm glad you think of your people, Elathlo."

I breathed a sigh of thanks that he was so generous. "Thank you, sir."

TWENTY-EIGHT

KEMEN

E lathlo's idea was intriguing, but I had too much to do to give it much thought immediately. I asked the men to pack the tents and gear and get the horses ready while I spent those last moments with Ria.

I brushed her hair for a few minutes, wishing I could be there in the evening for that cherished, sweet hour before we slipped into bed together. She sat on a chair and I stood behind her. There was a mirror off to the side, and in it I could see the curves of her cheek and jaw and neck, like a painting by a master. I smiled as she reached back to pull my arms over her shoulders and leaned against me, her head resting against my stomach. I bent to press my lips to the soft smooth skin beneath her ear.

She sighed in contentment and I smiled, inhaling the warm, sweet scent of her hair.

"Lani asked me something this morning, and I've been thinking about it. I thought you should know too," she said.

"Hm?"

"She said, and I think she's right, that Elathlo must care about her if the traitors chose to threaten him by threatening her." She turned to meet my eyes. "I can't think of another reason for her to be in the middle of it."

I sighed. "Probably. I hadn't seen it, but I shouldn't be surprised. She's pretty and kind, and they're friends. They're both very young, though. You shouldn't worry."

She caught her bottom lip between her teeth as she thought. "No, I'm not worried. He seems like a good boy, and besides, he's much too terrified of you to pressure her into anything."

"You think he's still afraid of me?" The thought stung a little, because I had tried not to frighten the boy. Surely by now he knew he could trust me.

"Not like he was, no. But he'd have to be blind and stupid not to realize that you care about Lani. I should have noticed before now. I wouldn't be surprised if she likes him as well. But she's not ready to make any kind of big decision."

"I should hope not." Lani was a sweet, beautiful girl, but she was only a girl, not yet fifteen. "You think she likes him back?" That could make our morning training sessions awkward, to say the least.

"A little, perhaps." Ria thought. "She's flattered and intrigued, but not in love."

I nodded, imagining Lani blushing as she asked Ria about it.

Ria smiled a little. "You really hadn't noticed he liked her?"

I shook my head.

Her smile broadened. "I have the excuse that I barely see him. You see them everyday. Together. Someone else noticed, at least. Someone who probably sees him less than you do."

"So I should have noticed?" I gave her a skeptical frown. "What in our history together makes you think I'm good at noticing things like that?"

She snorted. "Nothing. You're right."

I ached with frustration that I had to be away from her again. Even in silence, her presence was warmth and comfort after too many years alone. At least this trip would be short.

She showed me a painting she'd started that morning while I was in the palace.

"I opened the window and listened to the wind in the branches. It was cold, and I closed it again soon. But it made me think of summer, and sitting together in the garden." She smiled and leaned against me. The painting was all green leaves and pink and yellow flowers.

"It's beautiful," I said.

"No, it's not. But it was fun." Her voice wavered a bit.

I kissed the top of her head. "You're beautiful. And when you smile..." I kissed her fingers, then held her hand against my chest. "Feel my heart beating faster?"

She blushed and leaned her forehead against my chest. "I was almost afraid you'd grow tired of me. You're sure you're not bored with me yet?" Her voice shook.

"Ria!" I dropped to my knees in front of her, looking up into her face. "What's wrong?"

She brushed angrily at the tears filling her eyes. "I'm sorry. It's just... I feel sensitive and stupid these days. You're so busy, and I don't know what's going on. And I don't have anything to do all day. Citulali is nice but

258

she's barely a friend yet. I don't want to bother Kveta. Anyway, she's the queen. All my friends are servants and they have work to do. I'd help them, but I don't want to shame you. It's not really appropriate." She forced an unconvincing smile. "I'm sorry. I'm fine."

"Oh, Ria." I stood and put my arms around her, feeling tentative and ill-prepared to comfort her the way I wished to. When she leaned into me, I tightened my embrace and just held her in silence for a time. I felt her trembling as she tried not to cry, and slowly she relaxed, her arms warm around my waist.

I stroked her hair with one hand, my cheek against the top of her head. "Ria, I can't say that we'll never grow frustrated with each other, or that we'll never have difficult times. But as long as my heart beats, I will love you. I might not be good at showing it. I'll disappoint you. But I *will* love you. Always." I bent to look into her eyes. I wiped a tear from her cheek with one thumb, then kissed the damp trail it had left until I reached her eye, then pressed a kiss to her temple. "I'm sorry I have to leave. I'll be back as soon as I can. When it's over, I'll tell you everything."

She nodded with a tremulous smile.

In the courtyard, she bid me farewell with a smile and a wave, almost as if there was nothing wrong, but I knew better. When I returned in a day or two, I would do anything to lighten her heart.

We camped only eight leagues from Lord Daiko's estate, just off the main road. Matxin cooked a lavish meal; he was decent in a fight and had been recommended as perfect for this role. He'd agreed to the unusual request with a curious smile, then a satisfied nod when I'd explained to the men what we were planning. Gutxi, another man new to me, played on a lyrekt while we ate. A lyrekt is a stringed instrument not often brought on military campaigns, though the sound can be quite beautiful.

As we were finishing eating, a scout rode up and conferred with Kudret for a few moments. Then he dismounted and strode to me.

"General, you are not so far from Lord Daiko's estate. He is ready to welcome you if you arrive tonight. You can be comfortable," he looked around at the lavish camp, "well, more comfortable." He smiled. "It seems you've brought quite a cook. It smells delicious."

"Yes." I kept my face suitably somber. "I thank you for the invitation. But this is sufficient." I turned away and let Kudret play his part.

Although I couldn't hear him, I knew what he would say. The travel was meant to distract me from the tragic death of a young friend, and a cheerful camp was better than a lonely room in a palace at the moment. He would report back that our camp was extravagant, our food smelled delicious, and there was beautiful music. My men were trying valiantly to divert me from my grief.

That night in my tent I spent almost three hours on a drawing of Ria and me. It was the first time I had drawn people as anything other than human-shaped smudges in the background. It challenged me. It would have been better to spend that time with Ria and depart later, riding more quickly, but we weren't sure there were no other spies in the palace, and we had to be cautious. The ruse had to be convincing.

My shoulders cramped from sitting so long in one position, concentrating on drawing and forgetting to breathe. The smoke from the lamp burned my eyes. But at last the drawing was finished, or as finished as my meager skill could accomplish. We stood, arms entwined, beside the Silverfall, the waterfall where I'd taken her before our wedding. The waterfall itself was not detailed, only a jumble of rocks and splashing water. I'd spent most of my effort on Ria, on capturing the slender curve of her waist and the way she leaned her head against my shoulder, relaxed and comfortable. My figure was taller, with my shape quickly sketched, my hair pulled back with a bit of leather. I hadn't spent much time on my clothes, just enough to indicate that I wore a light shirt and dark trousers tucked into my boots. Ria wore a simple dress, with ornamentation only around the bottom edge. In my mind it was blue, but on paper it was a medium tone indicated by the shadowing of my black ink.

It was hardly an artist's drawing, but I hoped she saw in it what I meant to show. Her trust and comfort with me. My head leaned toward hers. The way my left arm circled her waist, and her right arm circled mine. How we stood looking at the waterfall, as I hoped we would look at everything in our future together.

THE NEXT MORNING we waited until an hour after the sun came up before breaking down the tents. The men were bored, but entertained themselves without complaint, sharpening their boot knives and chatting quietly as they ate breakfast. From long habit I'd woken before dawn, and found myself just as bored as the others. I amused myself by working on my drawing for Ria a bit more, adding detail to the waterfall and to our clothes.

Finally we began packing, and just as we had begun to take down my tent, a rider clopped up to the edge of the camp.

"General Sendoa?" he asked.

"Yes." I waved to him and strode over.

He looked over the camp and then down at me. "Lord Daiko sends his greetings. He received a message yesterday from His Royal Highness that you were coming. Lord Daiko wishes to know if you have any requests for your luncheon?"

"No. Thank you." I looked down and sighed heavily.

"I understand you've suffered a loss?" he ventured.

I nodded. "Yes." I let the silence lengthen, then added, "I think it best if we simply get to work."

"Understood, sir." He paused, then added, "I meant to offer that my lord's manor is more comfortable than any camp, but it seems you've been properly provided for. All the same, you are welcome when you arrive."

"Thank you."

I watched him as he bowed, then galloped away. Perhaps it was not kind to deceive him, but he would report back to Lord Daiko that all appeared as he might expect.

We arrived only a few hours later, a little before noon. Lord Daiko's manor house was just as I might have expected from a member of the highest nobility, full of luxury even more ostentatious than the manor house I now inhabited. Mine still barely felt like home, and I was only comfortable in it because Ria was there. Lord Daiko fully inhabited his luxury. He welcomed us wearing a ridiculous cloak of gold cloth; even Hakan's royal cloak was more restrained. However, he did me the courtesy of coming out into the courtyard to greet us when we arrived. There was no warmth in his eyes, but he was as courteous as protocol required.

We ate lunch in his hall, an awkward meal that all of us were glad to finish. The men were given seats at one end of the table, separated from Lord Daiko and me by a space of a few chairs in order to reinforce their common status and his nobility. I thought it rather rude, but perhaps it was not an unusual practice; I'd never eaten in a lord's house aside from the palace, and common soldiers rarely eat in a lord's hall at all.

He said that the men had been summoned and were ready to meet with me at my convenience.

"We should start immediately."

He nodded, and gestured for a servant to lead me to the smaller hall in which the men waited.

"I'd like to take the men outside for the discussion. We'll be demonstrating some of the training methods we're using in the school, and we'll need a little space."

He nodded again. "As you wish. The courtyard is large enough and protected from the wind. The men know the way out."

"Thank you."

We followed the servant and then moved out into the courtyard immediately. The veterans from Lord Daiko's house were all my age or older, with the oldest being near fifty. I didn't know any of them personally, and I introduced myself first. They bowed and gave me their names as well. Two of the eleven men we'd identified as retired military were missing, and there were three others who had been added to the group by Lord Daiko. None were visibly armed, expecting only a conference, not a fight, although I assumed they all carried boot knives.

I kept my voice low, so that they crowded closer to hear me. "I'm not here for the reason Lord Daiko thinks. Lord Daiko has been identified as a leader in a plot to assassinate His Royal Highness Hakan Ithel.

"My purpose here is to arrest Lord Daiko. I want to do it without bloodshed. He will be given a fair trial before the king and all evidence, both in his favor and against him, will be considered. The plot involved all four criminal guilds in Stonehaven, who were hired to gather information and assist in a direct attempt on the king's life. My concern is that Lord Daiko would order you, and his other men, to defend him. Without knowledge of his crime, you would understandably risk your lives, and those of the men you command, in defending him against the king's justice.

"Let me be clear. The king has the power and authority to arrest Lord Daiko, whether you support him or not. My goal is to prevent unnecessary bloodshed by honorable men. Assist me in arresting Lord Daiko quietly and ensuring that the rest of the guards stand with the king, not against him."

The men stared at me in silence, then their eyes began to dart around, evaluating their companions. The soldiers with me, including Kudret, had quietly arranged themselves in an effective formation. Kudret stood just to my left, half-turned so that we could guard each other's backs if necessary. The others stood in pairs at the edge of the group, spaced a little apart to form a rough perimeter. Our numbers were roughly even, but we were all armed and they were not. I would also have matched my men's skills against anyone else's; our advanced training had produced excellent results.

The eldest of the men said, "General Sendoa, I trust the king's justice. I stand with the king."

"And I," other men murmured, glancing around at their fellows.

I held the eyes of one of the men who was not on the list I had expected. Lord Daiko's man.

He hesitated, then finally said, "I'm loyal to the king. Lord Daiko told me to report back to him about this meeting. I don't know what he expected, but if what you say is true, he must be nervous. I assume they have similar instructions." He indicated the other two men whom Lord Daiko had added to our group.

One of them was already nodding. "Yes, and I don't plan to follow them. I'm the king's man, through and through."

The third scowled, and I held his gaze until he looked away. "Aye. I did as well."

"Understood. You four," I indicated another man with them who had volunteered his loyalty early, "will work with Kudret and these men on some grappling moves for a few minutes."

We needed to do something visible in case Lord Daiko was watching from a window. I turned to the others, and one man spoke up immediately. "General, I understand there is a banquet planned tonight with a number of guests. It's to honor you, I believe." His mouth twisted a little. "Well, mostly it's to show off Lord Daiko's wealth, but arrogance isn't a crime. Beck and I select the guards for banquets and other events, so arresting him then should be easy."

I thought a moment, then shook my head. "There are other lords involved as well, and if they are present, we don't want to alert them. They and their men might fight. We'll arrest him immediately. I expect more information about the others involved soon. We will not notify anyone that the banquet is cancelled. If any of the other conspirators are involved, they will come to us and be arrested in turn."

They nodded. "As you say, sir."

"Right, then. We'll demonstrate a little more, and then return inside. Kudret, your group will find a secure room and remain there until I come find you. The rest of you, we're going to arrest Lord Daiko. When we have secured him, we will ensure that the rest of his men will cooperate. Does he have family in the manor as well?"

"Yes," Hodei said. Hodei was the man I'd noted earlier as the eldest among the group, a stocky man of around fifty years. "His wife and son are here."

"How old is the son?"

"Nekai is twenty. A good hand with a sword too." He caught my eye, and I understood the warning.

I nodded. "We'll handle Lord Daiko first. I have no reason to believe his son is involved, but we'll be cautious."

We moved back inside and Kudret led his group off toward the conference room where we had met first. I expected no trouble for him; all but one of the men were loyal to the king, but it was best to keep them separated until Lord Daiko was apprehended.

The others followed me back toward the hall where we had eaten, and then through other halls as we searched for Lord Daiko. We found him in a spacious library, writing at a desk while his wife and son played at a game on a table nearby. Nekai was not wearing a sword, but Lord Daiko was.

I strode up to him and bent to speak in his ear. "Lord Daiko, you are under arrest for treason. Come quietly and your family need not be involved."

He shot to his feet. "You lying dog! I welcomed you into my house and you dare accuse me!" He swung a fist at my face, which I blocked. I stepped back as his hand dropped to the hilt of his sword.

"Lord Daiko, surrender your weapons and come with us. Your plot has failed. Don't embarrass yourself."

His son stepped closer, hands clenched.

Lord Daiko tried to draw his sword, and I stepped in, immobilizing his wrist in a grip that made his knees buckle. I drew his sword and tossed it to the side.

"Remove his boot knife and any other weapons."

One of the men stepped closer and did as I said. He patted up and down Lord Daiko's jacket and trousers looking for another weapon, but found nothing.

The boy wavered, indecision in his eyes. I caught his gaze and shook my head, and his shoulders dropped a little.

"Disarm the boy as well."

The boy grumbled but did not fight as someone removed his boot knife and searched him for other weapons as well.

"What is the meaning of this?" Lady Daiko finally found her voice.

"A lying dog tells lies," Lord Daiko spat. "There's no truth to these accusations."

"If that's true, then I'm sure the king's inquiry will find out. You'll be freed without any further trouble." I smiled coolly in the face of his anger. "Until then, the king requires your presence at the palace in order to investigate an attempt on his life. Come. We will depart after dinner."

I pushed him out the door ahead of me, and nodded that the men should follow with the wife and son. We left them in the care of Kudret and his men and another two from my group, to ensure that they caused no trouble. The men had their hands bound, but I didn't want to inflict that indignity upon the lady. Yet I couldn't trust that she wouldn't attempt to free her husband, so I had her sit on the opposite side of the room, unrestrained but far enough from her son and husband that she would be unlikely to cause trouble.

The rest of us went back to the main hall to await the arrival of the dinner guests. We used the time before they arrived to search the estate for other men at arms, of whom we found only two. One immediately professed his loyalty to the king, and the other merely stared at me with wide eyes.

"I didn't sign on for treason. I have no quarrel with Lord Daiko, but I want to stay out of this."

I nodded. "Understood. Stay with me." I'd keep an eye on him, but I doubted he would be any trouble.

Not long after, the rider I'd been expecting arrived with a message from Sirkhar. It contained a list of names of noblemen who were implicated in the treason. I had Hodei read it aloud so all the men could hear.

Six noblemen came for the banquet, with wives and attendant footmen and drivers. Three of the six were on the list from Sirkhar. I greeted them courteously and pulled them aside quietly, then arrested them with a minimum of fuss. One of them pulled a knife on me from his belt, but I disarmed him before he could do any harm.

Remembering Sirkhar's statement about how to identify the guild members by their tattoos, we also required that all the men bare their left ankles, right arms, and the skin behind their right ears. To my own surprise, we identified a Black Rat and a Snake among the servants as well. They glared at me murderously, but they did not try to fight.

The other noblemen and their wives we sent on their way with our apologies for the inconvenience but with no explanation.

Late that evening the carriages I'd expected arrived from the palace. We bundled the captured men inside, their hands bound. The wives were given a separate carriage, and their hands were free, though I doubt they were as comfortable as they might have wished. We gave both men and women blankets for the journey, but the men were too irritated to be grateful.

There was no use in trying to keep the men securely in Lord Daiko's estate. He had no cells, and the trials would take place in Stonehaven anyway.

We rode through the night to return to Stonehaven about an hour after dawn. The wind was biting, carrying the day's snow up into our faces and promising more to come. I spent much of the long, cold ride wondering whether I had been a fool to trust Sirkhar after all. Something about him was wrong. Broken. Yet the unease I felt was not fear; I didn't actually think he'd strike at Hakan. I tried to believe my confidence in him was not entirely misplaced.

We were all heartily glad to enter the shelter of the palace courtyard. Sirkhar and Hakan met us.

"All went well?" Hakan asked.

"Yes." I told him everything that had happened. Sirkhar looked as tired as I felt, his eyes a little bloodshot. He gave me an appraising look and a nod at the success of our mission.

The men were taken down to the prison and put in separate cells where they could not easily hear each other. I dismissed my men, with thanks for their steadiness. They bowed to me and headed to their quarters for some well-deserved rest.

Sirkhar, Hakan, and I spoke only when we emerged from the prison back into a hallway on the first floor of the palace.

Hakan said, "Did you have any difficulties?"

"No. You?" I glanced between him and Sirkhar.

He shook his head. "Nothing important. Everything is taken care of. Thank you." He smiled and clapped a hand to my shoulder. "I think you and Sirkhar both need some sleep."

"If you need me..." I held his gaze until he nodded with a warm smile.

I SLUNG MY PACK over my shoulder and jogged through the royal garden toward the manor. My breath misted in the frigid air before me. The door was locked, which reassured me. I was digging in my pack for a key when Glaw pulled the door open.

"Did you have any trouble?" I asked as I stepped past him.

"No, Lord General." He bowed. "Lady Sendoa is eating breakfast in the study with the Tarvil boy."

"Thank you." I smiled. "His name is Elathlo."

Glaw blinked, then nodded. "Yes, sir."

He heated a bath for me while I went to see Ria. She jumped to her feet and rushed to me, throwing her arms around me. I whirled her around and kissed her.

She smiled up at me, with no trace of the sadness that had darkened her eyes two days before. "I missed you," she said.

"And I, you." I glanced at the tray and her nearly empty plate. "If you're finished eating, you can come with me," I murmured into her ear.

She blushed and nodded.

Elathlo stood and bowed to me. "Welcome back, sir. I hope everything went well."

"Yes, it did. Thank you, Elathlo." I caught his gaze and smiled. "You did well. I think everything is almost done."

He ducked his head with an embarrassed smile.

"I'll see you at lunch."

Ria and I went to the bathing room and I nodded Glaw out. He'd left a tray for me, and my stomach growled in anticipation. Staying awake all night always makes me hungry, and it was late even for a normal breakfast.

I kicked off my boots and pulled my shirt over my head, then began to unbuckle my belt.

"Did I mention that I missed you?" Ria stepped closer and slipped her arms around my waist.

"Even though I stink?" I almost winced as she pressed her sweet head against my chest. "Oh, Ria, you shouldn't."

She giggled and snuggled closer. "I'm sorry I was so… whatever I was. Before you left. Erratic." She let me go, letting her fingers trail over my skin so that chill bumps rose. She smiled, licking her lips as she raised her eyes to meet mine.

"I just want you to be happy, Ria."

"I am." She nodded toward the bath. "Get in. I know you're tired and cold. I'll just watch from right here." She gave me an impish grin, then sat on the dressing bench a few feet away. I almost laughed at the idea she could possibly enjoy the view.

I scrubbed and rinsed in a matter of minutes, then Ria brought the tray of food closer. I raised my eyebrows at her. "This is extravagant, Ria. Even for a nobleman. And we both know I'm not noble."

She snorted. "Eat. You're hungry, and there's food here. Your water is still warm. Why not?"

I felt foolish, but I did eat a hearty piece of bread slathered with butter, crispy bacon, and the berries. Ria watched me, smiling, though not as much as I was laughing at myself.

Then I let myself relax in the warmth for a moment with my eyes closed. Ria's cool hands slipped into the water, caressing my shoulders and neck. I leaned forward and her thumbs described circles on my shoulder blades and the top of my spine, up to the base of my skull.

"Come, love. You need to sleep," she finally murmured.

"Yes." I dried and dressed, and we walked to our bedroom together, hand in hand. Perhaps another time I might have stayed up all day, pushed myself to continue working. But Ria slipped her outer gown off and flipped back the covers.

Ria lay down beside me and draped her arm over my chest. "I love you," she whispered into my shoulder.

"I love you, Ria. I wish you knew how much." I heard my voice slurring with drowsiness already.

She chuckled softly, her breath warm on my skin.

I WOKE ONLY a few hours later, a little after noon. Ria was sitting near the fire, which was low, and reading a book by the clear, cold light streaming in the window.

"You let me sleep too long." I sighed as I sat up.

"Too long for what?" She blinked at me innocently. "You've barely slept in three days, Kemen. Everything is fine. The king sent Tanith over to say that he didn't want to see you until dinner."

"Oh." I frowned. What about the interrogations?

She smiled and stood to come closer. She sat beside me on the edge of the bed. "I was going to tell you earlier, but you looked a little tired."

"Tell me what?"

She took a deep breath. "We're going to be parents."

Time thundered to a halt, and I stared at her with wide eyes. *Parents?* I picked her up and spun her around. She laughed at me, kissed me, and then we stood, our arms wrapped around each other.

"Really?" I had to ask.

"Yes, really."

"Have you been sick?"

272

"Only a few times. Mostly I just feel tired. It took me a while to realize. I think that's why I was so emotional. I had to count back the weeks."

"You're resting enough, aren't you? You should rest."

She laughed at me again, a silvery sound that made my heart thud in my chest. "It's not an illness, Kemen. Women's bodies are good at this."

"I know!" I felt my face heat, and I hid my embarrassment by pressing a kiss to her forehead. "Don't do too much, though."

"And you're one to talk." She frowned and ran her thumb under my eye and over my cheekbone. "I'm fine, Kemen. Really." Her smile lit the room. "This is wonderful."

"You are wonderful, Ria." I stepped back to look at her. "It must be early, then." Her waist was just as slim as it always was.

"Eight or nine weeks? Not long before you went north. We have months to get ready."

Neither of us stopped smiling all day.

I WAS PRESENT for the first few interrogations. Again, I was impressed by Sirkhar's skill. Although he apparently had a reputation as a man who knew how to torture when necessary, he did not resort to such methods in any of the sessions I saw, nor did I see evidence that any of the prisoners had been tortured in my absence.

Even so, he got the information necessary. Patient and clever, he smiled and he listened and he sympathized and he argued and he listened some more, until eventually he had a list of names as complete we could wish.

Hakan sent soldiers to arrest the men under Sirkhar's supervision and the authority of the court. Then Hakan requested a meeting while he was gone. "Kemen, I found some more information about Sirkhar. I'm a little troubled by it."

"In what way?"

He blew out his breath and pulled a stack of papers over. "This was written by Skadr Goro, who was apparently Sirkhar's trainer. I never met him, but from the records I gather his methods were harsh, to say the least. Sirkhar was apparently chosen and groomed from late childhood to be a tool of the crown. The records of his training are incomplete, but from what little is left, I'm surprised Sirkhar is loyal at all. He seems to have understood that my father did not know about, much less approve of, Goro's methods."

I frowned. "He was tortured? To train him for what?"

Hakan sighed. "It doesn't say that, exactly. Just that punishments for failing to complete assignments were appropriately harsh, given Sirkhar's predilection for doing exactly what he wanted to do, regardless of his assignment." He raised his eyebrows. "Sounds like he still does that. Basically, Goro's records paint a picture, and that picture frightens me.

"According to what he says, Sirkhar demonstrated no real sense of right and wrong. He demonstrated a poor ability to control his impulses, particularly towards violence and rage. However, he was not angered by the things you would expect. He once nearly killed some noblewoman because she, and I quote from Goro's report, 'sniffed at him.' Yet he didn't react at all when Goro punched him in the face hard enough to loosen a tooth. He smiled and spit out the blood and appeared to not hold a grudge at all.

"He seemed to show no remorse, guilt, or shame, and no empathy towards the pain of others. Keep in mind this is coming from Goro, who wasn't an empathetic man himself. Goro was concerned Sirkhar was so calculating that he would become more dangerous than he was useful. As Sirkhar grew up, he became better at containing his rage, but his skills at manipulation improved as well. Sirkhar could lie to your face and you'd never realize it."

"Where is Goro now?" I asked.

"Dead. He died when I was young, possibly by Sirkhar's hand. Sirkhar would have been about my age at the time, nineteen or so. My father never pursued the matter. I don't think he really cared." Hakan sighed and ran both hands through his hair. "I don't think Goro had any reason to lie. Sirkhar was his pet project, and he was proud of his progress for years, until he starts to sound more concerned. Sirkhar's doing good work, Kemen. He really is. These men were planning to kill me, and I wouldn't have known how to question them, much less break up the guilds, without Sirkhar. I don't know what to think."

I pulled out my boot knife and flicked it to spin around on the table. It was new, or newer, anyway; Hakan had given it to me shortly after the coronation. The long, slim blade winked and flickered as it spun. "Do you think he means you any harm?"

"Not at the moment. I don't think I like him. I don't think I can trust him. But I can appreciate his skill. I'm sympathetic towards him, but I don't think he'd care about that. What concerns me is his loyalty."

I don't know enough about Sirkhar to judge. I don't know enough about human nature to understand. I've felt, from the beginning, that something was wrong with him, but somehow it didn't concern me much.

Why?

"If he does not feel the difference between right and wrong, he's made an intellectual choice to do 'good' rather than pursue evil. Because he's had plenty of opportunities, and he hasn't taken them. I think he's calculating, and this has helped him set limits on his behavior."

Hakan glanced at me. "You think I can trust him?"

I shrugged. "Not as you trust Kveta, or me, or Riona. But yes, I think you can. If Goro was right about him, I think he's decided that patriotism is a worthwhile purpose. As long as he believes you're serving Erdem, more or less, I think you don't have anything to fear from him."

"Maybe so." He sighed, then raised his eyebrows at me. "I wouldn't have thought you'd be the first to tell me I could trust someone who has no conscience."

I felt my own wry smile. "I would't have thought so either."

TWENTY-NINE

ELATHLO

The fire crackled and I raised my voice as I read to my sponsor. He had invited me to his sitting room with Lady Riona after dinner, and asked me to read from my writings about my people.

"In winter, it is very cold. Not like in Erdem. If we have any horses or sheep, we keep them inside the tents to keep them from freezing. Some years we don't have any though, because they've died. Sometimes in winter we have to eat the sheep because we cannot find enough carabaa. Winter is very hard. The year my brother was born, in Erdemen counting 366, we called it the winter of the wolf. There were many wolves that year. We lost some of the men on a hunting party, one of my uncles and several of the other warriors. My father told me that if I did not obey well, he would take me out and leave me so the wolves would find me.

"I learned how to make snow goggles that winter, and I carved my own set and made the leather laces from the extra when my father finished repairing his snow-shoes. Snow goggles keep you from getting snow blindness, and they're very important in winter, because without them you can become lost and freeze to death." I showed him the picture I'd drawn of snow goggles, with the thin slit to see through, the rounded wooden eye coverings and the leather strap to hold them on. Wearing them frightened me, because I imagined wolves sneaking up behind me where I couldn't see them, but they were necessary.

"How old is your brother?" my sponsor asked.

"He's dead."

My sponsor blinked. "I'm sorry."

I shrugged uncomfortably. "He only lived a few weeks." I kept my eyes on the paper; I could feel him watching me. I added, "There was another child before me, too. A girl. She lived four years."

"So you're the lucky one." His voice was flat.

"Yes, sir! I am grateful." I added hesitantly, "I am also grateful that you have been so kind. Most sponsors are very different."

He flashed me a quick smile. "I have a letter ready to send to the schoolmaster at Ironcrest. They're almost ready to admit the first students. I'm going to attend the opening next month, and I'd like you to come with me to welcome the Tarvil students. I was planning to invite your grandfather and the other chiefs to attend as well."

"Thank you, sir!"

"You can speak to your grandfather then about re-placing aloka service with training at the school."

My eyes widened. "You want me to suggest it?"

"It's a good idea. You should get credit for it." He smiled again. "Speak to him privately, and make your

278

case with logic. Explain why it benefits him and the other warriors."

I considered this. My sponsor was placing me in a role to advise Otso-ka, rather than replace him immediately. He also considered my grandfather's pride, specifying that I make the suggestion privately. Perhaps he intended for Otso-ka to take the idea to the other chiefs. I expected that many of them would guess that it was my idea, or my sponsor's, rather than Otso-ka's. But they would like the idea and Otso-ka would not lose face before them.

"I understand, sir." I ducked my head.

IN ONE OF MY READINGS for Colonel Bekendi, I had read a quote from some military scholar whose name I could not remember. It said, "When a warrior and a soldier fight, the soldier dies. When warriors and soldiers fight, the warriors die." It was meant to explain the value of discipline and strategy as well as individual tactics.

A nation's military strength is built on more than its soldier's individual skill. But when I thought about my sponsor, I realized he was both a warrior and a soldier.

THIRTY

KEMEN

For the next three mornings, I exercised alone in our smaller courtyard. Although we believed the conspiracy was dismantled, I thought it safer to keep Elathlo out of sight for a little longer.

After breakfast with Ria, I walked through the garden to the palace. Sirkhar was interrogating the men, assembling all the information necessary to make a legal case against the conspirators. The second day, Hakan authorized the release of the women who had been captured with their husbands, as well as the teenage son of Lord Bretthaven, who had been captured along with his mother and father when they arrived for the banquet. Lord Bretthaven, unknown to his wife and son, had confessed quickly to his involvement, stating that he owed his life to Lord Daiko and had been pressured by guilt and moral obligation into complicity.

I imagined Hakan would look on his case with some sympathy; I know I did. But sympathy did not necessarily mean that justice would be denied. He had conspired to kill the king. That's treason, regardless of any mitigating factors. Lord Daiko's son had not yet been released; Sirkhar believed he may have supported his father's actions.

After lunch the third day I went back to the estate to see Ria again. Hakan and I had spoken about the potential for greater trade between the Tarvil and Erdem, and he agreed that it was likely to reduce the border tensions. Perhaps, because I had spent so much time with Elathlo, I felt more sympathy toward the Tarvil people. Or perhaps it was only because the pain of Yuudai's loss had faded a little in the intervening years, and the injustice of his death was as much Taisto's doing as any Tarvil's. I didn't like the Tarvil culture, but I saw them with more understanding now.

The day was clear, the sun glittering on the fresh snow that had fallen the night before. It crunched beneath my boots, the sound a manmade counterpart to the quiet creaking of the branches above me.

I didn't find Ria in the study, nor in her sunny little sitting room where she painted. Nor was she in our room.

"Glaw!" I finally found him. "Where is Ria?"

"I haven't seen her in some time, but she was in the study with Lady Gerrenti and her son."

I frowned. "Should I know that name?"

Glaw frowned as well. "I didn't recognize it. I hoped you would."

He followed me to the study. Ria was not there.

There was nothing to cause alarm, but somehow, inside, I knew something was wrong.

"Find her."

Glaw nodded and hurried out.

Some moments later he returned, while I was still standing in the middle of the room, my eyes searching for any clue for where she might be.

"Sir? The gateman on the far gate says he saw her walking out of the royal grounds with a lady and a young lord about an hour ago. He asked if they required an escort or horses, but Lady Sendoa said they did not."

"And they haven't returned?"

"No, sir."

"Stay here. Wait for her. I'll be at the palace." I ran back through the garden, trying to keep my heart from racing. *Ria will be fine.*

I OPENED THE DOOR to Hakan's office just as he was breaking the seal on a message.

"Ria's missing." My voice had an edge of tension that I couldn't hide.

"What?" Hakan looked up, the message forgotten.

"She walked out of the palace grounds with a woman and a man this morning and hasn't been seen since. I assume they threatened her."

He stared at me, glanced down at the message in his hands, then stopped and read more closely. He swallowed.

"The kidnappers promise her safe return if all charges are dropped against Lord Bretthaven. They say he was manipulated into participation by Lord Daiko, and that he's a good man. Lord Daiko destroyed him, saving his life only to take it back. Let it be known that he was innocent, let him keep his title and lands, and they will never cross me again." Hakan put the parchment down and rubbed his hands across his face. "We'll need Sirkhar. You need to stay out of sight."

"What?" My voice nearly cracked with anger. "She's my wife!"

He drew a deep breath. "I know. But you're easily recognizable. Sirkhar's face is more easily hidden. We'll find them, and we'll get her back, Kemen. Trust me." He held my eyes, and I tried to believe him.

He sent someone to the prison beneath the palace to retrieve Sirkhar.

"Let Lord Bretthaven go. He's not a threat."

He studied me. "Do you really want me to?"

I took a deep breath, and as I let it out, I realized I was trembling in fury and terror. "We make treaties with enemies we've fought in war. This isn't so different. They would never dare oppose you on anything again."

His steady gaze on me held a bit of hurt, but understanding too.

"Yes, we do. You negotiated with the Tarvil while you were dying. Maybe I should."

Then there was silence. My mind flooded with thoughts of Ria. Surely they would not dare harm her. Surely not.

"Ria's pregnant." My words fell into the tension between us, and Hakan looked up, his eyes wide and stricken. But he said nothing.

Do I really expect him to forget treason? If it was someone besides Ria, wouldn't I understand how absurd that is? But it is Ria.

A few minutes later, Sirkhar entered.

"Yes, Your Royal Highness?"

"Lady Sendoa has been kidnapped." He handed the note to Sirkhar, who read it expressionlessly.

My hands were clenched so hard my nails dug into my palms, and I forced myself to relax. Physically, at least; I could do nothing about the fury that burned in me.

Sirkhar gave a sharp nod. "I understand. Do you wish me to handle it?"

"Do you have a plan?"

"Im almost certain I'll be able to find them within a day or so. They aren't experts at hiding, they have Lady Sendoa with them, and they must be within the city, communicating with the palace. I expect I'll be able to kill them without harming Lady Sendoa, but I'll need to know more before I can be sure. They want an answer right away. Therefore, the best plan is to pretend to agree with their conditions, but kill them at the first safe opportunity."

Hakan frowned. "Lie to them."

"Yes." Sirkhar returned his look without expression.

Hakan sighed and ran his hands through his hair, leaving them locked behind his neck. He stared at the table for a moment before looking up. "No. I won't negotiate in bad faith, even in this situation. Nor can I allow a threat to someone I care about affect the decisions I make as king or as judge. We cannot deal with them."

Sirkhar nodded. "As you wish. Send a reply of some other sort. I will see who retrieves the message, then I will follow to see where the kidnappers are hiding. Then I will know more."

Hakan nodded. "Agreed." He glanced at me. "Then what?"

"What can I do to help?" I asked.

"Nothing," Sirkhar and Hakan spoke at the same time.

Hakan continued, "Kemen, I know she's your wife, and I know you're the best at what you do. But this must be kept quiet. You're too noticeable. If they're desperate, sight of you might put her more at risk."

Sirkhar nodded once.

Hakan continued, "Stay in the palace. Even being visibly concerned might encourage them, or others who might consider the same thing in the future. This ends now, with the Bretthavens."

He pulled a parchment from his desk and wrote quickly, then said, "I've said that negotiations with kidnappers are unacceptable. There will be no influence on how the prisoners are tried. The kidnappers are committing a capital crime and their only defense is that they are motivated by desperation, do not intend to harm anyone, and so far have not, as far as we know. If they come forward and ask for mercy, with Lady Sendoa unharmed, the matter will be forgotten. They may then ask for royal clemency for Lord Bretthaven, and present their evidence and extenuating circumstances in his favor. The kidnapping will not be held against them, or against Lord Bretthaven. I make no promises as to the outcome of his trial, but I promise to consider their pleas without prejudice. If they continue in this plot, they will be found and punished accordingly."

Sirkhar nodded. "As you wish. Bring the messenger in for a moment, if you will."

The boy was waiting outside under Drokan's supervision until he was allowed to go. He shook his head when Sirkhar asked if he knew who had given him the message.

"No, sir, just a man. I'm to bring the reply to the market and walk around near the well until someone finds me." He looked overawed and terrified.

Sirkhar nodded him out, and Sinta kept him in the sitting room with the message until later.

Sirkhar said, "The message says a reply is expected back within an hour. Wait the full hour. I'll go now with a team of men to watch the boy and track him; we'll be in place before he arrives at the well. We'll find out where

285

the kidnappers are hiding and proceed as seems appropriate."

Hakan glanced at me, then nodded. "Agreed."

A moment later, it was only Hakan and me in the room.

The hours dragged long.

HAKAN ENLISTED KVETA'S AID in his attempt to reassure me, but there was little they could do. I managed to distract myself from my thoughts for almost half an hour by holding little Kem and listening to the funny sounds he made. He did not soothe my terror and rage, but he enabled me to pretend for a moment, at least externally, that everything was fine.

Eventually I requested that Kudret, who had not gone with Sirkhar, bring some of the training pads indoors. Hakan, rightly, had suggested that I not be seen to be unduly upset, and an unusual training session in the courtyard might betray my emotion. I'd trained in the middle of the day before, but I wanted to be cautious.

Instead, Kudret and I took the training pads down to a large, empty stone cell in the prison beneath the palace. I didn't look in the occupied cells; I didn't wish to see the faces of the conspirators. Below ground, the cells were cold and slightly dank, but I took off my shirt and tunic anyway and let my skin prick with chill.

Kudret held the pads for me. After the first blow, Kudret told me to stop, saying that he was not strong enough and that we needed the heavy pad. I helped him carry it inside and we set it up in the middle of the cell. It was a wooden pole thickly padded with many layers of wool and cloth, and the bottom was a series of stacked heavy stones with a hole in the center for the pole, so it could be disassembled for transport.

Once we reassembled it, I vented my fury upon it with focused precision such as I had not exercised in a very long time. My knuckles bled, and Kudret shouted at me to stop long enough to wrap my hands in cloth before continuing. I knocked it over with my kick once, and that calmed me enough to realize that it would be inconvenient to break the stone base pieces. I turned my anger into greater precision, hitting the same tiny blood stain eight times in succession with the heel of my foot.

Kudret was standing in the doorway, apparently afraid to come inside, when I finally stopped. I wiped my face with the cloth around one hand and almost screamed in frustration. Ria was out there, and I could do nothing.

"Did it help any?" he whispered.

"No," I growled, and he flinched.

Kudret was not a coward, so seeing him flinch gave me a twinge of guilt. It was not Kudret's fault Ria had been kidnapped.

"Thank you," I muttered, and began unwrapping my hands. They were shaking, and I could not get the tightly knotted cloth free until Kudret reached out to help. The blood from my knuckles had soaked into the cloth, and it stung as he peeled the cloth away.

I washed my hands in the basin in my old palace room, where I'd realized I loved Ria and where Saraid had opened my shoulder and cut out the infection that was killing me. The blood swirled and disappeared into a faint rusty haze in the water, barely visible against the crisp white porcelain. I sat alone at the little table that looked out onto the courtyard. I'd eaten there with Ria the night I brought back word of Ashmu Tafari's consent to Kveta's marriage to Hakan. We'd stayed up almost to dawn, tired yet unwilling to leave the warmth of each other's company.

For duty, I'd sent men to risk their lives. I'd risked my own life in battle since I was fourteen, and I'd had command of men since I was sixteen. I'd sent men to actions that I knew were sacrificial, to distract enemy forces from the real push elsewhere. I knew, I thought I knew, what it meant to have the guilt of innocent, honorable blood on my hands.

But I had never expected anything to threaten Ria.

She was in danger because of me. Because of my position close to Hakan, because of my influence, because of my role in helping capture Lord Bretthaven. I could not regret those things, but I could not have imagined how much they would cost.

Sinta knocked on my door and told me that Hakan and Kveta awaited my presence at dinner. I asked her to convey my regrets, that I was not hungry and I wished to be alone a while longer. She nodded sympathetically and left. They would understand.

It got dark. I paced in the room, restless but unwilling to leave the solitude. My stomach growled with emptiness, and it meant nothing to me, only a reminder of life waiting to continue until Ria returned. Sayen brought a tray of snacks sometime after sunset. She frowned when I said I wasn't hungry and left it on the table. I had no desire to enjoy the dried fruit tart or chicken soup or rosemary bread or anything else. Enjoyment, the warm contentment of a well-fed stomach, was irrelevant without Ria.

I finally left the room because I remembered Lani and Ena, who would also be concerned about Ria's absence and would have heard nothing from me or anyone else about the reason. I found Hakan in his study and asked him to send a message to my estate, so that Glaw could give it to them. He wrote something quickly and sent it off with Noriso.

Hakan and I sat in silence. There was nothing to say.

MUCH LATER, someone opened the door and Ria stood there. In a moment, I held her in my arms. We were both trembling, and I heard her whisper into my chest, "I'm sorry. I had to."

"Had to what?"

She pulled back just a little and sniffled, tears in her eyes. "They said they had a poisoned knife. Even a scratch would kill me. I couldn't risk it, not with..." she shuddered and leaned into my arm around her shoulders.

"Of course not. You're not hurt?" asked Hakan.

"I'm fine." She forced a smile that crumpled immediately and she turned toward me again. "I just... I don't think it was necessary. I don't think they were going to hurt me."

I felt her arms tighten around me, as if to keep herself steady. She still wore her cloak, the thick fabric bunched around her neck against the chill winter air.

I held her in silence for a moment, then murmured into her ear, "Ria, I need to know what happened. Do you want me to wait until tomorrow, after you've had a little time to recover, or should I hear Sirkhar's report now?"

She nodded and brushed at her eyes. "I'm fine. It's just a lot to think about. I want to stay with you."

"Yes, of course." I tightened my arms around her and caught Sirkhar's eye. "What happened?"

He glanced at Hakan, who nodded that he should answer.

"The messenger boy was contacted by a hooded man. I followed him, with the soldiers, to an inn some distance from here. I spoke to the innkeeper and one of his staff. They said there were two people who were trying to remain hidden, and in doing so had attracted more attention than they should have. The shorter of the two had gone on errands several times, but the other one never ventured out. They did not allow anyone to deliver food or empty the chamberpots in the room. The innkeeper thought it was only the two occupants of the room, but he wasn't sure. When the one who left on errands returned, he always knocked on the door the same way, apparently unaware that it could be heard all down the hall.

"I had the soldiers wait in the common room at the bottom of the stairs. When the cloaked one came down, I clubbed him over the head. It was Santerit Bretthaven, the son. That meant the other one upstairs was likely Lady Bretthaven, but it could not be guaranteed that she had no other accomplices.

"I waited a few minutes, then went upstairs. I knocked in the prescribed fashion, with the idea that the occupant would believe I was Santerit and had returned for some harmless purpose. As the door opened, I immediately stabbed the person at the door."

Ria shuddered next to me, her face turned away from Sirkhar.

"Lady Sendoa was bound and gagged in a chair across the room, which was not large and mostly empty of furniture. I whistled for the men to come upstairs quietly, then entered and released Lady Sendoa, telling her to remain quiet. I asked if there were any others in the other rooms. She indicated there were not. I told the soldiers to escort her back to the palace immediately, keeping one soldier to assist me as I searched the rest of the suite and then the inn, and another to watch Santerit while we did so."

I swallowed. "Lady Bretthaven is dead?"

"Yes. She died immediately, as was my intent. Santerit is alive and more or less awake in the prison now."

Ria took a deep shuddering breath and let it out slowly, trying to control her voice. All the same, I could hear her anger and fear when she said, "You didn't have to kill her! She wasn't going to hurt me. She was almost in tears, telling me how frightened she was for her husband. She knew it was a bad idea, but they were desperate and her son insisted."

Sirkhar's face remained emotionless. I, too, struggled with the idea of a woman stabbed without even the chance to cry out.

Yet, in Sirkhar's position, what he did made sense.

If it had been me, I might have done the same thing. I might have felt more remorse for it than he did, but logically, what he did was sound. There was no way to be sure there were not other conspirators in the rooms or even behind the door. Sirkhar might have been outnumbered, trying to protect Ria from a poisoned blade wielded by an unknown assailant or assailants.

Sirkhar gave a faint nod. "Perhaps not. But I could not risk her alerting any co-conspirators in the adjoining rooms, if there were any. I could not even be entirely sure that the one who opened the door was Lady Bretthaven, and not an experienced combatant. I did what I thought best to achieve the goal."

Ria stared at him, tears welling in her eyes again. "Do you have no sympathy for her? She was wrong, but she was frightened, and desperate, and if you'd just talked to her…"

Sirkhar hesitated, glanced at me, then looked back at Ria. "Lady Bretthaven died almost instantly. Her son is likely to hang. So is her husband. And so would she, if she survived to be tried as her crimes demand. A public trial for treason is never a pretty thing, no matter how merciful the king is, nor is an execution.

"In what order should they be hung in order to minimize her pain? On balance, perhaps she will have the easiest death of the three."

Ria sucked in her breath and spun away from him. I felt, rather than heard, her words muttered into my shirt. "He's a monster."

I spoke over Ria's head, still holding her. "Thank you, Sirkhar."

"I did not do it for you. I did it for the law and for the kingdom."

"Then I thank you on behalf of the law, the kingdom, and whether you want it or not, from me."

He stared at me a moment, then gave a faint, surprised smile. "You're welcome then."

RIA WEPT in my arms that night. I wished I knew how to comfort her, but some things cannot be healed by words. So I held her in silence until her tears faded and she fell asleep, golden hair splayed across my chest and face pressed against my shoulder.

I WAS FINISHING the last round of strengthening exercises at the end of my morning training when I saw Sirkhar standing off to the side. His arms were crossed over his chest and he watched with clinical interest as I pushed myself up into the handstand yet again.

On my feet, I nodded to him as I moved toward the well. I needed at least a cup of cool water before I could speak with him with any intelligence.

"I understand you can't read," he said without preamble.

I nodded, swallowing irritation with my water.

He turned to lean against the well, looking across the courtyard as I did. "You are more intelligent than I had guessed at first, and more analytical. I assume you have no visual impairment, given your capabilities in battle."

"Correct."

"You have probably guessed there is something... wrong... with me." He glanced at me, neither embarrassed nor proud of the word. "I think differently than others. I realized it early, but I did not fully understand the consequences at first. Do you know of what I speak?"

I guessed, but I wanted to be sure. "You make intellectual decisions in advance to govern your actions. You don't allow your conscience or immediate feelings of right or wrong to affect your choices."

He gave a faint, wry smile. "Not exactly. I cannot be sure because the concepts mean so little to me. I believe I *have* no conscience, nor these feelings of right and wrong you speak of. I prefer to think of this as a difference rather than a defect... to me, everyone else seems intellectually impaired by these emotions and feelings, tossed about like so many flies in a hailstorm, unable to fully comprehend the decisions they make. And you're correct; that is why I disliked you. You made an emotional decision to support the prince before it was reasonable to assume it was wise.

"My condition predates my training; it may be why I was chosen. I decided, when I reached the age and level of capability to be dangerous, that I needed to understand how I was different and make a decision as to how to live my life. I spent considerable time trying to understand how I am different, and searching for a cure.

"I found none. However, in framing the issue, I decided that the real problem was that I wished to be 'good,' but I have no inner map to guide me, as others apparently do. So I formed strict rules based on careful study of philosophy and historical views of right and wrong. I carefully avoid temptation and plan as much as possible in advance.

"This is only a substitute for what comes naturally to others. My defect causes me no pain, although it is apparently disconcerting to others." He glanced at me. "Your wife, for example. However, from my viewpoint it is superior, at least in some ways. And it is the best I can do. It has proven to be of value to the kingdom.

"You also have something wrong with you. We are both broken in some way. Yours may perhaps be curable, or perhaps the problem is one that can be worked around. I have more experience in studying these kinds of problems than anyone else. In the interests of serving Erdem, if you wish for me to attempt to figure out how and why you cannot read, I will."

I studied his face for a moment. "You can be charming when you wish to be. You interrogated the prisoners with such skill that they didn't even realize what they'd told you. Why do you not use your charm on Hakan or me?"

"I use charm as I use any other tool. To get what I want. I don't want anything at the moment. Therefore it serves no purpose. I am merely offering my service in this regard because it may serve Erdem. It may prove to be a waste of time. In either case, charming you into trying will do little good."

"I agree then. I respect honesty." I couldn't help my bemused smile when he nodded without expression.

We spent the afternoon together in one of the sitting rooms. Ria stayed away; she said she understood what he'd done, but she could not bear to be in his presence yet. Sirkhar wrote out words and letters and had me try to identify them. He sketched the royal seal and had me tell him which way the eagle faced. We also looked out the window and watched the men doing a partner drill once, and he asked me questions about them.

I bit back my own frustration more than once. Sirkhar was just as matter of fact and devoid of emotion during those hours as at any other time, aside from the interrogations. Perhaps that was best. It was impossible to be irritated with him; despite his bluntness, he did not throw my difficulty in my face.

Finally he said, "I think I understand enough."

"And?"

"You have no problem organizing thoughts into a coherent order, nor with counting. I had expected counting to be an issue, but it is not. You seem to assign no importance to the direction a letter is facing, either left or right, which presents problems because many letters have mirror images that make different sounds. You also seem to accord little to no importance to the order of letters within a word, which means that many completely unrelated words have been indistinguishable to you.

"However, you know your left from right. If I reach for my knife with my right hand, you know how to react, and if I reach with my left hand, you know how to adjust your reaction. If you consciously looked for direction as a defining factor in every letter of every word, every time, you could probably overcome that difficulty.

"Order is a problem. If you see a line of ten faces, you know there are ten, and you know what order they are in. If you see a line of ten letters or digits, you know there are ten but you cannot tell me what order they are in. You did not reliably recognize the king's seal from its reverse. However, when I asked you which way the eagle was facing, you could tell me.

"I think the problem is almost entirely limited to appraising two-dimensional symbols, as opposed to a more general intellectual problem." He smiled, not the charming facade he'd put on for the prisoners, nor the faint imitation of a smile I'd seen several times before, but the smile of a man who has solved a particularly perplexing puzzle. "That means you might be able to learn to read. Not easily, not fluidly, but passably. You would do it by learning to recognize whole words, not reading phonetically. Even then, there are several possibilities for some words, given the directional flipping, but you could make corrections by context."

I nodded, not trusting my voice. If it was a matter of memorizing the shape of whole words... I did not know where to start. The Erdemen language has forty-two characters, along with accent marks that denote certain sounds. It is written with the characters flowing into each other, except for numbers, of course. How many words would I have to memorize to become even functionally literate?

He raised his eyebrows slightly. "I didn't say it would be easy. But I thought you should know if it could be done. We may be the two strongest allies of the crown. We should be as capable as possible."

I swallowed. "Agreed."

TWO MONTHS LATER, spring arrived in an explosion of flowers and birdsong. Elathlo was awestruck. The splendor of the royal garden barely hinted at the joy in my life.

The school in Ironcrest was finally ready to open, and I wished I did not have to leave Ria yet again.

"Could I go with you when you go?" Riona asked.

"To Ironcrest?" I blinked. "It's a long journey."

She bit her lip and looked at me. Finally she said, "I don't want to be separated again, Kemen. It hurts when you're gone."

"If you're willing to travel. It's not comfortable, not like here." I smiled when she nodded.

Ria had never been farther than the Silverfall. It would have been a more pleasant journey if the weather was warmer, but it was still too early for many flowers to bloom outside the protected walls of the garden and into the northern forests.

The morning of our departure, Ria and I ate an early breakfast with Hakan and Kveta. Ria had sometimes suffered from sickness in the mornings, but that had mostly passed. This morning, though, she said she felt a little ill, so she didn't eat much. I packed the food up for her, in case she wanted it later in the carriage. Some early strawberries, fried sausage and eggs, which wouldn't last long, soft brown bread, a little pot of rich butter, and steamed rice with sweet red beans. Ena added some things to the pack too, almond pastries and lemon cakes, so Ria would have plenty to choose from if she felt better later.

I asked her if she still wanted to come, and she frowned at me. "Of course I do! I'll feel better, don't worry. I won't slow you down. Much."

"I'm not worried about that." I studied her face and finally bent forward to kiss her cheek. She looked a little pale.

"I'm fine." She smiled at me.

I drove the carriage so I could be near in case she felt ill, and she sat beside me. I expected the movement of the carriage to worsen her nausea, but she said she felt better as the day went on, and the cool breeze in her face helped. I'd wrapped a thick blanket around her shoulders, so even in the chilly breeze she said she was comfortable. She leaned against me and sighed contentedly.

We drove in happy silence for some hours. I was thinking about the school when Ria spoke.

"What shall we name him?"

The thought of our son made me smile. "Hakan."

She laughed softly. "I was thinking Kemen."

"We already have two of those."

"I don't think you can have too many." She straightened and stretched her arms. "Doesn't Hakan mean ruler or something?"

"Yes." I added, "I asked Hakan if he minded. He was pleased."

"And for a middle name?" She watched my face. "Did you have something in mind?"

"Did you?" I glanced at her, and she smiled.

"I thought you should pick."

Sendoa means strong. Hakan means ruler. I considered the question; a man's name is important, and not a decision to be rushed. "Garaile means victor. Hakan Garaile Sendoa."

She smiled. "You like it?"

"I don't know. Maybe Eguzki. Hakan Eguzki Sendoa?" I tested the name. It sounded grand for a baby, but he wouldn't be small forever.

"What does it mean?"

"Sun." I glanced at her, and she wrinkled her nose.

"It's nice but…" she hesitated. "It's hard to say."

"It's a good name." But I was tentative too. It didn't sound right. Then, "Arkaitz. It means rock. Hakan Arkaitz Sendoa."

She blinked. "If you like it." She still sounded uncertain.

"I do." It sounded strong, solid. A name for a man who could be trusted. A man I'd be proud to call my son.

She smiled and tucked her arm in mine. "Then Arkaitz it is. Hakan Arkaitz Sendoa." She smoothed her dress over her softly rounded belly.

WE STAYED SEVERAL NIGHTS in inns, but our journey toward Ironcrest took us along the highways north. These roads, as Hakan had discovered when he first fled Vidar, were not as well maintained as the roads west and south. He'd improved the roads a little in the intervening time, but it was a big task and far from complete. The nobles did not travel often travel north; they preferred to visit the coast for summer weather. Without the nobles to demand and pay for luxury, the inns on the north roads were no more comfortable than the extravagant royal tents, and our food was at least as good as any inn could boast. In addition to the supplies Joran had sent with us, we also roasted hares and flat bread drizzled with oil and crushed herbs, one of my favorite campaign meals.

We traveled slowly, making the trip longer but less strenuous than it might otherwise have been. Ria was tired, and sometimes when we stopped for lunch she took a quick nap in the carriage or on a blanket with her head in my lap. Elathlo gave me a funny look the first he saw us relaxing this way. Even almost a year after he had come to Erdem with me, I was not one to often show my affection so openly before him or the soldiers. But I wasn't embarrassed. Instead, I felt an unexpected surge of happiness and pride.

Sometimes she chose to ride behind me. Her belly was rounded but not so big she couldn't lean against me, her arms wrapped around my waist. We both enjoyed it when she did. I know I smelled like sweat and horse and smoke from the fires, but she didn't seem to mind. When we camped beside the Silvertongue River, I gathered a bunch of early irises for Ria. Our group was too loud to see much wildlife, but I pointed out what I saw.

The soldiers saluted us when we arrived at Ironcrest and opened the gate with a flourish that made Ria's cheeks turn bright pink. The schoolmaster was a retired general named Kuro Biteri; I'd interviewed him myself some months before. He seemed to understand what Hakan and I imagined the school might accomplish. It was more than a place to learn academic subjects and fighting skills; it was meant to be a place for students to become friendly. Perhaps not the closest of friends, but for them to view each other with sympathy and understanding.

We slept that night in the officers' quarters. The rooms still smelled of fresh-cut pine and the walls were entirely bare of the maps I knew would soon grace them. I was pleased with the school, which had been established only a short distance away from the barracks in a new enclave enclosed by an extension of the outer wall. It was a lot of work to extend the wall, and the men were justifiably proud of their accomplishment. I thanked them at dinner and again in the morning, when I was asked to lead the morning exercises.

I thought Ria would be bored while we exercised, but she watched with evident interest. Once she caught my eye and gave me a proud smile, her hand resting on her belly. Elathlo kept up with the men. He was not as powerful as the soldiers, of course, because he was smaller, but his technique and speed were impressive for his age. Months of intensive, individual training could make anyone skillful, if they worked for it, and I liked to think I was a skilled instructor. He'd certainly worked hard, and now he saw the results.

The Erdemen boys had arrived two days before, and I took the opportunity to address them after the exercises. I told them of the purpose of the school, to foster understanding and friendship, as much as possible. I asked them to remember that the Tarvil boys who would be their fellow students were far from home and everything they'd ever known, and asked them show compassion. Compassion is a virtue of the strong, and we were strong. Their behavior, their compassion and generosity, would reflect on the king and on Erdem itself. They should make us proud.

Just before noon, the Tarvil arrived. The gates were closed, and they approached cautiously, waving a sash on the end of a pole to indicate their peaceful intent. We opened the gates and they rode in with wide eyes.

Otso headed their delegation, but there were eighteen other men, as well as twenty boys between the ages of nine and fifteen. I greeted them with Elathlo at my side.

"Welcome. I am Kemen Sendoa. This is General Biteri, the schoolmaster, and these are the instructors who will be teaching the first session." I introduced the instructors one by one, and they bowed to the men and to the boys separately. The boys all looked frightened, and one of the youngest boys looked near fainting with terror. I asked their names in turn and bowed to each one individually.

I asked the boys to line up by height, Erdemen boys in one row and Tarvil boys in another. Then I paired them, each Tarvil boy with an Erdemen boy of about the same size, and had them introduce themselves to each other. I asked Elathlo to translate for me, because I knew many of the Tarvil boys had only a spotty understanding of Common.

"This is your partner for the next session. Many of you may not speak Common fluently. If you don't understand something, ask your partner. Your Erdemen partner has been asked to be helpful and considerate."

Then I spoke to Elathlo "Let me speak with your grandfather and the other men for a moment. Stay with them and answer their questions if you can. Come in when you're finished."

He bowed, and pride flashed across his face.

THIRTY-ONE

ELATHLO

My sponsor stepped into the room with the warriors and men of our tribes sitting tensely on one side of some tables pushed together, and the schoolmaster and the other instructors sitting on the other. They'd been speaking, but the words stopped when my sponsor walked in. All the Erdemen men stood and bowed to him, their respect palpable. Otso-ka and the others belatedly followed, standing and nodding toward him before sitting down again as the door closed.

I turned back to the many eyes facing me. My pride in being asked to speak to the boys evaporated into sudden shyness, and I felt my face heating.

"What do you want to know?" I asked.

The first question came from one of the younger Tarvil boys, about ten years old. I recognized his tribal sash, but I didn't remember his name. His voice shook as he whispered, "Are they going to kill us?"

"No!"

He flinched at my answer, and I felt for the first time what my sponsor might have felt when I first served him. The child was afraid of me, and I meant only to reassure him.

"No. It is a school. I've never been in a school, but my sponsor is kind. I know he looks frightening. He's skilled, and he's strong, and he's faster than you can imagine. He's dangerous, but he's good." I thought of Tirta and his face when he'd spoken to me after our morning demonstration. I wished he'd been selected, but he was not there. "My sponsor is the supreme military commander of the country. He is a friend of the king. That's like their high chief but much more powerful. He makes the rules for the school, and he will not let you be killed. He has never even beaten me, and I'm his aloka." I licked my lips. Their expressions ranged from disbelief to hope to despair. "This is good. You will like it more than being an aloka to a Tarvil warrior. You'll learn so much. You can't even imagine."

One of the Erdemen boys asked, "Why are you allowed to study under Lord General and Ambassador Sendoa?"

I ducked my head, hearing the muted jealousy in his voice. "My grandfather is our high chief. He asked it as a favor at the treaty signing last year, and Lord General Sendoa agreed. I am very fortunate."

He nodded, and I knew the humility of my answer had been wise.

No one else said anything, though the Tarvil boys stood with hunched shoulders, still afraid but with no words to express their many questions.

I offered, "You'll see. Be grateful for this opportunity." Then I bowed and made my way to the door of the room where my sponsor and the other men were talking.

I knocked, and stepped inside when I was invited.

My sponsor stood and said, "I've been telling Otso and the men how the school will be run. Perhaps you would like some time to speak with him? I can lead the boys in their first training session."

"Yes, sir." I bowed to him.

I bowed also to Otso-ka as I approached, and we watched the men moving slowly out of the room into the courtyard.

Otso-ka turned to me. "You have something to say?"

"Yes, Otso-ka." I took a deep breath and let it out slowly. "But first I wish to ask about Tirta. He is not here."

He shook his head. "He fell from his horse the morning we set out. He hurt his leg and could not travel."

"Will it heal?"

He shrugged. "Tirta is not my concern."

"I care about him!"

Otso-ka flung an openhanded slap at my face. I blocked it without thinking, and he growled, punching with at me with more intent. I blocked again.

Otso-ka was as slow as my sponsor when we worked on half-speed sparring, and not half as strong as my sponsor. Every move was obvious to me as soon as he thought about it, his body showing me what he intended to do before he did it.

He stepped back and gave me a narrow-eyed glare. "You do not submit to my discipline."

I bowed slightly. "My sponsor would say that concern for a friend is not something that requires a beating."

Otso-ka grunted and relaxed a little. "You do not wish to strike me back?"

"No, Otso-ka. Why should I?"

He grunted again and studied me, as if I'd become something strange to him. Perhaps I had. Perhaps, two years ago, if I'd suddenly been able to strike my father or grandfather back when they beat me, I would have used that ability. I resented their beatings as unfair and unnecessarily cruel. Now, Otso-ka did not frighten me, and because I was not frightened, I also found myself not angered.

"You wished to say something else to me? Other than about Tirta?"

"Yes, Otso-ka." I considered my words. "I wish to suggest that you send all Tarvil boys to the Erdemen school instead of assigning them to warriors as alokas. The training can substitute for aloka training. It would happen at roughly the same age, and it would not be wise to do both. No warrior would want an older aloka, who is already trained in weapons, and moving the aloka training to a younger age would mean that warriors would have young children as alokas, too young to serve well or to benefit. Most warriors would probably be just as happy not to have to train alokas anyway."

He studied me, his head tilted to one side in an expression I'd never seen before. "I am pleased with your progress, Elathlo. I admit, I had no idea your placement would be so successful. You've gained much respect among the men." He paused, then said, "You have surpassed your father, I think. If not in physical ability yet, you are close, and your father had a temper like mine. He was feared and respected, a good combination. You are liked and respected. That might be better. I don't understand everything you are learning in Erdem, but I can see that it is valuable."

I bowed, trying to hide my smile. He sounded perplexed, both by me and by his own words. He was a smart man, but he was not one to often speak his thoughts aloud. That he did so made me think that he viewed me as a man, and one that he might trust, not like one of the tribal chiefs with whom he was always fighting.

"You are as tall as I am now, aren't you?"

"Yes, sir." Perhaps I was a hairsbreadth taller, but neither of us would say that.

"And strong, too."

I merely bowed.

"I've heard rumors that you might be enchanted by the general's demon magic."

"No, sir. He's human, like us. I think people of his color are taller even than the Erdemen Tuyets. But also we eat very well. The first day I traveled with him, I ate meat three times, in the morning, at lunch, and in the evening. There are all kinds of good foods, things I'd never heard of before."

He nodded thoughtfully.

He paced a few steps away and then back. "It is a wise suggestion. Unfortunately we have nothing to trade to Erdem for such training. Your sponsor's generosity with your training price was helpful, but we have spent all we have to meet this year's obligation."

I felt myself smiling. "May I suggest other goods? There are some things that are expensive in Erdem, but we have not considered them valuable before. White fox furs would fetch a good price in Stonehaven. A white bear skin could pay for many students' training! And also the blue stones that we found in the north, by the side of the dry riverbed... do you remember? Those are sold in Erdem for much gold."

He glanced at me. "You think so?"

"Yes, Otso-ka." I bowed again, relishing the question in his voice, as if my opinion mattered. "I have been bold, and I spoke to my sponsor about this already. He seemed pleased by the idea too. I believe he spoke to the king about it as well."

He gave me a sharp look. "You negotiated for us?"

"I suggested it to him, making it clear that I did not speak for our people, but that I thought you might find the idea interesting. I made no promises."

He nodded thoughtfully. "I will speak to your sponsor about it and ask how many students he is willing to accept into the school."

"Shall I get him?"

"I will wait until he is finished with the training session."

We stepped outside and watched the session. The Tarvil warriors stood in a row, their arms folded across their chests as they watched. The Erdemen officers looked more relaxed, murmuring to each other as they studied the boys. Otso-ka glanced at them and then back at my sponsor, who was demonstrating how to do a proper front stance and then how to shift into a back stance. I remembered how he had taught me, and how my legs had been sore for days afterward.

Otso-ka fidgeted beside me. "Is your training like this?"

"In what way?"

He frowned, but it was a frown of thought, not irritation. "He is spending much time on explanations and reasons. They are not doing anything now."

I hid my smile. "They are remaining in the stance. It is very tiring. He is explaining to take their minds off how much their legs hurt. Yes, he did that with me too."

The Tarvil boys were struggling more than the Erdemen boys. I guessed it was because the Erdemen boys, even the younger ones, were stronger. Good food eaten regularly makes one's body much stronger, with more energy. The Tarvil boys would strengthen, though; they would be fed well at the school.

A moment later, my sponsor told the boys they could relax and stretch for a minute with their partner. He gave the class to one of the instructors and headed toward us.

My grandfather gave him a clumsy bow and then the Tarvil salute; my sponsor returned both.

"Let us talk together," Otso-ka said.

Back in the room, my sponsor motioned for me to speak first. I explained what I had told my grandfather, and he nodded. My sponsor then pulled a parchment from his pack and placed it on the table.

"I hoped you would agree that trade benefits us both, and I have already spoken to the king about a possible trade agreement. It is not specific; we do not demand any particular goods from you, nor set prices for them. We merely state that traders are promised safe passage through Erdemen lands as long as they remain peaceful. Tarvil traders are permitted to sell their goods at any location in Erdem. I would note that your people are likely to get the highest prices in Stonehaven, but that requires more travel; they might find it easier to trade with the border towns. Trading with these border towns is likely to improve relations with our people." He flattened the curling corner of the parchment with one hand.

Otso-ka nodded cautiously. "I understand. I must ask about the price for the additional students. Many of our people see the benefit of training in Erdem, but we fear the cost. What cost do you require for each student?"

My sponsor pulled a second sheet of parchment from behind the first. "Tuition for each student is set at the value of one healthy lamb per year. This is an agreement between the schoolmaster, General Biteri, and me, stating that he is to accept any Tarvil student sent with your approval. Pay what you can, and I will pay whatever is lacking."

I had not known about this agreement, and I blinked in surprise.

Otso-ka stared at him. "Why would you do that?"

My sponsor smiled. "I believe it will benefit all of us. I have been honored with a good position by the king, and it pleases me to spend my money on something that serves Erdem and helps ensure peace between us. Also, I believe your pride will not allow you to take advantage of Erdemen generosity."

Their gazes met for a long moment, and finally Otso-ka asked carefully. "You would be willing to pay the cost for an additional three boys, then?" He sounded skeptical.

My sponsor nodded. "Only three? I thought there would be more."

Otso-ka hesitated. "There are. But they can wait."

"If you wish them to attend the school, send them. The cost is not too great."

Otso-ka glanced at me, and then asked in our language, "How rich is he? Will he be angry if I ask for nine more?"

"He will be pleased," I said.

In Common, he said, "There are twelve altogether. But that is much money for you to spend on Tarvil boys."

"Send them." My sponsor smiled again.

My grandfather blinked in surprise, and glanced at me again, then back to my sponsor. "I thank you for your generosity. The boys will be selected and sent for the next session."

"Good." General Sendoa smiled more broadly. "If you are pleased with the agreement, please sign the trade agreement. If you wish to speak with the others first, that is acceptable."

Otso-ka shook his head. "They will not object to what you have said."

There was a quill pen and a little pot of ink sitting at the end of the table, and he pulled them closer, then signed his name. It startled me to realize that I now noticed how he struggled with the letters, and how they were a little lopsided, not the fluid curves I had finally mastered.

"I thank you on behalf of the king Hakan Ithel," said my sponsor formally. "Let us go see what the boys have learned so far."

We ate dinner that evening together in the common room, the Tarvil on one side of a long table and the Erdemen officers facing them. The boys sat at another table. There were many awkward silences, but it might have been much worse. I had the feeling afterwards that everyone was relieved it had gone so well.

Otso-ka spoke to me again in a quiet moment after dinner, when the boys were being shuffled off to their new quarters. "The men are pleased with you."

I bowed a little. "Thank you, Otso-ka."

He turned to face me squarely. "I said before that you have already surpassed your father in some ways. It was true. But you are still very young to lead men. You know an aloka's training is generally three years. I did not want to ask so much from your sponsor when I asked him to take you."

"Yes, Otso-ka."

"I am pleased with your progress. But I cannot see how to assign you to a different sponsor when your time with the Erdemen general ends. It isn't much longer."

I swallowed. "Do you wish me to come back?" My fear rose, familiar and yet lesser this time.

"I want for you to lead when you are ready. That was always my goal. I am surprised, and pleased, that you do not want to remove me in order to claim power already. Your father and I had come to an agreement about when I would step down. Even that is unusual; most high chiefs never let go of power until they die. That is how the successor takes power. I had hoped to come to a similar agreement with you when you were old enough to keep the chiefs in line." He sighed, and I realized how much this had troubled him.

"Otso-ka, may I speak?"

He nodded.

"I believe there is much I can still learn in Erdem. I think also that my sponsor would agree to continue training me. He is generous, as you have seen. I am very young to lead the tribes, and I have no desire to do so yet."

He studied me. "You don't wish to take power as soon as possible?"

I shook my head. "No, grandfather. I need to learn more before I can lead well. Besides, maybe I can help our people from Stonehaven."

"Yes. I think you can." He smiled a little. "I like your sponsor. I don't always agree with his methods, but I think you're learning good things."

I SPOKE to my sponsor in a free moment just before dinner, when no one could overhear us. "Sir, my grandfather has reminded me that you agreed to take me as your aloka for a year. That year is almost gone."

He nodded. "Yes."

312

I couldn't help swallowing, the lump in my throat nearly choking me. "I wish to ask for permission to stay longer, sir. I have learned much from you, and..." I had to clear my throat. I knew I loved my sponsor, knew I loved my life in the palace, the strict discipline of training and the intensity of my studies contrasted with the gentle hospitality and kindness of the people. But I did not expect my desire to stay to bring sudden tears to my eyes. "I wish to serve you more, if you can think of anything for me to do."

His white teeth flashed in a quick, compassionate smile. "If you wish to stay, you're welcome, Elathlo. You don't need to do anything but ask."

I dropped to one knee in the Erdemen bow of a man before his king. I didn't think about it; I didn't mean to make so dramatic a gesture.

He let out a short, sharp breath, an almost inaudible expression of modesty and embarrassment. "Stand up, Elathlo. There's no need for that." He clapped a hand to my shoulder and steered me toward the door. Just before we emerged into the cool, bright sunlight, he gave my shoulder a squeeze and let me go.

That small gesture made me feel like my mother had hugged me.

LATER, WHEN THE MEN were readying to depart, Otso-ka said to me, "I was considering the Red Tarvil for your marriage. Not yet, of course, but in a year or two."

"Otso-ka..." I started, then stopped. He would care nothing for my protest of disinterest in a Red Tarvil girl. He knew I'd only met one or two, and we had little interest in each other. "Perhaps it might be wiser to wait," I finished, knowing the words were unconvincing.

"As I said, not yet." His voice held an edge of irritation.

Another brilliant idea struck me. "Have they been hostile since the peace with Erdem?"

Otso-ka shrugged. "Not especially."

"May I offer an idea?" I asked, keeping my voice humble and steady despite a sudden rush of hope, surprise at my own cunning, and youthful desire.

He nodded.

"We have always seen marriage as a way of binding the tribes together, haven't we? Choosing the more hostile tribes in order to bring them back into our influence."

He nodded again.

"But if the trade agreement with Erdem proves as successful as I hope it will, hostility with the Red Tarvil will diminish because they will be happy with the arrangement. Instead, we risk appearing to play favorites."

He studied me thoughtfully, waiting while I formed my vague thought into convincing words.

"So perhaps it might be wiser to choose a bride from outside the Tarvil completely. An Erdemen woman?" I let the question hang in the air between us.

He looked up at the sky thoughtfully. "It would be beneficial, yes, but impossible. No Erdemen noblewoman would want to live on the tundra, and no one but a noblewoman would bind the Erdemen king to us in any useful way."

I licked my lips and gathered my courage. "What if I could marry someone related to my sponsor? He has standing with the king, and with the Tarvil tribes."

Otso-ka sucked in his breath and looked at me squarely. "Have you spoken to him of this?"

I shook my head hurriedly. "Oh no! I haven't spoken to the girl either. In Erdem, she wouldn't be pledged against her will anyway, and I haven't dared mention it.

But if you thought it worth trying, I might see what she and my sponsor think."

He stroked his jaw and thought. "How is she related to him? I thought he had no children."

"She is the cousin of his wife. They are close though; they don't move around as we do, but you could say they live in adjacent tents. My sponsor also cares for the girl. They are friends as well as bound by marriage." I did not say that she trained with me in the mornings, nor that she worked as a servant. I almost said that the king knew of her, but I thought it might be stretching the truth a little farther than I should.

"I think it unlikely she or your sponsor will agree, but I see no reason for you not to try. I will not let anyone know, though. If an offer is rejected, it should not become rumor and gossip." He frowned at the thought. "It is a good idea." He glanced at me again, as if I had surprised him. Perhaps I had.

There was silence until I said, "My sponsor agreed to let me stay longer."

Otso-ka gave me another appraising look. "Good. I will announce your appointment as our representative to Erdem. It gives you reason to continue your training, as well as a promotion from merely aloka."

"Ambassador?" I asked, stunned.

He blinked. "Is that an Erdemen word?"

I nodded. There was no Tarvil word for ambassador. Representative was used to refer to the Tarvil warriors sent to negotiate and argue with Otso-ka, but it was not a formal title. He'd heard the word at our last meeting, but he must have forgotten. I'd realized by now that he did not understand as much Common as I used to think.

"Yes, that is what you will be." He smiled a little, and in it I saw his pride and satisfaction.

Thirty-Two

KEMEN

R ia and I had been married a little over a year. It was late summer, and the days were filled with heady warmth and brilliant sunshine, the scent of the flowers in the garden, and birdsong. Kem could walk now, but he still liked to grasp my fingers in his to steady his wobbling steps. He liked even more to ride on my shoulders around the palace, gripping fistfuls of hair to keep himself upright, although I clasped my hands behind his back so he couldn't fall.

One night I was nearly asleep in bed, one of Ria's perfect arms across my chest, when she gasped. "Kemen, the baby." Her eyes were wide, beautiful blue, and she smiled. "Get Saraid."

Hakan and Elathlo waited with me in the hallway while Saraid, Lani, and Sayen attended her.

The first time I heard her cry out, I think my heart stopped. Hakan glanced at me and put one hand on my shoulder. "Don't worry."

I swallowed. My wife's pain was more difficult to bear than anything in my life.

Later I learned that her labor was relatively short and the birth was simple. But it felt like eternity. I paced all night and past dawn with my heart in my throat.

Finally Saraid came with a smile. "Sir." She had a small squawking bundle in her arms, sputtering and furious. "You have a daughter."

Riona was flushed and smiling, her hair damp with sweat. She nursed the baby. I'd never seen anything so beautiful. I knelt by the side of the bed and watched them sleep for hours.

THE ORANGE RAYS of sunset slanted through the window and across the covers. My eyes burned, but I barely noticed. I sat beside the bed, my head propped on my hand, watching Ria sleep. The baby slept too, nestled close against her. I wanted to hold her, but I didn't want to wake them yet. Ria's hair was stiff with dried sweat at her temples. She was so beautiful I could barely believe I wasn't dreaming.

And the baby! Her face was red and crumpled-looking, so fresh and new she hadn't had time to become beautiful yet. Her hair had dried into a fuzz of black down. I wondered if all babies arrived with black hair and it lightened, or whether she would keep the color. I hadn't had a good look at her eyes, and I wondered what color they were. Her lips were so small, her ears so tiny! I reached out one finger and carefully ran it across her hair. The hair was so fine and the skin so soft beneath it I was surprised she didn't wake at my touch.

"You're here." Ria's sleepy voice sounded surprised.

I kissed her hand and sat up straighter, blinked and ran my hands across my face. "Yes. I'm here."

"Aren't you tired?" She took a deep breath and pushed herself up carefully. I stood and adjusted the pillows for her, leaned down to kiss her forehead.

"I'm fine." We smiled at each other.

"I thought she was going to be a boy," Ria frowned gently. "I don't know what to call her."

"Riona is the most beautiful name I've ever heard."

She smiled drowsily. "That's silly. You never told me what it means, anyway."

I almost laughed. "In Kumar? It means tender. But it sounds much like the old word for a torture device used in the Second Age, the rihon-ha."

She frowned and met my gaze. "Really? You never told me that."

"Should I have?" I smiled and looked down at the baby again. "I didn't think about it. What do you think of Riana?"

She looked at me doubtfully. "What does that mean? And it sounds so similar, won't it be confusing?"

"It means innocent one. We could call her Ani." I liked the name, both the meaning and the nickname. "Ani sounds like the word for a fresh spring in the forest."

"And her middle name could be Sareen, after my mother. If you like it."

"It's beautiful."

Riana Sareen Sendoa. I'd never imagined I might be a father. I'd dreamed it, but never truly thought it would come to pass. When Ria's belly had grown, I'd tried to tell myself it was real, that I would experience the joy of holding my own child, but my imagination fell short of reality.

I watched Ria fall asleep again, her tired smile fading into relaxation. When her arm slipped a little, I gently extricated my daughter. My daughter! The thought alone made me smile.

I held her close to my chest and tried out her name. "Riana. You'll be beautiful like your mother, Ani. She's kind and gentle, yet stronger than she seems at first. You'll be like that, I imagine. I hope so. You are loved, Ani. More than you can imagine."

Looking at her sleeping face, I thought suddenly of my own mother. What had happened to make her give me up? I would never know, of course. But now, feeling the fierce love inside me, I understood a little more of what it must have cost her.

THOSE FIRST MONTHS of being a parent were difficult in ways I had not imagined. Ria was tired, and there was little I could do to help. We enlisted Ena and Lani to help with the endless changes of the cloth diapers and the tiny clothes, but only Ria could feed little Ani. For months, Ani would not sleep anywhere but on Ria's or my chest.

As tired as we were, Ani's presence was a joy I had never expected to be mine. I'd always wanted a child, but I'd never imagined I would actually be a father. Ria's gentleness and love made my heart swell and tears come to my eyes.

Ani's newborn redness faded within days to a creamy tone closer to Ria's than mine, though still darker than Ria's alabaster tone. Her eyes took on a greenish tint, though they remained more blue than green. Somehow, in her soft, tiny face, the color was more beautiful than I could have imagined.

While Ani was sleeping on Ria or me, I spent hours every day memorizing words. Some few words I managed to sound out by the phonetics that Ria helped me with, but most I had to remember as units, whole combinations of symbols. If I attempted to disassemble them into their component parts, as my teachers had done when I was a child, the whole thing turned into a mess of illogic and confusion. Perhaps I was never more grateful for my memory. It was not easy, but with time and Ria's patience and a great deal of swallowing my own shame, I managed to learn enough words to read several children's books from Hakan's library.

It may not seem like much, but I'd accomplished something I'd believed impossible for me. Ria, to her credit, was as encouraging and gentle as I could possibly wish. Years before, if I'd thought of demonstrating my failure to read before a woman I loved, over and over and over again, the shame would have overwhelmed me. But with Ria, though I felt the shame, I also felt gratitude, and love, and warmth, and a thousand good feelings I cannot even name. She loved me despite the brokenness, and that made her love more real and more true.

My love also grew more than I could have imagined. Before, I had loved an ideal of her, believing in her love and gentleness but not testing the depths of her forgiveness.

Now I knew.

LANI AND ENA stayed on with us, and though they helped the servants often, they were not servants but family.

One morning, Lani walked back with me after our morning training with Elathlo. He was advancing in his studies more quickly now, and Bekendi had told me that he was impressed with the boy's progress.

Lani started to say something, then stopped, letting the silence fill up with the sound of birdsong above us.

Finally she blurted, "What do you think of Elathlo?"

I licked my lips, then said, "In what way, exactly?"

She stopped walking. "Can we talk here for a minute? I just want your opinion, not anyone else's."

I nodded. She must have felt the affection in my gaze as I studied her face. She blushed and looked down, scuffing her shoe in the gravel.

"He likes me. I know you know that." She glanced up only long enough to see me nod. "I think he *really* likes me."

I nodded, then said quietly, "Yes, I think he does."

She glanced up at me again, and I added, "Because you're beautiful and kind and smart and brave, Lani."

She choked out a sweet, embarrassed little chuckle. "What do you think of him?"

I smiled. "He's a good boy." I wasn't sure if she wanted more detail, or if she just needed time to get her thoughts together, so I waited.

"I think I like him too. A lot."

"You don't owe him anything, Lani."

She shrugged a shoulder. "I know. But I do like him. He makes me feel..." she blushed even harder. "He makes me feel funny inside." She rushed through the words, as if she didn't want to get stuck on the awkwardness. "I was just wondering what you thought of it. If it was stupid to think about maybe having a future together. Because you've been there and everything."

She was trembling a little, and I reached out one tentative hand to put on her shoulder. "Are you upset, Lani?"

"I don't know." She seemed to be on the verge of tears, but not sad tears. Just... tears. After spending more time with women in the last two years than in my previous thirty-three combined, I'd come to understand that sometimes women's tears did not indicate something so simple as sadness. Sometimes they meant overwhelming emotion of some other sort, or a confusing mix of emotions that welled up and found some sort of resolution in tears. Tears weren't bad, they merely *were* sometimes. It was best to be there with her and simply be kind.

I pulled her to the nearest garden bench and sat down, one hand on the bench behind her. She could lean against me or not as she wished. After a moment, she leaned into me, her head resting against my shoulder. She sniffled.

"It's hard up there, Lani. The people, the weather, the food... it's hard. I can't say I'd want you to go. But I want you to be happy, and if Elathlo is the one who makes you happy, and he truly loves you, who am I to say no? You're both young, though. You're sixteen, and he's barely fifteen. Feelings may not last. Don't make any big decisions yet."

She nodded and sniffled again. "I know. It's a long time off."

"It is." I thought about how Ria and I had met and loved without understanding each other. "Be friends first."

She nodded again, not looking at me. "If I'd asked my dad, he would have just said 'no' and that would be the end of it. I loved my dad, but sometimes he made me mad. I felt like I didn't have the right to be mad because he was sick, but sometimes I couldn't help it. You just make me think about things."

"He was concerned about you."

She sighed. "I know. But you care too, don't you?"

"You know I do." I rested my cheek against the top of her head for a moment, then straightened. "Come. It's time for breakfast."

TWO WEEKS LATER, at the end of Runsaasti, as the summer heat was fading but the leaves were barely beginning to change colors, Elathlo and Lani talked to Ena, Ria, and me together at lunch. Elathlo's face alternated between pale and flushed with embarrassment.

"We're both very young, and I know I can't offer Lani much right now. I wouldn't presume to make any promises about our future. But we do care about each other.

"I think, if there's any possibility of having a future together, we need to convince Otso-ka and the chiefs that it's a wise choice. Otso-ka has agreed in principle to an alliance through marriage, but..." he hesitated and glanced at Ena. "Marriage among our people is different than marriage here." He flushed even redder than before. "Your kind is better. General Sendoa is happier than my father ever was, and kindness hasn't made him weak. But my people respect strength above all, and they will respect Lani more if we can show her to be strong." He raised his gaze to hold mine for a moment. "Perhaps we could do for her what you did for me, General. The demonstration, I mean." He bowed, holding the respect pose for longer than necessary, showing his gratitude.

Ena glanced at me. "What happened?"

"We showed off a little." I smiled at Elathlo's proud smile. "Elathlo's skill earned him respect among the men of his tribe. We can do the same for Lani. We'll work on something before the new session."

Elathlo's demonstration had been spontaneous, and, if the Tarvil warriors had been trained Erdemen soldiers, they would have seen the beginner's sloppiness in his moves. He'd been good, certainly, especially for his age and the short time of his training, but there had been a few minor mistakes. Lani's demonstration would be more polished, more fluid.

If in the future Lani chose to make her life on the tundra, the Tarvil would respect her. She would have the skills to earn their respect herself, if they were foolish enough to respect only skill in combat. But they would be wise to understand that others stood behind her with love. And maybe, after a time, she would earn their respect in other ways too.

THIRTY-THREE

ELATHLO

T he school in Ironcrest had been formally named Ironcrest Academy, a word that the king said would remind everyone that the purpose was academic and peaceful, despite the military training the students would receive. It was starting a second session in the Erdemen month of Jaa, after a break of ten weeks for the boys to travel home, see their families, and help with the harvest if necessary. My sponsor said that additional Tarvil boys had been added to the students.

"Is Tirta there?"

"I didn't receive any names. Just that there were twelve new students." He shook his head apologetically. That no longer seemed strange to me. My sponsor's strength and ability to fight meant that he should never have to apologize, but he apologized to me because he knew I was disappointed, not because he was wrong. It made him seem stronger, not weaker.

I had learned many things in Erdem. Perhaps some of them could not be transferred to my people, or should not. Not yet. But some of them could. My sponsor treated Lady Riona with consideration, respect, and gentleness that I had never seen my father show my mother. That did not make him weak either; if anything, Lady Riona respected him more for it. When I was married, to whomever it might be, I would try that. I'd never had the aggression or self-assurance of many other Tarvil boys, so perhaps it might be easier for me to try this new idea than it would be for them. Maybe it wouldn't be weakness, either; maybe it would be a different kind of strength.

My sponsor took me with him to the opening of the second session. Lady Riona and baby Ani and Lani and her mother came too. It made the trip longer and slower than it might otherwise have been, but I enjoyed it. Each morning while the suvari escort packed the tents and Lady Riona and Ena talked and played with the baby, my sponsor trained Lani and me. Even when we traveled, he rarely stopped our training, unless we were in a hurry. We ran a few sprints, practiced the demonstration my sponsor had devised, then he had us race each other climbing up trees. Ena shook her head, and I tried to decide whether her expression was of pride, irritation, or merely confusion. Perhaps all three. Lani loved it, though, and I did too.

We arrived after a leisurely three weeks of travel. My sponsor had paid for us to stay in inns several nights for the comfort of his wife and infant daughter. Most nights we slept in tents though. I liked those nights. The soldiers no longer intimidated me; they were friendly and understood that I loved Erdem as much as they did, although my love was different. I had come to it later, and I loved my people too, but I did love Erdem.

The autumn evenings were long and slow and restful. My sponsor had us make camp early so as not to tire the ladies. The men sang around the campfires, and I liked to listen to their stories of Erdemen legends. My sponsor surprised me, and perhaps many of the others, by a recitation of some epic poem I had not yet heard. He was not a performer, like the entertainers who sometimes came to the palace to perform during banquets. But his subdued, intense voice rose and fell with the appropriate emotion at each part, and he knew the words by heart, over an hour, which he said was only a short section. When he finished, the soldiers clapped and shouted with admiration.

We arrived some hours after Otso-ka and the Tarvil boys, and they had already eaten lunch and begun their first set of exercises outside. My sponsor let me accompany him to the front of the exercise ground, where we watched them learn how to stretch after a hard exercise session. The new Tarvil boys looked a little frightened, but less terrified than the first group had during their first session. I found Tirta in the third row near the middle and smiled at him.

All the Tarvil boys looked tired and hot, suffering worse than the Erdemen boys. After over a year in Erdem, I didn't find the heat as stifling as I had at first, but exercising in the afternoon heat was still difficult. Although we were well into autumn, the afternoons were still much warmer than anything they had endured before, and only the crisp chill of evening reminded me that winter came to Erdem too.

My sponsor spoke to the instructor and then sent all the boys to get some water.

Tirta meandered over to me after he'd gotten his water and splashed some over his head, as the Erdemen boys were doing. I stepped away from my sponsor and the others for a moment, and we grinned at each other, feeling awkward and happy all at once.

"I'm glad you're here," I said.

He flushed and looked down. "So am I. My father had picked Terathlo for my sponsor when Otso-ka announced that the school would accept more students."

"Oh." I gave him a sympathetic look. Terathlo would have been a difficult sponsor, indeed. He was one of the few who might actually dare kill an aloka. It was every sponsor's right, but few actually did it because it tended to cause bad blood between the families. Terathlo had a temper that rivaled my father's though.

"That's what I thought." Tirta grinned. "So I don't mind the fact that I'm sweating like I never have before. How are you?"

"Good. My sponsor has a daughter now." I gestured toward where my sponsor stood, his head bent so that Lady Riona could whisper something in his ear. "I have a favor ask, Tirta." He nodded. I told him my plan in a low voice.

The men planned to stay only a few hours. I imagined that they were nervous at the thought of sleeping in an Erdemen fort, and perhaps the Erdemen soldiers were equally glad to see them go. The boys were divided by age into three groups, and the Tarvil warriors were invited to sit in the back of the classroom while the instructors taught their first lesson. My sponsor and I also stood in the back for several minutes.

The lesson was on arithmetic. The Erdemen boys were bored, but they were well-mannered enough not to show it rudely. The Tarvil boys were as confused as I'd been those first few months. I understood better why

Colonel Bekendi had been so baffled as to where to start with my education. This instructor was better prepared and started at the beginning, demonstrating addition and subtraction on the board at the front of the room.

Otso-ka and the warriors stayed long enough to eat dinner. My sponsor suggested that I eat dinner with the students. They were suitably impressed with the food, as were the warriors. Meat twice in one day! I knew they would not always eat meat at every meal, but my sponsor had told me that the boys would be provisioned in accordance with the physical training they would undergo. The training was intense, therefore the meals would be enough to satisfy them and fuel their growth. The fort had an extensive store of food, as well as three milk cows, a sow with a full litter of pigs, and a number of hens that provided eggs and meat. There were also farms nearby which benefited from the ongoing needs of the soldiers and the students.

The boys would return as the strongest fighting force my people had seen in generations. They might not all be warriors, as my sponsor was, but they would be something closer to soldiers, with some of the skills of a warrior. Their education would make them influential, even without the benefit of their fighting skill.

Otso-ka was a chief, and despite his harshness with me, he was not a bad one. But perhaps my people could benefit from another kind of chief, one more like the Erdemen king. If we could be united as the Erdemen people were, we would be stronger. And, if I were chief, we would not fight Erdem. The Erdemen king, and my sponsor, would have no reason to object to a stronger, more unified Tarvil people, as long as we remained friendly.

The students, both Tarvil and Erdemen, talked quietly among themselves, and some of them asked me questions about my sponsor. They asked where I lived, where we trained, and when I would go back to the tundra. Perhaps, if I had been less surprised by my good fortune, I might have boasted about my life, but instead I found that answering their questions only made me more grateful toward my sponsor.

One of the boys asked about Lani. He said she was pretty, and I nodded, feeling my face flush. He asked if we were betrothed.

"No. But I've thought about it."

He smiled sympathetically.

As we were ready to wave them off, Tirta called out in our language, "Elathlo-ka, are you sure that's a good idea?"

I blinked at him, not sure what he meant.

He held my gaze for a moment, and said, "She is a beautiful flower. But flowers are fragile. Is she too fragile to withstand life on the tundra?"

Oh. "See for yourself." I smiled at him. "Lani? Someone has asked if you are as delicate as the flower you resemble. Would you be willing to demonstrate some bladework?"

I bowed to her, a deliberate gesture to indicate that I, not yet a man but soon to be one, respected this soon-to-be woman. It was unprecedented, and I meant it to be so.

After the effect my demonstration had on the warriors, I knew it would be important to gain their respect for Lani. She had practiced for months with my sponsor. Tirta was the last one brought in on the plan.

Lani turned to nod at my sponsor, who drew his short sword and tossed it to her. The throw was carefully rehearsed, a graceful arc during which the sword spun exactly the right amount to reach her with the hilt foremost. She caught it and begun the whirling series of movements my sponsor had taught her, a flashy exhibition meant to impress the warriors.

The Tarvil scimitar is meant to be used from horseback, a long, curved blade that is of little use in close combat. It is too long and too heavy to be good for close, intricate movements. My sponsor had designed this demonstration to emphasize speed and dexterity, which were both foreign and frightening to the watching Tarvil warriors.

Lani's exercise was a whirling, weaving dance, with the blazing autumn sun flickering from the polished sword. Her long, fair hair had been left free, so it could fly out as she twirled, a golden mass of spinning hair and sharp blade, with the occasional chin-high kick snapping crisply out of the blur.

When she finished, she turned to present the sword to my sponsor again, who received it with a bow and a proud smile. I glanced around. Not only were the warriors awed, but there were more than a few stunned expressions on the faces of the Erdemen soldiers.

My sponsor put a protective hand on her shoulder. "Well done, Lani." He smiled at her as he'd smiled at me, pleased by our progress and our skill, and proud of what we had become.

Otso-ka glanced at me and I knew he understood that our demonstration was not entirely spontaneous. Not only did he approve of Lani, but he approved of me, and our planning. Overcoming the warriors' objections to her by persuasion rather than a fight, or bribery, would give me more influence later. I might not rule as he had, but when I led our people, he knew I would lead well.

The fact that Lani could kick and wield a sword with such skill impressed them. No Tarvil girl had ever done such things. My sponsor had obviously spent time and effort training her, as he had done for me; that also increased her standing and importance among the warriors. It also meant that my sponsor was not opposed to the idea of marriage; that too would have impressed my grandfather.

Lani and I were not yet betrothed. Perhaps we never would be. But when our eyes met across the exercise ground, I think we both thought it might be nice.

We would change things among my people.

Someday.

C. J. BRIGHTLEY

C. J. Brightley lives in Northern Virginia with her husband and young daughter. She holds degrees from Clemson University and Texas A&M. She welcomes visitors and messages at her website, www.cjbrightley.com.

THINGS UNSEEN

A LONG-FORGOTTEN SONG
BOOK 1

CHAPTER 1

Researching this thesis is an exercise in dedication, frustration, making up stuff, pretending I know what I'm doing, and wondering why nothing adds up. Aria swirled her coffee and stared at the blank page in her notebook.

Why did I decide to study history? She flipped back to look at her notes and sighed. She couldn't find enough information to even form a coherent thesis. The records were either gone, or had never existed in the first place. *Something* had happened when the Revolution came to power, but she didn't know what, and she couldn't even pinpoint exactly when.

The nebulous idea she'd had for her research seemed even more useless now. She'd been trying to find records of how things had changed since the Revolution, how the city had grown and developed. There were official statistics on the greater prosperity, the academic success of the city schools, and the vast reduction in crime. The statistics didn't mention the abandoned buildings, the missing persons, or any grumbling against the curfew. At least it was later now; for a year, curfew had been at dusk.

She glanced around the bookstore at the other patrons. A man wearing a business suit was browsing in the self-help section, probably trying to improve his public speaking. A girl, probably another student judging by her worn jeans and backpack, was sitting on the floor in the literary fiction section, completely engrossed in a book.

Aria flipped to the front of the book again. It was a memoir of someone she'd never heard of. She'd picked it up almost at random, and flipped to the middle, hoping to find something more interesting than dead ends. The words told of a walk in the forest, and for a moment Aria was there, her nose filled with the scents of pine and loam, her eyes dazzled by the sunlight streaming through the leaves swaying above her. She blinked, and the words were there but the feeling was gone. Rereading the passage, she couldn't figure out why she'd been caught up with such breathless realism.

It wasn't that the words were so profound; she was confident they were not. Something had caught her though, and she closed her eyes to imagine the forest again, as if it were a memory. Distant, faded, perhaps not even her memory. A memory of something she'd seen in a movie, perhaps, or a memory of a dream she'd had as a child.

Something about it troubled her, and she meant to come back to it. Tonight, though, she had other homework, and she pushed the book aside.

Dandra's Books was an unassuming name for the best bookstore in all of the North Quadrant. Dandra was a petite, grey-haired lady with a warm smile. She also had the best map collection, everything from ancient history, both originals and reproductions, to modern maps of cities both near and far, topographical maps, water currents, and everything else. She carried the new releases and electronic holdings that were most in demand, but what made the store unique was the extensive and ever-changing selection of used and antique books. If it could be found, Dandra could find it. Aria suspected she maintained an unassuming storefront because she didn't want demand to increase; business was sufficient to pay the bills and she refused to hire help.

Dandra also made tolerable coffee, an important consideration for a graduate student. Aria had spent hours studying there as an undergraduate; it had the same air of productive intellectualism as the university library, but without the distraction of other groups of students having more fun than she was. She'd found it on a long, meandering walk avoiding some homework. Something about the place made concentrating easier.

Except when it came to her thesis. Aria told herself that she was investigating what resources were available before she narrowed her focus. But sometimes, when she stared at the blank pages, she almost admitted to herself the truth, that she was frustrated with her professors, her thesis, and the Empire itself. She didn't have a good explanation, and she hadn't told anyone.

Something about this image of the forest felt true in a way that nothing had felt for a very long time. It was evidence. Evidence of *what*, she wasn't sure. But definitely evidence.

She finished her homework and packed her bag. She put a bookmark in the memoir and reshelved it, resolving that she would come back later and read it a bit more. It was already late, and she had an early class the next day.

SNEAK PEEK: THINGS UNSEEN

After class there were errands, and homework, and more class, and lunch with a boy who'd seemed almost likable until he talked too much about his dysfunctional family and his abiding love for his ex-girlfriend, who lived down the hall in his apartment building. It was a week before she made it back to Dandra's.

The book was gone.

Dandra shook her head when Aria asked about it. "I don't know what book you mean. I've never had a book like that."

Aria stared at her in disbelief. "You saw me read it last week. It was called *Memories Kept* or something like that. *Memory Keeper*, maybe. Don't you remember? I was sitting there." She pointed.

Dandra gave her a sympathetic look. "You've been studying too much, Aria. I'm sorry. I don't have that book. I don't think I ever did."

Aria huffed in frustration and bought a cup of coffee. She put too much sugar and cream in it and sat by the window at the front. She stared at the people as they came in, wondering if her anger would burn a hole in the back of someone's coat. It didn't, but the mental picture amused her.

Not much else did. The thesis was going nowhere, and the only thing that kept her interest was a line of questions that had no answers and a book that didn't exist.

Was the degree worth anything anyway? She'd studied history because she enjoyed stories, wanted to learn about the past. But the classes had consisted almost entirely of monologues by the professors about the strength of the Empire and how much better things were now after the Revolution. Her papers had alternated between parroting the professors' words, and uneasy forays into the old times. The research was hard, and getting harder.

The paper she'd written on the Revolution, on how John Sanderhill had united the warring factions, had earned an F. Dr. Corten had written "Your implication that Sanderhill ordered the assassination of Gerard Neeson is patently false and betrays an utter lack of understanding of the morality of the Revolution. I am unable to grade this paper higher than an F, in light of such suspect scholarship and patriotism." Yet Aria had cited her source clearly and had been careful not to take a side on the issue, choosing merely to note that it was one possible explanation for Neeson's disappearance at the height of the conflict. Not even the most likely.

For a history department, her professors were remarkably uninterested in exploring the past. She scowled at her coffee as it got colder. What was the point of history, if you couldn't learn from it? The people in history weren't perfect, any more than people now were. But surely, as scholars, they should be able to admit that imperfect people and imperfect decisions could yield lessons and wisdom.

It wasn't as if it was ancient history either. The Revolution had begun less than fifteen years ago. One would think information would be available. Memories should be clear.

But they weren't.

The man entered Dandra's near dusk. He wore no jacket against the winter cold, only a threadbare short-sleeved black shirt. His trousers were dark and equally worn, the cuffs skimming bare ankles. His feet were bare too, and that caught her attention.

He spoke in a low voice, but she was curious, so she listened hard and heard most of what he said. "I need the maps, Dandra."

"You know I don't have those."

"I'll pay."

"I don't have them." Dandra took a step back as he leaned forward with his hands resting on the desk. "I told you before, I can't get them. I still can't."

"I was told you could on good authority." His voice stayed very quiet, but even Aria could hear the cold anger. "Should I tell Petro he was wrong about you?"

"Are you threatening me?" Dandra's eyes widened, but Aria couldn't tell if it was in fear or in anger.

"I'm asking if Petro was wrong."

"Tell Petro I did my best. I couldn't get them." Dandra clasped her hands together and drew back, her shoulders against the wall, and Aria realized she was terrified. Of the man in the black shirt, or of Petro, or possibly both.

Aria rose. "Excuse me? Can I help you find something?" She smiled brightly at him.

He stared at Dandra for a long moment, then turned away. He brushed past Aria and out the door without looking at her, and disappeared into the darkness.

Dandra looked at her with wide eyes. "That wasn't wise, but thank you."

"Who is he?"

Dandra shook her head. "Don't ask questions you don't want to know the answer to. Go home, child. It's late."

339

10150276R10192